In the kitchen I found no sign of Miss Henley or the dogs. Not good. Somewhere in the distance Truffle and Sweet Marie set up a wild racket. The barking sounded like it was coming from the dining room. I ran, stumbling over bits of debris, old toy cars, empty cornflakes boxes, and a clothesline. I narrowly missed crashing into two oak beams leaning at crazy angles. I'd already made a note to get those put away safely as soon as the team showed up. I kept an eye out for more beams as I careened through the junk.

My red stiletto boots were not made for running. I tripped and snagged my best hose on a pile of rusty springs scattered on the floor. Finally I rounded a corner and spotted Truffle and Sweet Marie. They were yipping at a pile of newspapers that had toppled over and blocked the path. They must have cornered a mouse. Or worse, that cat.

"Come away and leave whatever it is."

Okay, so obedience is not their best thing.

"Miss Henley will tear strips off us for making this mess even worse, you turkeys."

I reached forward to scoop them up and stopped, stunned. I climbed over the fallen stack of paper. I pushed the dogs away and fell to my knees. Sticking out from under the toppled pile was a pair of shoes, black patent, with small gold buckles. Classy, expensive. Roberto Capucci's unless I was mistaken.

The shoes had feet in them, feet with nice-quality trouser socks. There were legs too, covered in charcoal wool.

Miss Henley.

# Organize Your Corpses

## Mary Jane Maffini

**BERKLEY PRIME CRIME, NEW YORK**

**THE BERKLEY PUBLISHING GROUP**
**Published by the Penguin Group**
**Penguin Group (USA) Inc.**
**375 Hudson Street, New York, New York 10014, USA**

Penguin Group (Canada), 90 Eglinton Avenue East, Suite 700, Toronto, Ontario M4P 2Y3, Canada
(a division of Pearson Penguin Canada Inc.)
Penguin Books Ltd., 80 Strand, London WC2R 0RL, England
Penguin Group Ireland, 25 St. Stephen's Green, Dublin 2, Ireland (a division of Penguin Books Ltd.)
Penguin Group (Australia), 250 Camberwell Road, Camberwell, Victoria 3124, Australia
(a division of Pearson Australia Group Pty. Ltd.)
Penguin Books India Pvt. Ltd., 11 Community Centre, Panchsheel Park, New Delhi—110 017, India
Penguin Group (NZ), 67 Apollo Drive, Mairangi Bay, Auckland 1311, New Zealand
(a division of Pearson New Zealand Ltd.)
Penguin Books (South Africa) (Pty.) Ltd., 24 Sturdee Avenue, Rosebank, Johannesburg 2196, South
Africa

Penguin Books Ltd., Registered Offices: 80 Strand, London WC2R 0RL, England

ORGANIZE YOUR CORPSES

A Berkley Prime Crime Book / published by arrangement with the author

PRINTING HISTORY
Berkley Prime Crime mass-market edition / May 2007

Copyright © 2007 by Mary Jane Maffini.
Cover art by Stephen Gardner.
Cover design by George Long.
Interior text design by Laura K. Corless.

ISBN: 978-0-425-21580-7

46523882

BERKLEY® PRIME CRIME
Berkley Prime Crime Books are published by The Berkley Publishing Group,
a division of Penguin Group (USA) Inc.,
375 Hudson Street, New York, New York 10014.
The name BERKLEY PRIME CRIME and the BERKLEY PRIME CRIME design are trademarks
belonging to Penguin Group (USA) Inc.

PRINTED IN THE UNITED STATES OF AMERICA

10  9  8  7  6  5  4  3  2  1

# Acknowledgments

I am indebted to Lyn Hamilton, Mary MacKay-Smith, Victoria Maffini, and Giulio Maffini for their help and comments on this manuscript. Many thanks to Sue Pike for her inspired suggestion of the model for the fictional counterpart to Charlotte's hometown: Woodbridge, New York. Linda Wiken of Ottawa's Prime Crime Mystery Bookstore has been unwavering in her support from start to finish. I am grateful to my agent, Leona Trainer, for her enthusiasm, to Tom Colgan of Berkley for being such a splendidly cheerful and accessible editor, and to Sandra Harding for bailing me out on more than one occasion. My miniature dachshunds, Daisy and Lily, have given me more than enough material for doggie devilment in the series. It goes without saying that any pesky errors are my own.

# 1

"Is this some kind of death wish?" Sally's question trailed off in a high wail.

I held my cell phone away from my ear. "She's just a client, sweetie. And I'm on my way now. Talk to you later."

"Hold on, hold on! Listen to me, Charlotte Adams. You're talking about Hellfire Henley, the same teacher who made our lives at St. Jude's a living torment. Have you forgotten physics class?"

"Actually, I believe I said 'Miss Helen Henley,' not 'Hellfire.' That's because she's a potential client. I'm not reliving high school."

"Are you *deranged*? That woman used to be able to make the jocks on the football team cry."

I moved the phone just a little bit farther away from my ear. "Then again, I never played football."

"You know what I mean. She got you suspended. And she treated me and Pepper and Jack like scum. And poor Margaret Tang. Whoa. It wasn't easy to be a Korean kid in Hellfire Henley's class. How can you forget all that?"

"Sweetie, that was sixteen years ago. We're not helpless kids anymore. You have three children of your own. I'm a professional organizer. Margaret Tang's a lawyer, Pepper's a cop for heaven's sake, and Jack is, well . . . whatever. Anyway, Miss Henley has a high-profile project. Just the kind of boost I need to make it in Woodbridge."

"Yeah, well, what if it's a trap?"

I let a chuckle escape.

Sally said, "Not funny, Charlotte. Hellfire was like a fiend for organization. What kind of help could she need from a former student? Think about that."

"She's inherited the Henley House from a cousin who was definitely *not* a fiend for organization. It's a disaster."

"Spare me. That moldering ruin at the top of North Elm Street? Yuck. You mean she lives there?"

"Of course not. She has a beautiful home, but she's responsible for this place. It's hard to imagine, but Miss Henley's overwhelmed. Henley House has huge historic significance for Woodbridge. So this project is bound to generate media interest."

"Blah, blah, blah. Girl, you are so deluded."

"Seriously, Sally, people will think if I can handle this horrendous job then I can solve their problems with chaotic offices or cluttered garages or—"

"You know what, Charlotte? She's just going to toy with you, then toss you aside to face public humiliation."

I massaged my temple. "If a client's not happy, she doesn't get to humiliate me. I simply walk away."

"Don't make me laugh. This is the meanest woman in the Hudson River Valley. It cannot possibly end well. After she's through with you, you'll be lucky if you can crawl into a hole. And anyway, I need you to help *me*. You know Benjamin's been crabbing about the kids' toys everywhere. He sprained his toe on a Lego project and now he's on my case big-time. So how about if I become your client? I'll pay you and you won't have to face Hellfire and I won't have to deal with Benjamin. You know how anal retentive he can be."

I felt a guilty twinge of sympathy for Benjamin with his sprained toe. That couldn't make running his busy medical practice any easier. I wasn't falling for the anal-retentive tyrant talk. I knew firsthand the chaos Sally and her three darlings could create. Never mind. Sally's been my friend since grade school. I love her, I love her kids, and I love her besieged husband. I said, "Tell you what. I'll give you a hand. Not as a contract, as a favor. I'll pop over tomorrow and take a peek. In the meantime, how about getting a jump start on it? Ask each of the kids to pick out their seven favorite toys."

"Seven toys? *Seven?* You're kidding. How can they narrow it down to seven? What is the matter with you?"

"Seven, max. Gotta go now."

"Do not go to that horrible Henley House alone, Charlotte. Wait for me! I'll come with you. Give me time to find a sitter."

Right.

Luckily Sally couldn't see me roll my eyes. "Catch you tomorrow." I squared my shoulders, flicked the ignition, and roared up North Elm Street to meet Miss Helen Henley.

—◆—

The three-story house hunkered on a huge lot at the rocky crest of North Elm. I decided to give the steep driveway a miss and parked my freshly washed Mazda Miata on the street. I marched up the endless stairs to the front door. Five minutes later, I was still shivering on the decaying verandah as the afternoon light faded. I hummed a few bars of "Who's Afraid of the Big Bad Wolf." It was the first of November and the wind bit through my skirt and collarless leather jacket. I sniffed wood smoke. I hoped it was coming from Henley House. With luck, I'd be standing in front of a warm fire soon.

Dead leaves swirled around the bare oaks. No one had made any effort to rake, pile, or bag them. I just hate that. A large brass plaque proclaimed the house had been built by Phineas Oswald Henley in 1898. Too bad for poor old Phineas. This was one historic home that had definitely gone all to rat shit.

I peeked around the end of the sagging verandah to the parking area alongside the house. A Lincoln Town Car in a pale metallic shade indicated that Miss Henley had already arrived. It was a lot of car for one retired teacher, but she'd always favored full-size domestic models. I stamped my feet to keep warm. What was keeping her? Probably just a typical Henley power trip. For the second time, I banged the brass door knocker.

"Try a little patience," said a peremptory and familiar voice.

Seconds later the massive oak door creaked open. I pulled myself up to my full height of four foot eleven and a half inches. The red knee-high leather boots with the stiletto heels and the killer points boosted me to five-three and a half.

Miss Henley didn't recognize me.

She hadn't changed a bit. She must have been well past seventy, but she had retained her splendid posture and the iron helmet of hair, hard enough to bruise your knuckles. Her grey eyes reminded me of a metal fence post on a winter day. Of course, she hadn't worn trousers in the classroom at St. Jude's, even charcoal, fine-tailored ones like these. The sweater was right though. Charcoal cashmere, unless I'm losing my instincts. Her only jewelry was a small pink and white cameo brooch. No rings, definitely no earrings. I glanced down and was not disappointed. Patent leather flats with small gold buckles, classy, well made, expensive. I figured they were Roberto Capucci's. Obviously, Miss Henley's Achilles' heel was in her shoes.

I smiled like a fellow shoe person and extended my hand. "Charlotte Adams. We have an appointment."

Two large tears trickled down her leathery cheeks. Tears are a part of this business although they don't usually start at the front door. But I was ready. I reached into my briefcase and held out a couple of man-size tissues.

"What can I do?" she asked in a slight tremolo, wiping her eyes.

"Well . . ." I said, filled with hope.

"My miserable cousin, Randolph, has left all this behind," she interrupted, twisting the tissues in her hands. "Look what he's done to this beautiful old house. Appalling. And the grounds." She gestured toward the neglected lawn. Shredded bits of damp tissue drifted to the floor.

"That's why I'm here, Miss Henley," I said. "Organized for Success. Remember?"

She snapped, "Of course I remember. Do you think I'm senile?"

"Not at all," I said, startled.

"It's all dreadful. Truly dreadful." She combined the sudden mood change with a sad glimpse at the grounds.

"We'll fix it," I said, glancing behind me to see nothing but swirling leaves. I turned back to face her.

"Weren't you one of my pupils?" she said.

I tried smiling again. "Yes."

The red-rimmed eyes narrowed. "I do believe I remember you."

"And I certainly remember you."

"Has your handwriting improved?"

"What?"

"Smudges all over your work."

I wasn't even in the house and already I was losing ground.

"You must have me mixed up with another student." Sally maybe or Margaret Tang or Jack Reilly or even my former friend, Pepper O'Day.

"Something else then. Math."

I stiffened. "A strong point."

"Social studies."

"Straight As."

"English language."

I raised my chin. "I should hardly think so."

"Oh yes, it's coming back to me. Attendance. Dismal record. You had that bizarre mother. Divorces. Scandals. It's a miracle you finished school. You were never there."

"I'm here now, Miss Henley."

"I thought you'd gone on to work in the city."

"Yes. Investment banking."

"Did you get fired?"

*"No."* Good grief. What had she heard?

"You have a pale line on your ring finger. I suppose that means you are recovering from a failed marriage."

Without thinking, I whipped my left hand behind my back. The pale line had been left by a square-cut diamond solitaire now lying on the bottom of the Hudson. Too bad my double-dealing dirty dog of an ex-fiancé hadn't dived in after it.

I said, "It does not."

"Well, what else would make you move back here?"

"Excuse me?" I said, frostily.

"I must ask myself if you could be equal to a task of this magnitude."

"You're right, Miss Henley. You should find someone else." I pivoted perfectly on my stiletto heels and stalked off toward the sweeping staircase with its rotting boards. I kept my nose in the air but gripped the banister on my way down. No point in ruining a perfectly good exit by plunging down the steps and snapping my neck.

"You were always a drama queen," Miss Henley called out. "You might as well come in and see what we have to contend with."

I said, after a slow reverse pivot, "Keep in mind this is a business relationship and I expect to be treated—"

"Yes, yes," she said, disappearing into the gloom.

Seconds later I got her point about magnitude. The narrow path through newspapers stacked at least six feet high filled a foyer that would have been splendid under normal circumstances.

The paper gave off a whiff of mildew. I also noted the unmistakable reek of mice. Miss Henley forged on as if she'd gotten used to it, although perhaps she just had a head cold. I stopped and stared around and up. Wall-to-wall, floor-to-ceiling junk. Boxes, tools, building materials, frames, even a few broken lawn chairs. Here and there, I glimpsed rich red wallpaper and elaborate crown moldings, half hidden by spiderwebs and grime. Several heavy oak beams leaned haphazardly against paper towers. I didn't see any sign of beams on the ceiling. Had these been salvaged from another historic property? For what? They'd be another challenge for my team if I got the job.

Every room was choked with paper, garbage, and trivia. I spotted the odd item that might be worth a few dollars to collectors, but by and large, any valuable items were smothered by a thick layer of rubbish. As we proceeded through the house, from the first floor with its formerly grand parlor and dining room, to the spacious second-floor bedrooms, and finally to the third floor that had probably once been the servants' quarters, one thing was clear: the place was a disaster. Okay, make that two things: it was also a firetrap.

"Forget the basement," Miss Henley said, as we descended from the second floor. "We'd never get down the stairs. I've cleared a space in the kitchen. And I've just made hot tea. There will be room for us to sit, while I define the task."

Miss Henley steered past a tangle of broken lamps. "Watch out for wires. You might trip and kill yourself in those ridiculous boots."

I could have suggested she find herself an organizer whose footwear suited her better, but I chose to watch for wires instead. The kitchen took me by surprise. It was hard to know what was most striking. The piles of rags on the antique stove? The row of truck tires? Or maybe the overflowing kitty litter?

Two chairs were pulled out from a crowded table. A small bit of surface had been cleared in front of each.

"Have a seat, Charlotte Adams," Miss Henley said.

I sat. After a minute I decided it might be safe to set my briefcase down. I kept my jacket on, since Henley House seemed even colder inside. The lovely smell of wood smoke sure hadn't come from here.

Miss Henley handed me a cup and saucer.

"There's no milk or sugar," she said

"Thank you. I'll take it as it is." Hot was all that mattered.

I reached into the briefcase for my red notebook and the Celtic-patterned pewter pen I've had since my sixteenth birthday. I opened the notebook to the page I'd already earmarked as *Henley House Project* and clicked my lucky pen confidently. Call me a young fogy, but I prefer my connection to paper over the benefits of electronics.

Miss Henley sat on the other chair. "Here is the situation. I have always been the poor Henley relation. I'm not complaining. I had a career I enjoyed. I have invested wisely and I have a good pension. My wretched cousin Randolph ran my grandfather's home into the ground. Now see what I have to deal with."

I had a flashback of how Miss Henley dealt with people she didn't much care for. I felt a flicker of sympathy for the late Randolph Henley. He was better off dead than facing his cousin. "I can recommend a good hauler to drag the garbage to the landfill," I said.

"It's not that easy."

"I think—"

"You think wrong, Charlotte Adams. Randolph is laughing at me from beyond the grave."

"What do you mean?"

Miss Henley gave me a triumphant grin. "I mean he set me up. So if I followed your advice, I'd be in real trouble, wouldn't I?"

I sensed I was about to lose a point. "Why?"

"Are you going to let me finish or not?"

"Go ahead." I tried to sound magnanimous.

"Randolph was born nasty. Always playing mean games on the other children. He could ruin any celebration. Thanksgiving. Birthday parties. Christmas was his specialty."

"What did he do?"

"Toys disappeared. Whatever you cared about. Your shoes. Your gifts. Your puppy."

I gasped. My sympathy for Randolph evaporated.

Miss Henley took a minute to pull herself together. "He was an evil child and he grew up to become a wicked man."

I had a hazy memory of a shriveled man in a stained three-piece suit and a yellow bow tie. Suit and tie were always dotted with stains. For sure he'd been a sloppy eater and a pack rat. But given Miss Henley's critical nature, I gave him the benefit of the doubt on the evil label.

"Are you listening?" Miss Henley said.

"Of course," I said.

"There are papers I need. Documents. Randolph has hidden them."

"What kind of papers?"

"Legal documents. Several items. Not necessarily valuable, but of great historical significance."

"Well, if you tell me exactly what we're searching for . . ."

A flash of steel from the grey eyes. "If I knew what and where, I wouldn't need your services, would I?"

"How do you know he hid these documents?"

"For reasons I don't wish to go into, I believe that Randolph was playing a very dangerous game. He had the use of this property for his lifetime. In trust. After his death, the property was to pass to me."

"Also in trust?"

"No. I am the next oldest and inherit it outright. My cousin Olivia Henley Simonett is the only other relative left. She's richer than God, so Grandfather didn't feel she needed more money. And rightly so." She sniffed. "I plan to transfer the deed to the Woodbridge Historical Society, once we've found the documents. Of course, we'll have to ensure it's in better shape than this. The Henley name is attached to it."

"Do these documents have to do with your inheritance?"

"All that should matter to *you* is that *I* require them."

Right. I wrote down "missing documents???" and left it at that. "So to recap, you want me to recommend a way to eliminate this chaos while searching for documents that can't be described or discussed."

"I want you to find them."

Something snakelike brushed against my ankle and I screamed.

"Have you never seen a cat before?" Miss Henley said. "Another miserable legacy from Randolph, but hardly worth shrieking over."

I'll decide what's worth shrieking over, I thought. "Do you have any idea where these, um, documents might be?"

"They'll be someplace inconvenient. Possibly dangerous."

"Ah. In that case, I imagine your cousin planted them in the newspapers."

"That sounds like him."

"Maximum inconvenience."

"I see that you're getting the point."

"Of course, he might have put the newspapers here to slow your search. Not to mention providing a handy fire hazard. I recommend you deal with the newspapers first. They impede access to other potential hiding places. I'll hire a team to comb through the papers, carefully. Since the team members won't know what to look for, I'll get two people to check each newspaper. Then we can discard them."

She frowned. "Not until I have the documents."

"No problem. After they've been checked, we'll stick them in temporary storage. When the documents turn up, we dispose of the newspapers."

Miss Henley gave her familiar snort. "As long as I find what I want in time."

"With the papers removed, we can move on to the clothing, concentrating on pockets and linings. We'll have easy access to furniture. We'll check under tables, beneath beds and sofas. We'll hunt for items sewn into cushions or upholstery."

Miss Henley brightened. "Sewn into cushions. I hadn't thought of that."

"Next, we'll check loose wallpaper and examine the backing of paintings and photos. I'll get the artwork valued, if you want."

She sniffed. "And if the documents aren't found?"

"At some point, we'd inspect the china, crystal, and silver, if there is any."

"Of course there is. Randolph kept all the family heirlooms. After all, this was the Henley House."

"Then the china and silver might be worth a lot. You don't have a security system here. You should get one or have valuables moved until your search is completed. Before they've been removed, we'll look between the plates, in the felt wraps for the silverware, inside the coffee and tea services, under trays."

"You've done this type of job before?"

"It's my job." Maybe not exactly like this.

"Not that organizing drivel," she said. "I mean searching for missing documents."

Well, I'd read enough Nancy Drew in my childhood to get the drift. "It's all a matter of logic and planning."

"Fine. You're hired."

"Great," I said, jotting down the requirements for sorting and disposal. "I'll draw up an itemized contract with a timetable for your signature tomorrow morning."

"Then you can start immediately."

"As soon as you've signed the contract."

Miss Henley reached down and picked up her handbag. She snapped it open and extracted her checkbook. I watched as she wrote out a check, in my name. She waved it under my nose. "A retainer. To engage your services. It should be enough to get you started."

I said, "First, we need to get a liability insurance rider set up to cover the site. I wouldn't want one of my sorters or movers to get hurt."

"You're already stalling. You've got two weeks to get it done. No more. You can name your price, but that deadline holds. Take it or leave it, Charlotte Adams."

You'd think, at some point, I would have asked myself why anyone would want this job. I imagined my mother's voice, shrieking, "Wait. What's the catch?" But who listens to her mother?

"It's a deal." I slid the check into my briefcase. Now why didn't that make me feel all warm and fuzzy?

# 2

By the time I deposited Miss Henley's check through the ATM on Hudson Street, I was in desperate need of black and white fudge from Kristee's Kandees, which was right around the corner. But, oh crap, Kristee's was unaccountably closed. That was very bad. The meeting with Miss Henley had depleted my serotonin levels. Black and white fudge would have raised them. I formed Plan B, which was to head straight for Hannaford's and the candy aisle. But that was before the line of police cars shot by with roof lights flashing and sirens wailing, splashing my clean car and taking my mind off fudge.

I kept my eyes open in case I spotted trouble in the form of the upturned nose and expensive blonde hair of Pepper Monahan, née O'Day. At home, Pepper had been Mrs. Nick Monahan for the past two years. And about Nick Monahan, the less said the better. At work, Pepper had been recently promoted to detective sergeant in the Woodbridge Police. Once she'd been my very best friend in the world. But that was then.

The cop cars were clustered around a battered baby blue
Honda Civic, crumpled nose first into the guardrail. I swung
past, keeping my head low. Another patrol car, lights flashing, blocked the intersection. So much for getting to Hannaford's.

Plan C. I turned left to avoid the problem, drove around
the block, and pulled up in front of Tang's Convenience. I
was grateful that attempts at trendy redevelopment uptown
hadn't changed Tang's much. It had ten times more stuff
than you'd expect to find in a store that size, plus many intriguing concessions to the changing demographic in Woodbridge. Inside, I picked out some nice navel oranges and
headed to the back for the ice cream. I'd just turned by the
ten-pound sacks of basmati rice when a guy with light
brown hair and sad eyes careened into me. We both claimed
to be sorry and kept going. I ignored him when I arrived at
the cooler and found him there ahead of me. I was angling to
reach the Ben & Jerry's when he fumbled a tub of ice cream.
I yelped in surprise when it landed on my foot. I teetered on
the four-inch heels.

"Gosh, I'm sorry," my attacker said. He grabbed my
arm just in time to keep me from toppling backward into a
detergent display.

I latched onto his leather jacket as I tried to get my bal-
ance. Maybe I was just thrown off by a man who said "gosh."
I found that sort of charming. Now that I got closer, his eyes
were more like a shy woodland creature's. Large, dark, and
vulnerable. My weakness.

Here was a man who would easily pass inspection by any
of my girlfriends. Even Sally would have approved. I knew
that his simple leather jacket and faded jeans were the current trend in the city. He was carrying a camera case. That
seemed interesting.

His forehead wrinkled. "I don't usually throw ice cream
at unsuspecting women. Or not Neapolitan anyway."

"These things happen," I said with as much dignity as the situation permitted. "Especially with Neapolitan."

He managed a lopsided grin that went straight to my knees.

I blushed.

How dumb was that? Hadn't I sworn never to think about another man after my craptacular engagement? If not, I certainly should have.

He picked up the tub of ice cream and said, "No broken toes?"

"My feet are fine."

I watched him amble away and wondered where my notorious wit was when I needed it. *My feet are fine?* Not that it mattered because here was a guy who made my knees melt on first sight, so naturally I'd already spotted his wedding band. I didn't need a man in my life. Not even one who fumbled ice cream and said "gosh" and looked really good in those faded jeans. This jerk had a wife he should have been thinking about.

Five minutes later, I headed to the counter with two tubs of Ben & Jerry's New York Super Fudge Chunk ice cream and a fistful of Mars bars.

I smiled bravely at Mrs. Tang. She never acknowledges me even though her daughter Margaret has been my friend since grade school. Margaret has never been big on small talk either.

"Hang on a minute." I scurried back to the cooler and grabbed a third tub of ice cream. I believe it pays to be prepared.

I slid my business card across the counter along with my cash. "Mrs. Tang, can you tell Margaret I'm back in town? Ask her to call me, please."

Like me, Margaret had returned to Woodbridge. She was supposed to be setting up a law practice, but she wasn't in the phone book yet. Mrs. Tang's expression remained unchanged. This was the third card I'd left with her. Three times lucky maybe.

"Already paid," Mrs. Tang said.

"What?"

"Man paid." Mrs. Tang pointed toward the window. I saw Mr. Gosh I'm Unavailable amble out of sight.

I left swinging the plastic bag and whistling bravely.

On the sidewalk, I froze. There were now seven patrol cars at the corner of River and Hudson. I didn't think we had that many in Woodbridge. I spotted an unmarked black sedan with a snap-on round red light. Sure enough, Pepper stepped out, thin as a whippet and wearing a form-fitting black coat that made her seem more like a model than a detective. She glanced around elegantly.

I wasn't about to find out what was going on. On a day where I'd had to deal with Miss Henley, I couldn't face Pepper without a chocolate fix. Call me chicken, but I slipped discreetly into the alley next to Tang's, unwrapped a Mars bar, and ate it in two bites. I waited where I could see but not be seen. I stayed there until Pepper disappeared down the block, accompanied by a cluster of uniformed officers. They kept their hands on the butts of their weapons. But whatever they were doing down at the end of Hudson Street was none of my business.

I made a dash to my car, made a first-rate U-turn, and raced like hell for home. I took some mean-spirited pleasure thinking that Pepper probably couldn't chug-a-lug New York Super Fudge Chunk with impunity and keep that figure.

Seemed only fair.

---

I pulled into the driveway and felt the warm glow that comes from getting home on a wet November workday when it's already dark in the late afternoon. The pale yellow wood-frame Victorian with the gingerbread trim was starting to feel like my own place. A welcoming light burned in the window of my tiny, perfect second-floor apartment.

I spotted a face in the first-floor bay window as I parked and struggled out of the car with my purchases and brief-case. Dim streetlights reflected off rimless glasses. The glasses suited Jack Reilly. They were just right for his cute old-young-guy look. Perfect for a onetime dweeb with an equal interest in nineteenth-century European philosophy, high-end racing bicycles, and animals in need of rescue. Normally, I would have loved to stop and chat with Jack. But I needed a few minutes alone to calm my spirit. I planned to put my medicine cabinet in order. Or maybe fluff my towels.

I wasn't fast enough. Jack's door swung open. He leaned his six-foot-two lanky body casually against the frame. Be-hind him, where anyone else would have living room furni-ture, I could see the stock from the cycle shop he was planning to set up. I reminded myself that Jack is my good buddy and landlord, not my client, and the state of his liv-ing room is none of my concern. Who knows? Maybe hanging tires from ceiling hooks is a cutting-edge trend in interior design.

"By any chance, could I interest you in a dog?" he said.

I wasn't fooled by his expression of extreme innocence. From behind my door on the second floor came the unmis-takable sounds of the last dogs Jack had tried to interest me in.

"I'm trying to cut down. But thanks for asking."

"It's not a terribly large dog. Not huge," he said.

"Nope."

"Harmless, affectionate, well behaved." He leaned over and called up the stairs.

"Actually, I'm good for dogs right at the moment," I said over my shoulder.

Jack was undeterred. "The kind of dog who could save your life in an emergency."

Like what? A St. Bernard? "It's so not happening, Jack."
I scurried up the stairs and stuck my key in the lock. I felt a
bit silly with a brand-new, high-end dead bolt now that I
was back in Woodbridge where a fender bender brings out
seven cop cars and a police detective.

Jack's size-thirteen Nikes thumped on the stairs after me,
although it was hard to hear above the yipping. I opened the
door and braced myself for the assault. Two small velvety
creatures launched themselves at me, their metronome tails
working hard. Truffle, the black mini dachshund, and Sweet
Marie, the tan one, were ready with homecoming kisses.

Unconditional love. I needed that.

The phone screamed. Naturally, I reached for the receiver. A lifetime of conditioning is a curse.

"Are you all right?" Sally shrieked.

I stood in my tiny front entrance, with the door open to
the stairs, holding the phone with one hand, while the dogs
leaped joyously, tugging at my grocery essentials. I dropped
my house keys. The bag from Tang's followed. The dogs
went after the spilled goodies.

"Can I call you back? This isn't the perfect time. You
two leave those Mars bars. I mean it."

"Come on, you must have been traumatized. Remember
how terrified we used to be? That hideous old bat. I hope
you told her to take her stinky old project straight to hell."

"I'm not traumatized and I am taking on the project."

"How could you after everything she did to us?"

"Can we talk later? I just got in."

The fact was I didn't think I could explain to Sally why I
wanted this. It wasn't just the potential media exposure. It
was Miss Henley herself. Sure I'd been terrified of her.
Everyone had been. But I'd been impressed too. Miss Henley's classroom had been a model of order, her desk a work
of art. Her lesson plans were done a month in advance;
color-coded highlighting illustrated her board notes. Her
files were the same size, with crisply printed labels. She was

never late, never flustered, and never chaotic. I was sure she'd never missed deadlines or had awkward man trouble, like say, for instance, my mother. I couldn't imagine that Miss Henley's underwear ever turned up draped over lamps. She understood the value of written goals and milestones. And she always wore such lovely shoes.

Sally said, "I want to hear all the gruesome details. I was so afraid for you."

"I'll fill you in tomorrow."

"I won't be able to stand the suspense."

"Be strong."

I bent down and snatched a Mars bar from Truffle. Luckily, an orange rolled under the hall console and both dogs raced after it, teeth bared. They lost interest in a few seconds and made a bid for the Ben & Jerry's containers. Sweet Marie spotted the keys, and I had a serious tussle to get those back.

"I have to get my ice cream in the fridge. It's already melting."

"Remember who your friends are, Charlotte," Sally said before she hung up.

Meanwhile Jack had arrived and repositioned the chair in my entryway. He was sprawled, waiting, with his long legs stretched out. Bike boy was wearing shorts in November. Still he'd been kind enough to lift the Ben & Jerry's out of harm's way. "Wow. Three tubs," he said.

"You betcha."

"Ben & Jerry's too."

"Nothing but the best for the best people."

"Maybe it's time for me to get out of the bike business. Where'd you get it? On sale somewhere?"

"Tang's."

"You must be kidding. You bought three containers of Ben & Jerry's from Tang's? Did you win the lottery?"

"The cops were blocking the way to Hannaford's."

"Really? What was going on?"

"Just a lot of flashing lights."

"More than that. The radio said it was some kind of shooting," Jack said, staring with longing at the Ben & Jerry's.

"A shooting? In Woodbridge? Unbelievable. That explains why Pepper was there."

"Pepper? No way. You talked to her?" He attempted to remove the lid from one of the containers.

"Hands off the treats, Jack. And no, I didn't talk to her."

"You just let her walk by?"

I must have looked a bit sheepish because Jack said, "Baaaaa."

I threw a Mars bar at him. "Cut it out."

"Did big scary Sergeant Pepper speak to you then?"

I said, "She didn't see me. Now get out of my way. I have to walk the dogs."

"You want me to put this stuff in the freezer?"

"Thanks. Make sure it's uneaten and unopened."

"Take your time." Jack is always patient. That's more than I can say for Truffle and Sweet Marie.

"Are you kidding? It's pouring rain out. These cream puffs will be back in a New York minute."

I picked up the dog leashes and made a lunge for Sweet Marie. She's the hard one to catch.

Jack said, "Why don't I make some dinner and we can talk about that other dog opportunity when you get back?"

Jack's an enthusiastic cook. The problem is, his kitchen's so full of bike parts he can't reach the stove. He creates a cyclone in my miniature galley kitchen every time he gets the urge to sauté. Anyway, my plan was to have a large bowl of Super Fudge Chunk for dinner. It's my signature dish. I thought Mars bars would make an elegant dessert.

"No thanks to dinner and dog."

Jack said, "Let me know if you change your mind."

I snapped the leash on Sweet Marie. "There will be no other dog, Jack. See these two? They're quite enough."

Jack picked up the rest of the oranges and deposited them

on my tiny kitchen counter. "No harm in trying. This poor fella is due to be euthanized."

"Low blow, Jack. I didn't just fall off the ice-cream truck, you know. And, speaking of ice cream, you stay away from that Ben & Jerry's."

"You think you can't trust me? I'm your friend."

"Leave it. This means you."

I thumped down the stairs with a dog under each arm. Okay, I was smiling. There are way worse fates than having a couple of souped-up pooches and a landlord who is big in pet rescue. And who could fix your bicycle and engage you in a conversation about Heidegger at the same time. If that was what you needed.

Most women would be driven nuts by the fact that Jack rarely opened his mail, or that he loved to cook but never had any ingredients. Any woman with a tendency to plan might think Jack should finish his PhD, ditch the bike shop, get a real job, and start contributing to a 401(k). He might be damned cute with that lean body, the mussed-up hair, and that lopsided goofy grin, but he'd be a serious relationship challenge. If he were your boyfriend, your first task would be to change him.

But friends accept each other the way they are. So five minutes later we were curled up in my cozy living room. Jack took my word for it: aside from unconditional dog love, sometimes the only solution to getting your life back on target is the right ice cream. This was one of those times. I decided I could refresh the medicine cabinet and fluff the towels later.

Of course, if Jack were a girlfriend, by this point we both would have chucked our bras, and jumped into flannel pajamas and fluffy slippers. We would feel we could cry if we needed to. Even after all these years, I wasn't on crying terms with Jack.

He said, "I can't imagine you stuck in a creepy old building with Hellfire Henley."

I shrugged and poked at my container to get the last chunk stuck in the corner.

Jack said, "I'm impressed. To go right into her lair, without backup. That took guts."

I said modestly, "Sally offered and I turned her down. I don't know what you two are going on about. She's just an elderly lady with a problem."

"I remember how you stood up to her in class to save Pepper's butt. You earned the undying respect of everyone in the class at that point."

"Pepper would have done the same for me, back then," I said.

I did not add that she wouldn't have needed to. I didn't go to school with long sleeves on to hide my bruises. My mother might have made the tongues wag, but she never would have let one of the many men in her life beat me.

Jack said, "Yeah, but you were the only one with the nerve. Tell me you're not going to do that job."

"Let it go, Jack," I said, scraping hard at the bottom of the ice-cream container with my spoon.

Jack patted my hand. Soothingly.

That caused me to blurt, "Miss Henley's just a troubled old woman with a sadistic streak. I'm way more upset by nearly running into Pepper at Tang's."

Jack said, "But you said you didn't speak to her."

I blushed. "I dived into that alley by Tang's to avoid her. How brave is that? She didn't even see me. Stop laughing. It is so not funny."

"One of these days, you're going to run into her for real. Then what?"

Jack doesn't know what really went wrong with Pepper. Maybe someday I'll tell him.

We both jumped as the telephone trilled.

"Hey, let it ring," Jack said. "Might be Hellfire."

I laughed and reached for the phone. "Probably just

Sally. I forgot to call her back. Or Margaret Tang. I've been trying to reach her."

"Charlotte Adams, please."

Crap. "Oh, yes, Miss Henley."

"Told you so," Jack mouthed.

I turned my back. "What can I do for you?" I said.

"You can meet me at the Henley House in ten minutes."

I have been in business long enough to know that if you don't put limits on what your clients can ask, you're dead in the water. It's best to set boundaries early and firmly.

"I'm afraid I'm tied up, Miss Henley."

"That doesn't matter. I must see you immediately."

"Sorry," I said. "I can be there tomorrow."

"That won't do."

"What's wrong? Can we discuss it by phone?"

"I gave you a check."

"And I can give it back to you." I bluffed.

"Fine. I'll have to deal with it myself."

"I'll see you in the morning. How's ten o'clock? Your place or the Henley House? Hello?" I frowned at the phone. "Well, how do you like that? She hung up. Now I have to call her back and settle on a time and place."

Jack peered up from his ice cream and grinned. "Your point. Don't ruin it by calling her back tonight. That's what she wants."

"You're right. I'll deal with it tomorrow." I fished out my agenda. "Let me just make a note to do it first. Hey, have you seen my lucky pen?"

Jack shook his head.

"I didn't mean you," I said, giving Truffle and Sweet Marie a look. "I meant the resident thieves."

"Innocent until proven guilty. It'll show up," Jack said. "It doesn't really matter what you use, does it? Try mine."

It did to me, but I kept that to myself.

Jack was saying, "I'm glad you didn't let her push you around. Hey, weren't there three tubs of this stuff?"

"Maybe."

"Why don't we split the third to celebrate your close call? And then we can move on to the Mars bars."

"Someday, I hope to find a man who values me for myself and not my Mars bars," I said. A face popped into my mind. Big sad eyes. I nipped that in the bud. I deserved better. So did his wife.

Truffle and Sweet Marie wagged their tails.

"You're right, guys. I have you."

⸺ ❈ ⸺

What possessed me to flick on the local news before bed? I should know better. My routine is to tidy up my apartment, polish off any e-mails, and turn off the computer. Then I write out my next day's to-do list, lay out my clothes, brush and floss, slather on green tea face cream, and curl up between my yummy silky sheets with a book. Not too exciting, I admit. Just relaxing, fragrant, soothing activities to ensure a good night's sleep. But for whatever the reason, that night I flicked the remote and sat back.

WINY hotshot Todd Tyrell flashed his super-white phony smile across the screen. I flinched, but then I always do when I see his face. My finger automatically moved toward the Off button, when I spotted the scene behind him. My finger stayed suspended as the camera panned to the crumpled blue Honda I'd seen that afternoon. Usually I tune out Todd Tyrell's irritating voice. He hypes up every mundane event in the region.

Todd ran a manicured hand slightly over his gelled hair. "Police in Woodbridge have confirmed that the body found in a vehicle in uptown late this afternoon was the victim of a drive-by shooting."

This time the camera panned to Pepper as she barked orders to uniformed officers around the car. The camera lingered on her a bit longer than was absolutely necessary for news value. She put up her hand to wave them away, but I couldn't help but notice she turned to show her most flattering angle. I'd seen her practice that in front of the mirror often enough.

Ignore Pepper, I told myself. I thought the nonuniformed people must have been forensic technicians or crime-scene investigators. Thanks to television, I know way more than I want to about stuff like that.

Todd's mouth hadn't stopped moving. "Police have not revealed the name of the deceased, but WINY has learned unofficially that the victim, a fifty-nine-year-old female Caucasian, had been shot a short time before crashing her 1986 Honda into the parking gate near a busy grocery store. A dying woman was able to weave her car down a major street without being seen, without the police being called, and without a single soul coming to help. When respectable women are being murdered in this town, has Woodbridge become unsafe for its citizens? Stay tuned to WINY as details of this gripping story unfold."

As a recent resident of New York City, I had a tendency to roll my eyes when Todd Tyrell went on his pet rants about personal security in the area. Leave it to Mr. Toothy to turn a tragedy like this into yet another opportunity for self-aggrandizement.

But while I tossed and turned that night, I did wonder what was going on in safe little Woodbridge.

*Never place a large object over a smaller one.*

# 3

Miss Henley didn't answer her phone when I called right after breakfast to confirm the place for our meeting. It was just like her not to have an answering machine. The ball stayed in my court.

I'd been up since six with plenty to do. I whisked the dogs down the stairs and outside for their early-morning routine. While I had a quick shower and shampoo, they slithered back to bed.

I worked out the project plan on paper first, using my second-best pen. I polished up the contract based on my estimate, using the boilerplate form in my computer. I added the unique details and included a formula for extra fees if the job held any surprises. In this case, surprises wouldn't surprise me. At nine I made a few calls and got my sorters and packers lined up, subject to the signing of the contract that morning. I arranged for a truck and got a great deal on short-term storage plus a quote for the insurance rider to cover my staff. At nine thirty, I pressed Print.

Things were moving along. I called Sally to set a time to drop in to see her, the kids, and the wall-to-wall toys. I didn't mention I was heading out to see Hellfire Henley first.

She said, "Dallas and Madison are so excited about the toy project. Even baby Savannah. They've got it narrowed down to fifteen favorite items each."

"Seven," I said. "Absolute maximum."

"What a kidder. By the way, bring your puppies. That will be great."

Oh, sure it would. There are good reasons why Sally's life is full of love and chaos. I tried Miss Henley a half hour later. No answer. No machine. I made several other attempts in between other tasks.

I doubled-checked Miss Henley's home address and then reached for my car keys. I am always careful to place them in the attractive lacquered tray on the hall console near my door. The tray was empty. I whirled. Two small intelligent faces watched me with interest. I raised my voice. "Not again!"

A pair of streaks vanished from view.

"No damn wonder you two had to be rescued. You're nothing but thieves."

From under the sofa four wicked eyes gleamed. Two sets of pointy teeth grinned.

"How could you get up on that console to get . . . oh, right. Jack just has to move the furniture around every visit. And he thought I'd be up for another dog."

This was an excellent game as far as the pooches were concerned. Perfect, if you had four feet and no prioritized to-do list.

After five minutes of checking behind the hamper, under the sofa, and in my newspaper basket, I said, "Okay, I give up. Find the keys and we'll drive to the park."

Well, who would have thought to check in my slippers? Next time, I'd start there.

I gave Truffle and Sweet Marie a stern finger wagging. "But there'd better not be a next time."

———— ++ ————

I turned on the car radio and caught the tail end of the news. "Woodbridge Police have released the name of yesterday's shooting victim. Fifty-nine-year-old Wynona Banks was gunned down while at the wheel of her car, which later crashed into a barrier at the end of Hudson Street. Mrs. Banks was pronounced dead on arrival at Woodbridge General Hospital. No further details are available."

I shivered. I'd never heard of Wynona Banks, but I felt a wave of pity. What a terrible way to end your life. I flicked off the radio.

Ten minutes later, I pulled up in front of Miss Henley's small, neat federal-style house on the historic fringe of uptown Woodbridge. I left Truffle and Sweet Marie in the car with the window down an inch. Any more and they could wiggle out and head for Vegas.

"Just a quick visit, you guys," I said. "Then we hit the park. Not that you deserve it, but there's no rain today."

I buzzed and waited, knowing how she liked to keep people waiting. Ten minutes later, I concluded that no amount of buzzing and knocking would get an answer.

Fine. Time to try the Henley House. I headed straight for the car, where the dogs had managed to knock over my briefcase and drag out the contents. Luckily, I'd had the quote and contract for Miss Henley with me. Your fault, toots, their expressions said. You were gone soooo long.

I reassembled my briefcase, lectured the dogs sternly, and gunned the Miata.

———— ++ ————

Miss Henley's Town Car was parked at a dashing angle near the far end of the long driveway outside the number one moldering ruin in Woodbridge.

I took the dogs with me. I didn't feel like putting my briefcase back together yet again. This would be quick. We marched toward the massive front door. Oddly enough, I was feeling well disposed toward Miss Henley. Thanks to her, I'd learned to stand up to people I was afraid of. I could stare down the most deranged client, the vilest colleague, the slimiest ex-fiancé. This was truly a gift that kept on giving.

The heavy front door stood open. Truffle and Sweet Marie bounded up the stairs.

"Miss Henley," I called when I reached the door. I waited, shivering a bit in the nippiness. Winter was already in the air. The dogs shivered too. This would be our first winter together. Maybe they were going to need little coats.

"Miss Henley," I called louder this time. The dogs added their voices to mine, not that this was helpful. "Sorry I'm late. I thought you were at your home.

"Shh, you guys," I said to the dogs. "This is hard enough."

Nothing.

"Hello?"

At least the dogs had stopped barking. I stepped inside and shouted. "Miss Henley! It's Charlotte."

As I waited, Truffle and Sweet Marie dashed past me and tore through the path in the mile-high newspapers lining the hallway, knocking over a garden rake propped next to one of the stacks and sending a baseball bat rolling.

Oh crap. That was all I needed. What if Miss Henley flattened them with a broom?

"Truffle! Sweet Marie! Come back."

I narrowly avoided stepping on the rake and probably knocking myself out. I pushed the baseball bat off to the side.

In the kitchen I found no sign of Miss Henley or the dogs. Not good. Somewhere in the distance Truffle and Sweet Marie set up a wild racket. The barking sounded like it was coming from the dining room. I ran, stumbling over bits of debris, old toy cars, empty cornflakes boxes, and a clothesline. I narrowly missed crashing into two oak beams leaning at crazy angles. I'd already made a note to get those put away safely as soon as the team showed up. I kept an eye out for more beams as I careened through the junk.

The stiletto boots were not made for running. I tripped and snagged my best hose on a pile of rusty springs scattered on the floor. Finally I rounded a corner and spotted Truffle and Sweet Marie. They were yipping at a pile of newspapers that had toppled over and blocked the path. They must have cornered a mouse. Or worse, that cat.

"Come away and leave whatever it is."

Okay, so obedience is not their best thing.

"Miss Henley will tear strips off us for making this mess even worse, you turkeys."

I reached forward to scoop them up and stopped, stunned. I climbed over the fallen stack of paper. I pushed the dogs away and fell to my knees. Sticking out from under the toppled pile was a pair of shoes, black patent, with small gold buckles. Classy, expensive. Roberto Capucci's unless I was mistaken.

The shoes had feet in them, feet with nice-quality trouser socks. There were legs too, covered in charcoal wool.

Miss Henley.

What was I doing thinking about shoes and socks and worsted wool? The unimaginable had happened. Frantically I tugged at her feet. A shoe came off in my hand. For some reason, the foot was rigid. I scrambled to free her from the pile of paper. The dogs raced around yelping.

First things first.

I reached into my handbag with one hand and fished out my cell phone. I tried to pull the piles of paper from Miss Henley with my free hand.

911.

"Woman under a pile of rotting newspaper," I shouted.

"Can I have your name?"

"Charlotte Adams. This is an emergency."

"Charlotte Adams. Wow. I remember you. I heard you were back in town. This is Mona Pringle."

"Mona Pringle? I don't think I—"

"Yeah, yeah, St. Jude's. Grade eight. I was Mona Jones then."

What the hell? Even in Woodbridge, emergencies should be taken seriously. "There's an emergency here, Mona."

Mona got the point. "Sure. Can I have your location?"

"We're in the dining room. I don't know if she's breathing," I said. "Her feet aren't moving. They're . . . I think she may be . . ."

"Calm down, Charlotte. I mean the address."

"Sorry, sorry, sorry. I'm at the Henley House. Top of North Elm at Washington Avenue. It's the big house on the corner."

"I know it. What exactly is the situation?"

"Miss Henley is buried under a stack of . . ." I paused. Perhaps newspapers would sound insufficiently dangerous.

"What?"

"Debris," I said. "She's buried under debris."

"Charlotte?"

"Yes."

"Is that Hellfire Henley you're talking about?"

I raised my voice. "I have to put down the phone and try to dig her out. Hurry up and get someone here!"

"The paramedics are on their way. Is she breathing?"

"She might be suffocating." I dropped the phone and hoped Mona could hear. An unintelligible crackle came from the phone.

With both hands, I tossed papers over my shoulders. The dogs raced around in circles, happy to play. My shoulders ached as I yanked layer after layer away. The smell of rotting paper and rodents was overwhelming. What must it be like for Miss Henley buried under there? How had the paper fallen over on her?

I kept shouting, "Miss Henley. I'll get this off you in a minute. You can make it."

The question I didn't really want to ask kept surfacing in my mind. Had Truffle and Sweet Marie caused the paper to cascade, trapping Miss Henley? As I yanked another stinking chunk of paper away, I whacked my hand on something hard.

I yelped.

With my other hand, I pulled off another clump of paper. I stared at an oak beam stuck in the middle of the paper pile.

The beam was too heavy for me to move. I swept away a bit more paper and jerked back. Part of Miss Henley's charcoal sweater was clearly visible. But the beam lay on the point where her head would be.

My vision clouded. My head swam. My stomach turned. I screamed long and loud. No one heard, except for two small, very alarmed dogs.

"Stay away, guys," I yelled.

I tugged off more paper until I could see more of her chest and part of her arm. I sat back on my heels and tried to breathe. I stared at the small pink and white cameo brooch on her sweater and shook like a wet poodle.

It took every ounce of courage I had to reach forward and touch the arm. It was horribly cold. A ripple of relief shot through me. At least the dogs hadn't knocked over the paper and the beam. The relief was followed by a rush of guilt. Miss Henley was dead. An awful accident. I didn't want Truffle and Sweet Marie to be responsible for it. It would be my fault for letting them run loose.

There was no sign of the paramedics. I grabbed the cell phone. Mona seemed to have disconnected. My hands shook as I dialed Jack's number. Please don't screen this call, Jack, I prayed.

"Get over here quick," I said as soon as I heard his voice.

"Where's here?" he said cheerfully.

"Henley House. Miss Henley's buried in paper and I just got her partly dug out and her head's crushed and the paramedics aren't here yet."

"Try CPR."

"She's already cold and stiff."

"On my way."

As I hung up, I heard the shriek of an ambulance. I knew it was way too late.

Had she been there since last night when she'd called and asked me to meet her? Good grief. Maybe it really was my fault.

By the time emergency services arrived, mascara streaked my face. I smelled of mice poop and mold and I was starting to hyperventilate. Naturally, my dogs took a demonic dislike to the paramedics.

The paramedics didn't seem to hold a grudge. One of them draped me in a blanket and patted my shoulder.

The other one said, "Better watch out for shock. You don't look so hot, miss."

Truffle snarled at him. Both dogs struggled in my arms. Twenty-two pounds of combined fury. I used the blanket to keep them confined. I sat there sniffling while the paramedics worked to free Miss Henley's body.

Where was Jack? I wanted Jack there. Right that minute.

But next, a pair of police officers arrived, all business.

"What the hell happened here?" one of them said. "It's like a horror movie."

"Hellfire Henley," his partner said, glancing my way.

"Huh. Some kind of payback, I guess."

Minutes later, Jack burst through the door, covered in sweat from biking across town. My lower lip wobbled. I absolutely hate that. But that wasn't the worst part. The worst part was stepping along the cluttered hallway, heading toward us, svelte and willowy with elegant blonde high-lights and a form-fitting black wool coat.

"Why, Charlotte Adams," Pepper said, showing her sparkling teeth. "Isn't this a surprise?"

—◆—

"But why was she there at all?" I whimpered to Jack, once we were home, long after I'd given my statement and waited for Pepper to say it was all right to go. I was surprised at just how terrible I felt. Jack had dragged me off to Benjamin's office to make sure the shock wouldn't kill me. I now had a small vial of mood-altering substance in case I had night-mares, plus a pat on the head from a teddy-bear man with a white jacket, a stethoscope, and a sprained toe.

It was nice of Jack not to mention that my voice was still a bit funny hours later. Even though the heat was turned up to blast, I couldn't seem to get warm. I was bundled on my sofa and covered in a pair of Jack's mother's heirloom quilts, sipping hot cocoa prepared by Jack's own hand. The drinks had arrived on a tray with a plate of tiny shortbread cookies. The kitchen looked like a bomb had gone off. Jack had thoughtfully taken the phone off the hook and switched off my cell phone.

Jack had been entertaining Truffle and Sweet Marie by making paper airplanes. Apparently paper airplanes are fun to chase and chew up. Jack seemed to be enjoying himself too, except when I asked questions.

"Why was who there?" he said.

"The person we're talking about. Pepper."

"Take it easy. I wasn't sure if you meant Hellfire."

"Don't call her that, Jack. She's dead. You can't call her Hellfire anymore. And she had a good reason to be there. But why did Pepper show up?"

"I think you might be in shock."

"I can't get that sight out of my mind." I shivered.

"Drink your chocolate. It will help."

"If only I'd gone last night, it could have made a difference."

"We've been all over this. It is not your fault."

"But if I'd agreed to meet her, then it might not have happened. Maybe she felt overwhelmed and decided to get started on the project."

"When did you turn into a crazy lady?"

"It bothers me. I wish I knew when she died. Maybe it was right after she called me and—"

"I'm going out to get you some Mars bars."

"Well, I don't care what you say, Jack. It creeps me out that Pepper stuck her nose in so fast."

He paused at the head of the stairs. "She's a cop. It's her job to show up at accidents."

"It is not. She's a detective. It's her job to find crimes and blame people."

"What's your point? You go so over the top about Pepper."

"You're right. Maybe Mars bars will help."

"Coming up. One of these days you should make up with her."

"Maybe."

If hell froze over.

———

Hell froze over the next morning. I woke up and peered out the window to see an inch of snow covering the ground and a thick swirl of white in the air. Whee. Another November surprise. Apparently, Truffle and Sweet Marie do not do snow. They burrowed back under the covers. I gave up on my efforts to drag them out when they jumped onto the floor and scrambled under the bed.

Fine. I needed a cup of coffee before I crawled under the bed to catch them. While the coffee brewed, I squinted around at the mess in my living room. Empty Mars bars wrappers. Socks. Quilts tumbled from where I had fallen asleep on the sofa. Chewed-up paper airplanes on every surface. Except for the paper airplanes, it looked like the aftermath of a very kinky party.

How could I have gone to bed and left the place like that? I was shocked to realize that I hadn't even made my to-do list the night before. I could not remember the last time that had happened. I reminded myself that it wasn't every day I found a body.

I shook my head to clear that image and went about picking up the mess. Clean up first, drag out dogs second, make breakfast third. I tried not to think about Miss Henley and the horrible way she'd died. I'd promised Jack not to obsess.

As I was picking up the dog toys, I remembered Sally and her kids. I needed to apologize for not being able to sort out her kiddy chaos the day before and to make a new date before the day got away from both of us. It's never a good idea to put off apologies.

The aroma told me the coffee was ready. I poured a mugful and called her.

"Charlotte," Sally squealed. "I know. Benjamin told me. It's so awful. Turn on the news!"

"But—" I said.

"WINY," she said. "Todd's on. I'll call you back."

I sat on the sofa with coffee, picked up the remote, and despite my better judgment, clicked on WINY for the news. That must have been a sign of how upset I was about Miss Henley. I rarely turn the TV on during the day, particularly in the morning, and very most particularly WINY. But I should have known that Miss Henley's death would be news all over Upstate New York.

An understatement, as it turned out.

Woodbridge was in a major tizzy. Todd Tyrell stood outside Henley House, a light snow swirling around him. Not a single hair on his styled head moved, although the bare trees were practically snapping in the background. He was wearing his serious look. Todd has two expressions for his handsome made-for-television face. Serious and happy. Occasionally there's a third expression, best described as stunned, but I'm pretty sure that's not one of the official ones.

Obviously Todd isn't my hero, but Sally has had a crush on him since she was thirteen and he was a strutting senior. Marriage and motherhood haven't made much of a dent in her adulation. Go figure.

Todd adjusted his eyebrows to appear a bit more solemn and said, "Woodbridge is facing its second tragedy in less than two days with news of the death of beloved local schoolteacher, Miss Helen Henley."

I spewed a bit of coffee. "Beloved" had caught me off guard. As I mopped up, Todd went on. "Miss Henley perished in what, at first glance, seems like a tragic accident at this historic property in Woodbridge. Police are investigating but so far have not indicated foul play. Miss Henley was a formidable influence on generations of students at St. Jude's Catholic School. She will be deeply mourned by all whom she touched in life. That includes me, folks."

Todd screwed his face up a bit. I think he was trying for a new emotion. Could it have been grief? Or just a bad case of heartburn?

I sat there openmouthed. *Deeply mourned?* I'd been horrified by what had happened to Miss Henley, but it had never crossed my mind that she'd be mourned, that family and friends might grieve over her loss. And what did he mean by "so far"? I'd just flicked off the news when I noticed the loud banging at my door.

I assumed Jack was responsible for the racket. He's always keen on breakfast at my place. But why didn't he just walk in like every other time?

"Coming." I took another gulp of caffeine and flung open the door. I wore my old blue-striped flannel pajamas and my hot pink bunny slippers. My nose was red, my eyes bleary, and my hair stuck out in several directions, all of them just plain wrong.

Crap. Jack was nowhere to be seen. Instead, Pepper Monahan stood on my doorstep, looking coiffed, buffed, waxed, and very official.

"Good morning, Charlotte," she said.

"Glurk," I said, choking on the coffee.

"Problem?" She raised a professionally shaped eyebrow.

"No."

"You seem unsettled."

I said, "Huh?"

Of course I was unsettled. I could have had a cardiac arrest at the sight of Pepper at the best of times. Damned if I'd tell her that, although I was guessing she knew.

"Yes. Rattled even."

At that point Truffle and Sweet Marie remembered they were in charge of keeping strangers out. They shot into the room and hurled themselves at Pepper's legs. For added drama, they snarled, growled, and snapped.

Pepper paled.

"Well," I said, getting a grip on myself, "I *am* a bit surprised to see you."

"Are you?" she said.

In all the years that Pepper and I had been closer than sisters, I never remembered having the urge to smack her face. I had it now. Big-time.

"What happened to Miss Henley?" she said.

"You saw what happened. A beam fell on her."

"I'd like to hear all about it. Perhaps you'd be more comfortable talking at the station."

I gawked at her. "Talking at the station?"

"Yes."

"But I don't have much to add. That beam must have tumbled over with some newspaper and killed her."

"And you had nothing to do with it?"

"What?" Had the police concluded that Truffle and Sweet Marie had dislodged the mountain of paper that buried Miss Henley? Was I, as an irresponsible dog owner, guilty of some kind of negligence?

I gulped. "She was dead when we got there. She was cold. The dogs had no connection to it."

"You'd been there before?"

"Yes."

"And you had quarreled with Miss Henley?"

"Of course not. I was supposed to organize the chaos at Henley House for her."

"Hmm. Nice new career. Cleaning. She hired you?"

"Not cleaning. Organizing. And yes, she did."

"And you can prove that?"

"Why would I need to prove it? I had drawn up a contract. She was about to sign it that morning."

Pepper smirked. "There's more to this accident than meets the eye, Charlotte."

"There is? What do you mean?"

"I mean, the postmortem indicates that something is not quite right." Pepper gave me another smile. This one practically left freezer burn on my nose.

"She's dead. That's not quite right."

"Why don't you save it for the station?"

"I'm in my pajamas for heaven's sake. If it's absolutely necessary, I'll go and see you after I get dressed and walk the dogs and have breakfast and—"

"You actually don't get to pick the time."

"Why are you acting like this, Pepper?"

At that moment, Jack thundered up the stairs and into the already explosive situation. "What's going on?" he said.

"Police business." Pepper shot him a warning glance. "Do you mind?"

"What kind of police business?"

"The kind that's none of yours. We're taking Charlotte in for a statement."

"But I gave a statement at the scene!" I squeaked.

"We need to verify your version of what happened."

"My version? I don't have a *version*. I told you what happened. I went to see Miss Henley and I found her under the pile of collapsed paper. She was dead, cold."

"You don't have to say anything, as I'm sure you know. However, it's my duty to inform you that whatever you do say may be held against you in a court of law."

I gawked at her. "What's that supposed to mean?"

"Keep quiet, Charlotte," Jack said.

I flashed him a dirty look. "What could I say that anyone would hold against me in a court of law?"

"That's what we intend to find out," Pepper said.

"Wait a minute." My knees wobbled. "You think someone killed her?"

The perfectly tweezed eyebrow arched.

I said, "But who would want to harm Miss Henley?"

Pepper burst out laughing. As glad as I was to see she was human, that laugh seemed very wrong under the circumstances.

I said, "Okay. But she'd become harmless. Sort of. Who would kill her?"

Pepper said, "I'm guessing someone with an old grudge, someone in the vicinity. Someone vile and untrustworthy."

"Vile and un . . . ? You mean me? Well, that's just horrible, Pepper."

Jack said, "Stop talking. I'll call Margaret Tang."

"You're arresting me?" I turned to Jack. "What will happen to Truffle and Sweet Marie?"

Pepper's eyes glittered. I hadn't remembered them having that metallic quality. "It's just a statement. Of course, you are entitled to a lawyer."

All I heard was a buzz of words from Pepper, because, at that instant, Truffle shot forward and sunk his sweet little teeth into her elegant ankle.

# 4

Forget what you see on cop shows. There can't be many activities in this world more tedious than a police interview. To start, the interview rooms are bland without a single interesting feature or object, designed to bore you into shouting out a confession, I suppose. But at least when I was hustled into the downtown station, I'd been able to change. If Jack hadn't shown up in my apartment and mentioned Margaret Tang's name loudly, I might have been dragged out in my pj's and bunny slippers.

An hour after I arrived, there was still no sign of Margaret. Time ticked by slowly as I waited alone. I have nothing good to say about that room. Hard molded-plastic chairs that put your bum to sleep. Harsh yet ineffective lighting, protected with some kind of wire guard. No windows or posters. Nada. Paint the color of a mine shaft. Ick. One lonely, pathetic, disposable ashtray in the center of the boring rectangular table. I tried drumming my fingers on the table, but that didn't help much. The space needed a makeover from a skilled decorator. I could have recommended someone.

How did they expect a person to be at her best in these surroundings? You don't even get a cup of coffee. But then again, I was pretty sure Pepper didn't want me at my best. She'd prefer to deal with a sobbing wreck, eager to confess to anything. Maybe everything.

When she finally sashayed through the door, wearing that familiar smirk, I decided not to give her any satisfaction. I did my best to find the state known as calm, cool, and collected. She was followed by a red-faced, middle-aged man. His shirt gaped between the buttons when he sat down. He smelled slightly of coffee and doughnuts. Well, maybe I just imagined that. Did I also imagine that he gave me a tiny, sympathetic smile?

At a nod from Pepper, he got up again, turned on his heel, and left the room, taking his imaginary sympathy with him. He wasn't gone long. The next time the door opened, he'd returned with three cups of coffee, packets of cream and sugar, and little stir sticks. Perhaps the encounter would be all right after all. It was only a statement. I suppose there was a good reason to tape-record it.

Despite the coffee, Pepper's mood declined as the morning wore on. For starters, she kept rubbing her ankle. For another, she asked me the same questions dozens of different ways. I gave my statement and gave it again. And then I got to give it again. It came out pretty much the same way every time. Different details and emphasis, maybe. But no contradictions. Lucky me, I'd been telling the truth. What did she want from me? What did she think had happened?

"Why am I here, Pepper?"

"How about I ask the questions and you answer them?" she said.

That set the tone.

It was a long morning. At least ten times, I mentioned the documents that Miss Henley had wanted. "If there is something odd about her death, it has to be connected to them," I added. In case she hadn't picked up on this the first nine times.

"Get real. This is a police investigation," she said, "not a made-for-TV movie for kids." Then to add insult to injury, she stifled a yawn. That really bothered me, because I was the one who had a right to be bored. Pepper could just get up and leave.

Finally she did. I waited for her to say, "Don't leave town." But all I got was, "You'll be hearing from us."

I didn't doubt it.

Five minutes after Pepper left the room, the rumpled detective showed up and thanked me for my time. I found myself cut loose, wondering if the whole interview had just been a power trip from Pepper. I skittered along the hallway, craving fresh air and feeling like a felon. I kept my eyes down until I got out of the building, in case I ran into Pepper again, or equally bad, her husband, the well-known himbo, Nick Monahan.

I used my cell phone to call Jack, but he was already waiting across the street. He seemed very informal compared to the passing uniformed officers. But if he found it cold in those biking shorts, you would never have known it. He leaned against the Miata, grinned, and tossed me the keys.

"Thanks, Jack."

"Hey, what are friends for?" he said, unstrapping his bike, which he had managed to secure to my roof. "I couldn't reach Margaret. She was in court in Albany. But speaking of friends, I dropped Sweet Marie and Truffle off at Sally's, in case Pepper succumbed to her mean streak and sent the animal control officer in."

As rattled as I was, I knew that the best strategy was to just keep going. I headed for Sally's place. She needed my help with her toy jungle, and I needed her project to keep my mind off Miss Henley's death and the police station.

No one answered when I arrived. I could hear kiddy music blaring and the children shrieking, even from outside. Sally's doorbell plays "The Farmer in the Dell," but apparently that wasn't enough to attract attention over preexisting conditions. I peered through the glass side panels into the foyer and kept my finger on the bell. At ring number thirteen, Benjamin limped through the toy-strewn entrance to the front door. He glanced up in surprise and smiled when he saw it was me.

"Your doorbell might not be working," I said. "Oh, I see you have your MP3 player on."

Benjamin held the door as I entered the toy-festooned foyer. "That doorbell is working way too well. I hate that sucker so much that I just tune it out with whatever I can. But never mind. You had a terrible shock the other night. How are you doing, Charlotte?"

"Hanging in."

"Hope so, because you're in commotion central now. Listen, I appreciate you helping Sally, Charlotte," he said as he grabbed his briefcase. "There was never a house that needed more sorting out than this one, that's for sure."

I could think of at least one, but I didn't want to talk about that. "My pleasure."

"Good luck. I'm just heading out to give a lecture. And, of course, I'm late."

"Thanks, but I'm fine. Make tracks."

"Watch out for that toy truck. Make sure you can see the floor. I wouldn't want you to break your neck," he said, shrugging into his overcoat.

"When you have time, Benjamin, I'd like to get your input on the great toy project."

"You mean I get a vote?"

That came as a surprise; Benjamin had always adored

his wild, noisy, messy wife. And been a proud and playful dad to his three exuberant offspring.

"Of course you get a vote," I said. "I'm a practical girl. I always want my doctor to be happy."

"Here goes. All I want, really, is a room, one room, one miserable room, four walls, and a door, without a pile of bleeping toys, without screaming, without jam sandwiches stuck on my notes, without wastepaper baskets scattered. I could go on. I want to be able to sit in a clean, quiet spot and hear myself think, for half an hour a day. Is that so wrong? I just wasted twenty minutes hunting for my briefcase before my meeting, because my desk, the only spot I can call my own in this house, has been turned into a pretend dog-house with a blanket. So all my useless professional stuff had to get dumped somewhere. Does that make any sense in a house this big?"

Benjamin's round friendly face was turning an alarming shade of red.

I said, "Oops. Sorry if my pooches made you late."

"You're not the problem and neither are your dogs," he said. "They didn't make the tent. They didn't move my speaking notes to the laundry room."

"Got ya," I said as the door banged behind him.

Ooh. Trouble in paradise.

From upstairs I heard the thunder of tiny feet, squeals, shouts, and sharp little barks. Truffle and Sweet Marie practically tumbled down the stairs to meet me. They were pursued by two shrieking preschoolers. Sally followed, carrying the baby. The baby wailed, distressed at not being able to chase the dogs, I suppose.

The house might have given the impression of a recent explosion, but Sally, as usual, looked fabulous, with her halo of blonde curls. She was born for bare feet and jeans with spandex.

"Thanks for keeping Truffle and Sweet Marie, Sally," I said as I swept a pile of stuffed animals and a book of baby names from Sally's white leather living room sofa and plunked myself down on it. Truffle and Sweet Marie leapt onto the sofa and hid out behind me. Normally I wouldn't allow my animals on someone else's furniture, particularly white leather, but Sally's sofa already had popcorn scattered on it, tiny sneaker prints, and a bright fuchsia stain that might have been Kool-Aid.

As usual Sally didn't notice. "No problem. Jack was worried Pepper might toss them in the slammer so he asked if I'd provide a witness protection program. The kids love them. We need a dog, but Benjamin's being poopy about it."

The children, squealing, attempted to climb over me to get at the dachsies. I gave each kid a cuddle and turned them in the opposite direction. It didn't help much.

"I wasn't too worried. You know how much Pepper cares about her public image." I had to raise my voice a bit to drown out the shrieks. "I don't imagine she wants to have her new reputation as a hotshot detective tarred with the image of a ten-pound dog getting the best of her. Especially if Truffle's picture made the media. Can you imagine Todd Tyrell getting hold of that story? No, no, sweeties, the doggies don't want to play."

Sally's green eyes gleamed. "Todd is very good at this, isn't he? Anyway, don't just sit there. Dish. What happened when they took you in?"

I preferred to just sit there, guarding my traumatized pets. "Not much. Pepper took my statement. She didn't think much of the information about the documents that Miss Henley needed. She said it sounded like the plot of a kids' movie."

"Well, it does, kind of," Sally said.

"But it's true. Anyway, she kept asking if I'd had some kind of a falling out with Miss Henley."

"Everyone who ever went to St. Jude's had a falling out with Hellfire," Sally said. "Including Pepper."

"I didn't mention that."

"But it's true and you know it."

"In high school, sure, but not as adults. I can't speak for the rest of Woodbridge, but I didn't have any kind of dispute with her when she died."

Sally gasped, "Of course not. I didn't mean to suggest that."

"The project would have been great. Except that I felt guilty about not meeting her that night."

"How could you have known?"

"I might have found her in time to call 911."

"I doubt that. If an oak beam falls on your head, there's not much 911 can do for you. That's what Benjamin said and he should know. So what else happened at the station? What was the interview room like? Is it the same as television?"

"It was just a room. Pepper sort of filled it, and she made me very nervous."

"But why would you be nervous?"

I shook my head. "I'd like to get started on our project. We should have fun getting these toys sorted out."

Sally said, "We don't have to do that today. We shouldn't just jump right into it."

I nudged a broken doll with my foot. "It's a good time to start. It will take my mind off Miss Henley."

"Okay. You want a snack?"

"I'm good. Let's take a couple of minutes and think about what you want to accomplish with our little organizing problem."

Damn. That just slipped out. I'd meant to say organizing project. So much less judgmental.

Sally said, "I don't have a problem."

"But, Benjamin . . ."

"Yeah, *Benjamin* has a problem. I don't. I don't even know why I called you about it in the first place. I told you Benjamin's being really anal lately and it was getting on my nerves."

I didn't plan to tiptoe through that particular marital minefield. I kept my mouth shut. For once.

Sally said, "I want my kids to be happy. I want them to have food to eat when they want it, and where they want it. I want them to have music and fun and toys and love. I want them to have lots of friends. I want them to be cuddled and valued and . . ." Sally choked up at this point.

I could have finished the sentence for her. She wanted them to have everything she'd missed. I remembered Sally letting herself into a dark house after school, never having me or Jack or Pepper or Margaret visit in case we left a glass out of place or a smudge on a piece of furniture. Sally keeping quiet so Mom's headache didn't get worse or her step-grouch didn't get behind on his sleep.

This was going to take some pussyfooting on my part. I remembered Benjamin's glower as he left. Whatever it took, it would be worth it.

"That's all part of my plan too, Sal. Hard to argue with kids being happy and loved."

"How would we know, right?" she said. "No wonder we were all such freakin' misfits."

"Hey," I said.

"The truth always hurts, Charlotte. Hang on, let's catch the news. Where's that stupid remote?"

"What? Please don't . . ." I wanted to say don't add the racket from the television to the chaos we already have. Instead I said, "How about we wait for that? I brought these really neat boxes for the kids to keep their favorite toys in. Benjamin says he wants one room without toys. What do you want, Sally?"

"I want the remote."

Both the kids started to blubber. "We want to keep our toys. Don't let Charlotte take our toys." The baby joined in, a wordless accusing shriek.

"I'm not taking your toys," I said, but nobody was listening.

Sally clicked on the remote and Todd Tyrell's giant teeth flashed across the screen again.

"He's so gorgeous," Sally said.

I stared at her. Had she lost her mind? She had Dr. Benjamin Janescek, an intelligent humanitarian, a fine doctor, a good father, a rumpled, cuddly teddy bear. She had three beautiful children and enough family income to stay home with them. She had a five-thousand-square-foot house and a trillion dollars worth of sharp-edged toys. Why would she give Todd Tyrell a thought? Maybe he had been a total stud muffin when he was head boy and we were in eighth grade, but surely a mother of three children should be long past that stage.

"You think?" I said.

"Just look at him. That gorgeous smile."

"Oh yeah, the teeth. I was wondering if he plugged them in at night."

Sally shot a scowl in my direction. "Very funny."

"How old do you think he is?" I said. "Fifty?"

"What are you talking about? He was only three years ahead of us at St. Jude's. Remember he was head boy?"

"I had forgotten," I lied. "Maybe the fake tan just makes his skin seem that much older."

Sally had developed a small pout by this time. "It's not like you to be mean, Charlotte."

"Maybe I'm changing. Necessity is the mother of invention and all that."

"Shh! He's saying something important."

"I doubt that."

"Pay attention. It's about Miss Henley. You would have heard that if you hadn't been so . . ."

I plunked myself on the sofa and paid attention.

Todd Tyrell had lowered his voice about an octave. That's always a bad sign. "In breaking news, Woodbridge Police have revealed that the death of Woodbridge's beloved teacher, Miss Helen Henley . . ."

I blinked twice at that. Beloved teacher?

"... was not a freak accident as previously believed. Police have revealed"—Todd lowered his voice into the basso profundo range—"foul play was involved."

"Foul play?" I said. "That's craptacular, but what does he mean?"

Sally gave me a condescending smirk. "He means murder, silly."

The children danced and sang, "Murder, murder, murder."

Truffle yipped in panic, and Sweet Marie shook like a dying leaf in the November wind.

———

"That's as far as we got," I said to Jack when I arrived home. I was more than a bit shaken by what I'd heard. I'd banged on his first-floor door and walked in to blurt out the news. I plunked myself down on the floor, surrounded by bikes, wheels, and racing gear, and box after box of supplies for the shop he hoped to set up. Truffle and Sweet Marie snuggled up to me. There were no other soft surfaces in Jack's place.

Jack slid down to the floor and sat cross-legged facing me. "What did Sally mean, 'misfits'? I thought we were just the weird kids."

"Come on, Jack. Consider the families we had. Remember the kind of stunts Margaret's mom used to pull to keep her away from the rest of us? The dying relatives who weren't really dying. The crisis of the day at the store?"

"Mrs. Tang was a pussycat compared to Sally's family. What a sour bunch they were. Supercritical. Mean."

"Oh yeah. They were miserable, all right. It's a miracle that Sally turned out to be such a warm, affectionate person."

Jack said, "And Pepper's were just as bad."

"Worse. Remember the bruises on her arms? Miss Henley

always used to pick up on the bad days and make life harder for her."

"She could sure sniff out vulnerability. And there was no way Pepper could complain about it at home. She'd just end up with more bruises," Jack said. "Made my folks seem normal."

I hadn't mentioned Jack's swarthy, roly-poly mom and dad, barely five feet tall and perpetually terrified some disaster would befall the blue-eyed, white-blond beanpole they'd adopted.

Jack said, "They had nightmares about me starving to death."

I had to laugh at that. "Hey listen, the rest of us didn't mind. All those pies and cookies. They just kept coming. Endless snacks. Sally and I used to eat until it hurt."

"I didn't have such a bad deal, I guess."

"I adored your parents. Maybe that's part of the reason I like living here so much. I have really nice memories of this house from when we were growing up."

"Yeah, I think the folks would be real happy to know you were living here too."

"You're probably right." I didn't add that they probably would have been just as happy that Jack had totally filled one entire floor of their lovely old Victorian with bicycles and parts, with a side order of philosophy books and university assignments. As long as he was eating lots.

"They were pretty cool, weren't they?" Jack turned his face away, and I felt a catch in my throat.

I said, "For sure. And they thought you were the sun, the moon, and the stars."

"You mean I'm not?"

"Of all of us, you were the lucky one, Jack."

"Thanks, Charlotte. It's hard for me to talk about them since the accident."

I gave his hand a squeeze.

Jack produced a half-hearted grin. "Come on, your mom

was pretty neat. She was so glamorous, and she sure could get the rumors flying around Woodbridge. And you can't complain about the way she treated you. You got all those neat trips. Paris. London. Venice. L.A."

"But life was always all about Esme Adams, best-selling author. Right through four marriages, each one wackier than the one before. And I never even got to know my own father. And I can't even remember the name of this latest guy. No wonder I can't pick a decent human being for a fiancé."

"Never mind our parents. We had a lot of fun. I don't think we were misfits. That's harsh."

"Let it go, Jack. That comment was just Sally's way to distract me. Although the WINY news took care of that."

"Whoa. Suspected foul play," Jack said.

"But it's almost impossible to believe. Who could have wanted to kill her?"

"Surely you jest," Jack said.

I stared, astonished. "What do you mean? Jest. It's murder."

"She had tons of enemies, Charlotte. Think back. How many kids from her class would have nurtured anger and re-sentment over some humiliation at Hellfire Henley's hands?"

"Kids are always being humiliated. It's a rite of passage. How are you going to cope with adulthood otherwise?"

"Hellfire went way beyond. She could twist the knife and make a kid's life a living nightmare. I know it. You know it. Everyone knew it. We were *just* talking about how she treated Pepper when her life was already the pits."

"Even so."

"But you had the guts to stand up to her. Imagine all the kids who couldn't because they'd get in trouble at home if they did. Or expelled. Or just have to endure more and more bad treatment from the old witch."

"We're talking murder, Jack. *Murder.* I don't care what you say. I don't believe people commit homicide because they're mad at someone who taught them way back."

"Face it, the list of people who never felt like killing Miss Henley would be a lot shorter than the list of people who did. Just about everybody would have had some reason. Even Pepper."

I shivered. "They're not releasing the body yet."

Jack said, "They're not? But I heard on the radio that there's a memorial service planned tomorrow afternoon, at St. Jude's."

"Really? Tomorrow?"

"Yeah. That's kind of fast, isn't it? I wonder what the rush is."

"I guess they figure a lot of people can get there on a Saturday afternoon. We'll have to go."

Jack rolled his eyes. "If you say so."

# 5

As memorial services go, Miss Henley's had a festive air. And why not? According to the latest rumor rocketing through Woodbridge, all the instructions were in her will, right down to choice of the organ music. If you believed the wagging tongues, Father Timothy wasn't all that happy to take orders from beyond the grave. True? Who knows? But Saturday turned out to be an excellent day to hold a memorial. People sure made a point of getting there early to get the best seat. When Jack and I drove up in my Miata, it was impossible to find a place to park anywhere near St. Jude's. Jack is the proud owner of an ancient Mini Minor in an alarming shade of mud brown. It is currently experiencing technical difficulties, so mine is always the vehicle of choice.

We circled the block three times before spinning off to find a spot four blocks away.

"Well, crap. I can't believe it," I said. "We're a half hour early. Who are all these people? You'd think it was a rock concert from the crowd."

Jack said, "Told you we should have biked."

"Not in this outfit, buster."

By the time we reached the wide stairs to the church, I was doing my best not to limp in my black suede pumps with the four-inch heels. Sally and Benjamin were right behind us.

"It's the place to be," Sally said merrily. She was one of those blondes who were born to wear black and she knew it. She fluffed her corkscrew curls as she spotted Todd Tyrell in the clump of media types surrounding the church.

A crowd flowed behind us and swept past up the stairs. Eager beavers took the stairs two at a time. We were lucky enough to elbow our way into the last pew. I recognized quite a few people, from school and just from living in Woodbridge. Kristee from Kristee's Kandees, Mrs. Tang, and Margaret were sitting closer to the front. I saw the two constables who had come to Henley House, the paramedics, and a pixielike woman with a sleek ponytail who I finally recognized as Mona Pringle, former schoolmate and now emergency services operator. She gave me a conspiratorial wink. I really, really hoped that no one else had spotted that.

I could feel the buzz in the air, like a midnight madness sale at the Woodbridge Mall, a swirl of excitement that seemed just plain wrong at a memorial service. Especially when the service was for someone whose body I'd found myself.

To add to the buzz, there was plenty of police presence. Sally elbowed me and pointed toward Pepper and her husband, the noted boy toy, Nick Monahan.

"There he is, God's gift to the girls," Sally snickered.

I kept my mouth firmly shut. The less said about Nick Monahan the better. But there was a good reason he'd earned the nickname "Nick the Stick." It was just hard to believe that Pepper, with all her guts and brainpower, couldn't see past that handsome face and athlete's body. It had cost her my friendship. What else would it cost her?

"Bed-hopping slacker," Jack said cheerfully.

Sally added a bit too loudly, "I suppose they deserve each other."

Benjamin turned his head and furrowed his teddy-bear face. "Sally, for heaven's sake. We're in church."

Pepper turned around at that exact moment.

Sally caught her breath.

I felt myself blanch.

Benjamin whispered, "When will you two learn a bit of control?"

Luckily Pepper's attention was diverted by the arrival of several elderly women, in navy skirts and sweaters, wearing large crosses. They could only be nuns, in those outfits. I remembered some of the faces from St. Jude's. It wasn't like nuns to be late, but I figured this batch was probably from out of town. They were being ushered toward the front of the church to join the rest.

Although the new arrivals seemed quite solemn, even the somber church and the nature of the event couldn't mask the upbeat mood of the congregation. Miss Helen Henley was dead. Murdered it appeared. But, as Jack kept insisting, who had never wanted to kill Miss Henley? Tra la la.

By the time Olivia Henley Simonett, the sole surviving relative, was escorted in her wheelchair to the front of the church, it was standing room only, with stragglers sulking outside on the stairs. Everyone strained to see the fragile figure in the wheelchair. Her long, wavy white hair was held back by a pink ribbon. Each cheek had a spot of rouge like a target, and her bright lipstick had overshot the mark on her upper and lower lips. She wore a strange, shy smile, alternated with an expression of stunned surprise. On her way toward the front, she began to wave coyly at the crowd. Muffled laughter swept the church. Near the front, she began to try to get out of her wheelchair and was promptly shoved back in her place by the sturdy, dark-haired woman who was wheeling her.

Benjamin shook his head. "Oh, poor Olivia. This kind of circus won't do her any good."

"Do you know her?" I whispered.

He nodded. "I was her GP before she went to Stone Wall Farm. She's very fragile."

I hadn't known Olivia Henley Simonett was one of Benjamin's patients. Of course, I didn't know much about her at all. I wanted to ask him what he meant by fragile. But I knew Benjamin well enough to know that he wouldn't spill the beans on anyone under his care.

The memorial was uneventful. I couldn't imagine what people would find to say that would be all that heartwarming about Miss Henley. I had admired her passion for order, her spectacular self-discipline, and her shoes. But that would hardly bring a tear to anyone's eye.

There were no tears in the church that day. Imagine spending seventy-plus years in one town, and when you die, the church is packed and everyone's in a mood to party.

Six St. Jude's students carried a half dozen large arrangements of lilies and green mums up the center aisle. As the flowers neared the front of the church, Olivia Simonett leapt to her feet, staggered away from her wheelchair, and waved her arms in what appeared to be jubilation. I guarantee you just about everyone in that church experienced a most un-Christian thrill. The dark-haired attendant was knocked sideways. Her glasses flew through the air. Olivia blew kisses to the crowd. The attendant recovered in time to grasp Olivia by the arms, just as the elderly woman staggered and sank out of our sight, with a crash that must have been wheelchair related.

"Holy shit," Sally said.

Benjamin pressed past us and hurtled toward the front of the church.

"He's great in doctor mode, isn't he?" Sally said. "That's what I fell in love with."

"He's great in any mode," I snapped. "What do you think was going on up there?"

Jack climbed on the seat of the pew and stretched to see over the hundreds of craning heads. "A celebration, for sure. Seems to have ended badly though."

As I strained to see the ongoing commotion, I caught sight of a pair of dark eyes. And they caught sight of me. I found myself staring once again at the man from Tang's. Mr. I-may-have-the-eyes-of-a-shy-woodland-creature-but-I-also-have-a-wedding-band was heading toward the front of the church too. I turned away but not before Sally noticed.

"Who's that stud muffin?" she said.

"What?"

"Don't get all coy, Charlotte. The guy with the leather jacket."

"Nobody."

"Come on, Charlotte."

"Actually I have no idea, and I don't need to know, Sally. Remember we're in church. Pay attention to the ceremony."

"Since when do you care about ceremonies? Anyway, it's stopped, as you must have noticed."

Benjamin gave us both another of his irritated teddy-bear frowns as he hustled by with the attendant wheeling Olivia Simonett. The attendant still seemed pretty dazed, her glasses tilted at a definite angle. Olivia, her long white hair hanging loose, waved to the crowd. The hair ribbon had vanished.

As soon as they were out the door, the organ music swelled and the memorial service was under way.

At least Sally shut up. I tried to pay attention to a succession of retired school principals for St. Jude's. Each one of them gave the impression that unseen marksmen had high-powered rifles trained on their foreheads. I could almost imagine the red dot from the laser. If you chose to believe them, Miss Henley had brought much joy to their lives by her immaculate record keeping and maintenance of classroom order.

Sally said, "I hear the old witch left a serious bundle to the school, and the catch was they had to have all the living principals speak at the memorial."

"That would explain it," Jack said. "Principals losing their principles."

Benjamin's face was pale as dust when he ducked back into the pew. When Sally opened her mouth, he said, "What is the matter with you people? Keep your voices down."

Jack gave me a nudge. I refused to make eye contact with him for the rest of the memorial. The high point continued to be the fracas at the front with Miss Henley's fragile elderly cousin. By the time the last representative of St. Jude's wiped his brow with a handkerchief, the crowd was pleased to exit and head for the bread portion of the circus.

By the time we reached the bottom of the stairs, the big white wheelchair-accessible van from Stone Wall Farm had arrived, the attendant had her glasses straightened out, and Olivia Simonett had shipped out. The eager crowd could surge toward the reception without distraction.

The reception was held, not in the church hall with the parish's Women's League traditional egg-salad sandwiches, but in the ballroom at the Woodbridge Arms, Woodbridge's recently renovated historic hotel. It was a two-block hike from the church. I suggested we skip it, but Sally and Jack nixed that idea. The chocolate brown van from Kristee's Kandees was parked by the hotel.

I pointed to it. "That's good news, at least."

"Get a load of that." Jack smirked, staring around in wonder as we walked in. "Everything but the disco ball."

But I approved. The ballroom was quite splendid. Tables of canapés and tiny pastries, chocolate truffles, huge silver coffee urns and tea services. Small glasses of quite tolerable white wine were handed around by busy servers in black and white uniforms. Miss Henley had made sure her memorial would be one to remember, even if she couldn't have counted on her cousin to give it that little extra touch.

I spotted Margaret Tang frowning at some canapés. She radiated expensive professionalism in a severe navy suit, with just a whimsical bit of lace camisole showing. There was always more to Margaret than you'd expect. There was no sign of Mrs. Tang. I figured she'd hustled back to the store. I slipped up behind Margaret and said "hi."

She turned and squealed, "Charlotte Adams."

"That's me!" I squealed back.

"Did you come back for this happy event?" she said, picking up a small plate and adding a few sandwiches and a pastry.

It didn't take a genius to figure out that Margaret's mother hadn't been passing on messages. I figured that was typical for the Tang family.

I said, "I've been back in Woodbridge for more than six months now. I've set up a business."

"No kidding."

"I heard you'd set up a law practice. That's great. I left you a couple of messages at the store. I left my business card too. I figured you were too busy getting settled to get in touch."

She shook her head. "Mom's weird. You should know that after all these years."

"Jack tried to reach you too, when Pepper hauled me in for questioning. You were somewhere in court."

The hand with the sandwich froze. "Pepper hauled you in?"

"Yeah. She questioned me about Miss Henley's death. I think she wishes I'd done it."

"Unbelievable."

"Yeah."

"Sorry, I didn't even hear about that. I've been up to my ears with a deposition in Albany. And I didn't get that message. Of course, that's what happens when you have your cousin working in your office. Mom probably issued a 'no message' list. This kid's scared to death of her. Anyway, here's my cell number if you ever need me again. I'll give it to Jack too."

We went through a juggling act with plates and wineglasses until we'd completed the ritual exchange of business cards. It sure felt strange to do that with an old friend like Margaret.

I said, "Let's hope. Listen, why don't we get together? Come on over and catch up with Sally and Jack. It'll be just like old times."

Margaret made a face. "Hope not," she said.

I took it the way I thought she meant it. I couldn't blame her. Margaret had been a chunky, brilliant Asian in a small town that didn't value any of those attributes in a girl. She'd complicated matters by wearing glasses and winning school medals. Her science projects had been jaw-dropping. All that wasn't quite the kiss of death, but close. I never remembered Margaret having a date or even a conversation with any of the popular kids in our school. She'd worked hard at the store under the eye of her sour mother, and endured ethnic slurs and cracks about her weight at school, when she wasn't being completely ignored by prom queens and football players with half her brains. Except for Jack, Sally, Pepper, and me, no one ever spoke to her. And of course, no matter what Jack said, we were the misfits.

So what on earth had possessed her to return to Woodbridge now that she had a size-two figure, a thousand-dollar suit, a law degree, and a pair of contact lenses? Knowing Margaret, I decided it was better not to ask.

I slipped my new business card into her pocket. "That was then, this is now. You know what they say: doing well is the best revenge. Anyway, we had fun together, you and me, Sally and Pepper and Jack."

"You're right," Margaret said. "We did. Maybe the only fun I've had in my life. I'll call you. And you call me."

The reception turned out to be the social highlight of the year. I was taking it all in when I felt a tingle on the back of my neck. I turned to meet the gaze. The one person I didn't want it to be. I felt a flush rising on my neck. Oh crap, how seriously uncool. I turned away and bumped into Sally.

Damn.

"I figure this sucker cost about seven grand, easy," Sally said, sipping a sparkly drink. I watched as she flitted from person to person, catching up on news here, air-kissing there. Of course, her little black dress was perfect for a funeral. I just hoped she hadn't seen the flash between me and Mr. Wedding Ring.

I snatched up my fourth truffle. I quickly stepped backward to avoid a cluster of chocolate lovers and bumped into Kristee Kravitz of Kristee's Kandees. "These are fabulous. Did you supply them?" I said, pointing to the truffles, which were vanishing fast.

"I sure did. It's the first time I've ever felt grateful that a person died," Kristee said with a giggle. "Oh that's awful, isn't it?"

I made a noncommittal noise.

"Thousands of dollars, just today," Kristee was saying. "She loved her chocolate truffles."

"Did she?"

"For sure. She was a steady customer ever since I opened the shop. You'd never think about her being kind to anyone, but she was, in her own mean sort of way. She bought a half dozen black and white truffles for herself and one for her cousin every week. You saw that poor lady at the funeral? That's Olivia Henley Simonett. She's a few chocolates short of a gift box, to put it mildly, but Miss Henley was always really nice to her. I guess old Hellfire wasn't always awful, the way she was to us in school. Well, all right, she was awful. A nasty old bat."

I said inanely, "But I suppose you'll miss the business."

"Won't have to. She even left a little fund so her cousin still gets the truffles every week. The best part is, I still get the business and I won't have to put up with all those remarks she always made. The left-handed compliments and the digs. And that special way she had of looking down her nose at you. Remember?"

"Who could forget?"

"She had a lot of power over people." Kristee shivered.

"You're telling me," said a pink-faced woman with a silver brush cut and earrings to match. I recognized her as Ramona, the librarian from the Woodbridge Library reference department. "I saw her when I went to the doctor for my annual checkup last week. Just the sight of her was enough to raise my blood pressure. And I'm a tough cookie. But it was like when you barely avert a car accident by slamming on your brakes. There were a couple of scrapes she never caught me out on at St. Jude's, and all of a sudden I panicked. That's crazy, I know. I can't believe I was afraid of her, but . . ." She shivered and her silver earrings jingled. "These truffles are fabulous though, Kristee."

Sally edged her way in between us and gave me an oversized wink. She followed it with a playful nudge in my ribs.

"What's that about?" I said.

"He's very yummy."

"Who?"

"You know who." She glanced over my shoulder.

I jerked my head around, and sure enough, there he was, leaning against a wall and watching us. Sally gave him a flirtatious little wave.

"What is the matter with you? He's married. I need to get involved with a married man like I need . . ." Words failed me. A periscope? An ant farm? A weather vane?

"That's just it, my tiny single friend," Sally said. "He's not married."

"Is."

"Was."

"I said *is*. Oh. Was?"

"Yep."

"Well, I'm not looking for a recently divorced man either."

"His wife died. Plane crash."

"That's awful. But what did you do, stroll up to him and ask? Oh crap, Sally. I hope you didn't mention me."

"The topic just came up. We are at a reception for someone who died. I didn't tell him that you have been blushing every time he so much as glances at you."

"Not true. They have the heat blasting in here."

"His name, in case you're interested," Sally breathed, "is Dominic Lo Bello. That's kind of romantic, isn't it?"

I shrugged.

"He's new in town. Remember, any time you need the facts, just put Sally on the trail. See you later."

The party atmosphere continued. The room was jammed with former students and teachers, many of whom seemed jubilant in the extreme. I even thought I caught a glimpse of Mr. Kanalakis, the art teacher who'd been fired in the middle of his first year at St. Jude's. Yes, for sure, it was Mr. Kanalakis. At six foot six, he towered over everyone else. His long, thick black ponytail had a bit of grey in it now, and maybe he was showing the beginning of a paunch, but nearly fifteen years later, I would have recognized him anywhere. Perhaps I just imagined that cloud of testosterone in the air. Amazingly, he was having an animated conversation with two retired nuns from St. Jude's. They had obviously been to a hairdresser for today's send-off.

"Get a load of that," Sally said, stopping for second. "That's Kanalakis. He's sure having a hell of a good time."

"Yes," I said. "There was a time when they were all ready to run him out of town. Oh look, there's Mrs. Neufield too."

"Time heals all whatevers," Sally said, drifting off into the crowd.

Everyone seemed eager to talk about the last time they'd seen Miss Henley and how she'd been able to put the fear of God into them. The conversation was punctuated with squeals and nervous laughter. Tales of fear at the gas pump, the bakery, the post office. The last time I'd seen Miss Henley she was dead, and I didn't want to revisit that.

I drifted back to the food table, all the time trying to dodge Todd Tyrell, who was working the room. I found myself picking up a truffle, then another. What is this connection with food and funerals?

I scanned the room for a friendly face and spotted Benjamin standing alone. I scooted over as fast as I could.

"Was Mrs. Simonett all right?"

"As all right as she'll ever be, I guess."

"What's the problem?"

"Come on, Charlotte," he said with a hint of exasperation. "You know I can't discuss former patients with you."

"I was just being polite," I said. "Well, I wasn't really trying to pry into your patient's private life."

"Former patient," he said.

"But you must admit, standing up and doing the wave at the funeral of your only surviving relative is a bit odd."

"Poor Olivia. Just leave it."

I said, "Well, I can't just leave it. Miss Henley was murdered. You know that. What if Olivia killed her?"

Oops. I hoped that rise in Benjamin's color didn't signal high blood pressure.

He sputtered, "Listen to me, Charlotte Adams. Olivia could no more plan and execute a murder than she could fly a commercial airliner. It simply could not happen."

"She stood to inherit all that money."

"She already has more money than she can use. And what good would another inheritance do, if you were confined to a rest home with . . ." He caught himself just in time.

"Okay, don't get excited. I just thought she's the only person who stands to gain."

"Gain? The woman doesn't need money or property. She's lost her last relative now that Helen's dead. For heaven's sake, some people are saying you did it, Charlotte."

"Me?"

"That's right. Now how do *you* like it?"

"Are you serious? Why would I do it? That's not fair."

"Of course it's not fair and it's preposterous. But it's no more unfair than insinuating that a helpless, sick woman committed a heinous act of violence. I would expect a bit more compassion from you, Charlotte. I would be very upset to learn that Olivia had been badgered by anyone wanting to explore that ridiculous idea. Now, excuse me. I have to find Sally."

I looked around. Where *was* Sally? Had she left the reception? Sally loves a party way more than I do. It's not like her to head out early, not with the babysitter engaged for the afternoon. I reminded myself, this was not a party. Somehow the revved-up mood seemed more like a school reunion than the aftermath of a death. Easy for them; they didn't have the image of Miss Henley's damaged corpse floating in their brains.

I didn't notice Dominic Lo Bello anywhere, so I didn't have to worry about awkward encounters. Who knew what Sally had said. It gave me the shivers just thinking about it.

I was feeling pretty down by the time I located Jack. He was busy talking up his new retail plan with his accountant. Very animated. Plus he was in no hurry to depart while there were still chocolates on the premises.

I abandoned Jack to his accountant and left the hotel. The November wind tossed my hair, and the thin sprinkle of drizzle added just the right air of misery. I had plenty to think about. Who had killed Miss Henley and why? Maybe if I could find that out, I could get rid of that truckload of guilt. In the meantime, I had my dogs to worry about, and an evening of doing laundry was starting to look good. But my mind kept drifting back to the church, remembering Olivia Henley Simonett and her strange little victory jig.

What was that about?

# 6

Don't ask me why I swung by the Henley House the next day. Perhaps because it was Sunday and I was at loose ends. Maybe the Miata had a mind of its own. But more likely it was guilt about refusing to meet Miss Henley the night she died. Not to mention the fact I'd cashed her substantial check without earning it.

I headed for North Elm and drove slowly up the hill in second gear to the Henley House. The temperature had plunged dramatically. A few lonely flurries floated randomly in the late afternoon sky.

I stared up at the dark, hulking building. What had gone on in there? Long strips of police tape surrounded the property. The vivid yellow plastic snapping in the wind made a cheerful statement in the late November afternoon. Slashes of fresh graffiti stood out against the front of the house. Graffiti artists aren't deterred by ribbons of yellow tape. *Police line. Do not cross.* That just gets them going.

How had Miss Henley's life ended? The police were being tight-lipped about what kind of foul play. Was it really

possible some former student wanted revenge? Or was it a
robbery gone wrong? Who would expect to find valuables
in all that clutter? There had to be an easier way to rip off
some homeowner.

I wondered if the police had gone door-to-door on North
Elm looking for information. They must have, I decided.
Pepper was thorough and efficient. She never wasted any
time. Out of the corner of my eye, I noticed a solitary figure
standing across the street. A man with a camera. He turned
this way and that, snapping pictures. He got down on one
knee and twisted to get a different angle.

When he lowered the camera, I caught my breath. None
other than the new man in our town, Dominic Lo Bello. He
climbed into a dusty red Jeep Cherokee and disappeared
around the corner. Had he seen me staring at him? Would
he think I was some kind of whacko stalker? That would be
just craptacular. Get over it, I told myself firmly before I
stepped out of the car.

I sniffed the air. There it was again, the scent of wood
smoke I'd noticed on my first visit. Where was it coming
from? I continued down the street, slowly, peering around. I
smiled when I spotted the thin swirl of smoke from a chim-
ney, across the street and down five houses. I got out of the
car and headed down the hill.

Up close, the sturdy wood-frame house was well kept,
including a newly installed yellow metal door, every bit as
bright as the police tape up the road. A fat grey and white
cat was parading in front of the door, yowling.

Luckily I didn't have Sweet Marie and Truffle with me.

The cat brushed against my ankles as I stood ringing the
doorbell. After a while, I figured out the bell wasn't working, and I banged on the door. I could see lights from the
inside. The smell of wood smoke was tantalizing. I strained
to hear and thought I picked up banging noises as well as
squeaks. Squeaks? Squeals? I'd be lying if I said the hair

on my arms wasn't standing straight up. Never mind the action on the back of my neck.

When the door finally opened, I had to look down. A wizened woman with deep blue hair stared at me with interest. She was wearing a purple jogging suit, oversize bright white running shoes, and a wheeled oxygen-support apparatus.

"Oh," I said.

"Oh yourself," she said happily.

"I . . . was worried about your cat."

"My cat?"

"Yes. He seems distressed."

She gave a long wheezy chuckle. "Distressed."

I am such a bad liar. Why do I even try?

She said, "Are you distressed, Hairball? That's too bad, because you're not my cat and you're not getting in. And here's me thinking: this nice young lady wanted to talk about what happened at the Henley House."

"Possibly that too," I said.

"Follow me, hon. I don't need to add another case of pneumonia to my medical file." She turned on her slipper heel and shuffled down the hallway. The grey and white cat made an attempt to join the party. I guess he didn't hold the name Hairball against her.

"Get rid of that creature, will you, hon? Or get ready to dial 911. I'm really allergic."

Right. I popped the cat outside and closed the yellow door. I followed her as the wheels squealed along the hallway. I suppose I was expecting another junk-filled uninhabitable space. But except for a pizza ad on the floor by the front door, the place was clear and clean. From force of habit, I bent and picked up the flyer.

"You can put that flyer right in the basket," she said, making a quick right turn. The wheeled oxygen tank squeaked after her.

What? Did she have eyes in the back of her head?

I turned too and found myself in a small living room, where a merry fire burned in a brick fireplace with a glass insert and an antique television with rabbit ears was tuned to WINY. Todd Tyrell stood outside in the wind and rain. As usual, not a hair on his head moved. Lucky for me the sound was muted and I didn't have to listen to his play-by-play of Miss Henley's memorial service.

"Right there, thank you, hon," my hostess said, nodding toward a small wicker container on the seventies-style coffee table. "And make yourself comfortable," she added, pointing to the bright orange plaid sofa, with the brown and cream crocheted throw neatly draped over it. The throw matched the cushions on the orange recliner. The colors might have been alarming, but every surface in the room that could shine did. The carpet had obviously been vacuumed, and the orange net curtains looked fresh and clean. Somehow it all meshed with the purple jogging suit. Come to think of it, the purple jogging suit matched the small portable plastic filing box on the floor near her chair. Bills, envelopes, and stamps sat on the TV tray in front of the recliner.

I plunked myself down and said, "My name is—"

"I know who you are, Charlotte Adams. You found Helen Henley's body."

"Yes."

"Have to follow that story, don't I? Since it pretty well happened in my backyard."

"Thank you, miss, um . . ."

There was that wheezy laugh again. It made me want to dial Mona Pringle at 911. "It's Mrs. Um, actually. Rose Skipowski. But you can call me Rose. I'll call you Charlotte. Now, let's not beat around the bush anymore. What can I do for you, Charlotte?"

"I suppose you could tell me if you know anything about what happened to Miss Henley."

"Don't know much. I know that damned cat out there was Randy's. But that's about it. I didn't see anyone sneak up there and whack her on the head, if that's what you mean."

"Well, no. I never—"

"Come on, admit it. You were hoping. But I have nothing better to do than look out the window. I know everything that goes on on this street. If I'd seen a thing out of the ordinary, I would have told the police. But I was in the hospital. Bit of a heart scare. Happens every now and then. Missed the whole thing. You wouldn't believe the tests they put you through. You want to kiss the ground if and when you get out."

"Sounds rough. I'm glad you're out of the hospital and feeling better."

"As far as that goes."

"I'm wondering if any of your neighbors might have seen anything."

"Not from Florida, they wouldn't have."

"Oh."

"They're out of here as soon as the first leaf falls. Both sides. They leave me watching their houses." She pointed to a key rack by the door. "As if I don't have anything better to do. And I don't. And they do plenty for me the rest of the year. Check and see if the old car's still running, arrange for my wood."

I was about to protest this thoughtlessness on the part of the neighbors when she said, "Would you like a cookie, hon? Don't be fooled by this contraption." She pointed to the oxygen apparatus. "I haven't lost my touch with baking. Just made a batch of my own special sugar cookies. And the coffeepot's on fresh too."

Oh no. Cookies are right up there with chocolates as my drug of choice. I love homemade cookies. Love them. Perhaps because my mother had never made a cookie in her life. Except if you count some of the ones that crumbled.

"Thanks. But I had a few too many chocolate truffles at Miss Henley's funeral reception yesterday."

"You sure now? These are still warm from the oven."

It would have been rude to refuse.

Rose slipped a plate of sugar cookies onto the coffee table and shuffled back to the kitchen for the coffee. She turned down my offer of help. She said, "Chocolate truffles served at the reception? That's special."

"I hear Miss Henley left instructions."

"Just like Helen. Doesn't surprise me."

This was good news. Strong opinion about Miss Henley. First-name basis. Exactly what I needed. Plus Rose's sugar cookies were to die for. Too bad she made the worst coffee I'd ever tasted.

"Just like her in what way?" I said encouragingly.

She snickered. "Helen always figured she was special. Better than the rest of us. I would have enjoyed that service, but I couldn't get there under my own steam, as you can tell. And yesterday was a real bad day for me anyway. Couldn't take a chance with all that perfume people dose themselves in. Goddam fragrances should be illegal in public spaces."

"Did you know Miss Henley well?"

"Knew the whole family well. Every one of those Henleys."

"You did?"

"Sure, hon. I grew up less than a mile away, and they grew up right up the hill." She nodded in the direction of Henley House.

"You mean Miss Helen Henley and Mr. Randolph Henley? And Mrs. Simonett?"

"That's what I said. The cousins, of course. My mother worked for old Mr. Henley before she got married, and she helped out a lot at the Henley House when I was a girl. Whenever there was a special event on, they'd need extra hands. Back then, there was always a party or some kind of celebration. Ma used to get called in, and I went along for the ride."

"Wow. Oh sorry, I was just trying to imagine Miss Henley as a little girl."

"Don't waste too much of your imagination, hon. She never changed all that much from the time she was a little girl. Always a bit mean-spirited, liked to have her own way, be the center of attention. She used people, including me from time to time. All I can say about Helen, she was never cheap. She liked nice clothes, good cars, and fine food."

"Did it run in the family?"

"What? Not being cheap?"

"Mean, controlling, and a bit cruel."

"The rest of them were fine. Crazy as coots in recent years, but pleasant enough."

"What about Randolph?"

"What about him?"

"Didn't he torment the other children? Destroy their new toys? Hurt their kittens?"

"First I ever heard of it. Randy had his head in the clouds, but he was a harmless fool."

"Oh. It's just that Miss Henley said he could ruin things for other children. Birthdays, Christmas."

"The only way Randy could have ruined a birthday party would be if he accidentally fell in the cake." She stopped to chuckle at her own joke. I waited and worried until she caught her breath.

She said, "Seems to me that did happen once. Randy was jumping around and being a clown, and he tripped and landed on the table with the cake. What a ruckus. It was Helen's birthday and I thought she'd never stop howling. She gave Randy a bloody nose over that. They both ended up being sent to their rooms by old Mr. Henley. I remember thinking how stupid it was. They were lucky to have everything they wanted, and then one of them would spoil it by acting like a brat. I got an extra piece of cake that day,

so it was all right with me. Of course, back then, I didn't
realize that I was the lucky one. I had Ma to tuck me in at
night and give me a hug."

"Where were their parents?"

She shook her head. "The Henley family was always
plagued. Olivia's mother ran off when Olivia was a toddler.
Left with a piano player. Just sent cards from Paris and
Berlin and places like that. Must have been quite the life in
Europe before the war. No one ever heard from her after
war broke out in Europe. Helen's parents died in a car accident. Another boy died of TB. And Randy's father hung
himself during the Depression. So . . ."

"That's terrible."

"Sure was."

"And their grandfather took care of them?"

"I suppose you could say that. Along with a small army
of maids and nannies and governesses."

"Was he a fierce person?"

"Not at all. He was a hard-nosed businessman, ran a suc-
cessful foundry. But he loved those children. He just wasn't
much for physical affection. Even at the time, I knew I was
better off with my hand-me-down clothes and my own
mother."

"I had no idea. I never thought about Miss Henley as a
sad little girl without parents."

"Well, don't start now. She was never sad."

"So Randolph didn't make Miss Henley's childhood
miserable?"

"The other way around more like it. Can you imagine
Helen Henley putting up with someone treating her badly?
Even when she was a child?"

I thought about it. "Not too likely. Do you remember
hearing about a puppy? Does that ring a bell?"

"Another dustup. But I thought it was Olivia who had
the puppy. Never mind. I don't even remember what kind
of dog it was. But I do recall Ma saying that Randy left the

gate open—just like him, really. And the puppy ran out into the street. End of puppy. A childish mistake. Anyone could have made it. Helen never forgave him for that, even though poor Olivia did."

I shivered, thinking of Truffle and Sweet Marie. Maybe Jack needed to fence the front yard as well as the back.

Rose continued. "Randy, though. He was such a foolish dreamer. He loved reading and writing and art. He wanted to travel the world."

"Did he end up doing that?"

"Not really. He had health problems. Never was all that stable. In the end, I think he lost his marbles. He turned into a pathetic old pack rat, ruined that house. I remember when it was grand. Lots of parties and fun. So many beautiful people."

"Did you ever visit Randolph?"

"I couldn't breathe up there. But he'd drop in from time to time for tea and cookies. He had that sad, sweet, goofy smile. I felt bad when he died. It's a shame, for sure." She closed her eyes. "I remember the food they'd serve for the parties. And the dresses. Boy. Those Henley girls always had the fashions first."

"Tell me about the other cousin, Olivia."

"Ah, poor Olivia."

"I guess she's not well either." Maybe Benjamin wouldn't tell me about the Olivia problem, but I figured Rose wasn't bound by any oath of confidentiality.

"No. She was never the same after the accident."

"What accident?"

"You don't know that story, hon?"

I shook my head.

"That was the saddest thing ever. Olivia had only been married a few years. Oh, that was the wedding of the decade. I'll never forget it. Of course, it was back in the fifties, before everyone and his dog had a big fancy wedding they couldn't afford. But old Mr. Henley, he put on a show for his favorite girl. Olivia was very beautiful, you know. Even with that Henley nose, she was lovely. I can't forget her in acres of white taffeta, all that ivory skin, that silver blonde hair piled high. Olivia had such beautiful hair. I think her veil stretched for half a city block. I can recall the scent of orange blossoms. Olivia and John Clinton Simonett. Those Simonetts were steel money, way more wealthy than the Henleys, and John Clinton was their only child. A real good catch and a fairy-tale couple they'd say today. The bridesmaids wore mint green taffeta and flowers in their hair. Now how many bridesmaids were there? Oh brother. Seven? I'm trying to think."

I cleared my throat. "The accident?"

She jerked herself out of the memories. "What? Oh right. Well, that came long after. A couple of years."

"A car accident?"

"No, no. A boat. A canoe. Olivia and J.C. and the babies were . . ."

"Babies?"

"Well, yes. You got to let me finish, hon. What exactly is your big rush?"

"Sorry."

"Olivia and her husband had twin boys. Silver blonde like the mother but big and strapping lads like their father."

I found myself holding my breath.

"They had a summer place up the river a ways. It was a beautiful day in the fall. I remember it like it was yesterday, trees just starting to change and we had a bit of Indian summer. They were out on the little bay in canoes. It was late in the season, but Olivia always loved the water."

I found my hand pressed to my mouth.

"Who knows if it was a random wave or if one of the children tumbled over and that upset the canoe. Back then, there weren't any, what do they call them?"

"Personal flotation devices," I whispered.

"The children drowned, of course, and John Simonett

died trying to save them. Randolph hauled Olivia out. She was half-drowned herself. He gave her mouth-to-mouth, but I guess it was too late. She'd been underwater too long. Her poor brain was never the same. She's been in one institution or another ever since. Always expensive places. Always the best of care. Of course, her grandfather made sure that she was well taken care of."

"What an awful story."

"You said it. Old Mr. Henley died less than a year later. I think his heart broke because Olivia hardly recognized him, after the accident. He loved that girl in his own way. Of course, losing those beautiful little boys too. And Randolph never forgave himself. He always said if he'd jumped in the river two minutes earlier, he might have saved one of them. Silly boy. He was always so afraid. I'm surprised he could even swim, let alone know anything about mouth-to-mouth. He didn't have common sense at the best of times. No one could ever tell him that, of course. He made himself miserable over it. Ruined his life too."

"Was Miss Henley there?"

"No. If she had been, she probably could have saved those babies. Helen was an excellent swimmer. But like I said, it was fall, and she'd gone back to college. She missed the tragedy. Maybe that tragedy turned her into the kind of person she became. Cold, bossy, mean. Who's to say? She talked to me about it at her grandfather's funeral. That was quite a splashy event too. Randy was in charge of flowers and he always went too far, poor boy. They said he bought up every lily in the state."

I didn't want to get off topic and onto splashy funerals and flowers. I steered us back to Miss Henley. "What did she say to you?"

"Well, I had a new fella at the time, and I was over the moon over him. Helen said to me. 'You know, Rose, why bother getting close to people? They're only going to die on you.' "

"Maybe it explains her attitude to others."

"Probably does. But she was wrong. I married that boy. I had fifty wonderful years with him. And I didn't regret one single minute. Not while he was living and not afterward, rest his soul. He might be dead this past six months, but I have lovely memories."

"That's nice."

"Practical too, hon. He built this house himself, on a scrap of a lot. Worked two jobs to buy it. I wish Ma could have lived to see us in our own home on North Elm Street. Good investment too. Worth a pretty penny now. If I'm lucky, it will pay for a decent nursing home for my last days."

I was starting to feel a bit depressed, but Rose seemed happy enough. I said, "The house means a lot to you. And you keep it nice too."

"Well, maybe I'm crazy to stay here when I can't even manage the stairs anymore. Luckily, my late husband put in a full bathroom on this level a couple of years back. Then when he was sick, we turned the dining room into a bedroom. Means I can stay here anyway. I just wish I could get to the second floor. I've got some furniture I'd like to keep for my daughter. She's out on the West Coast. Course, most of it's junk—my husband's clothes, old tools, magazines— but I can't even get up there to throw it out. I guess if I end up in what they call an assisted facility, the upstairs will become someone else's problem."

I didn't want to forget our discussion. "Olivia is in a home. Would you go to that one?"

"I'd never be able to afford Stone Wall Farm, where she is. That's out of my league. In fact, pretty much out of everyone's league. Folks call it Millionaire's Manor." She chuckled. "But, never mind. I'll do all right. I like to have some nice people around. I like to have a chat now and then."

I could see that. "Olivia had an attendant with her at

St. Jude's for Miss Henley's memorial. She had to be sub-
dued a bit."

Rose's eyes glistened. "Did she now?"

"She got out of her wheelchair, waving and blowing
kisses to everyone."

"Poor old crazy Olivia. I think that's good news. Lucky
she can stand up. There was a time she couldn't get out of
bed. She's a lot better than she used to be. They got better
drugs now, I guess."

"Did she get along with Miss Henley?"

"Helen was good enough to her, I guess, in a practical
way. Weekly visits, I heard. Not a warm person, Helen, but
dutiful. Why are you asking, hon?"

"I was just wondering."

"Wondering if poor Olivia killed Helen? Because if you
are, you can forget that. Even if she could have, she wouldn't
have hurt her. Olivia thought the world of Helen."

"But she seemed so . . . overjoyed at the service. Like a
victory dance."

I waited until Rose finished one of her long, scary chuck-
les. I raised my eyebrows encouragingly. "Olivia would have
seen flowers and heard music, and seen all those people in the
same church she was married in, and she would have thought
it was a party. Most natural thing in the world for her to get
up and try to dance and wave. In fact, I'm darned glad to
hear that she was able to do it."

"Wouldn't she associate the church with the funerals?
Her husband and her children? Her grandfather?"

"Olivia wasn't able to attend any of those. She was in bad
shape for a year. And if she had been conscious, well . . . no,
whatever you're thinking about poor Olivia, you're wrong.
You'll have to look somewhere else to find out who killed
Helen Henley."

"Not that I'm trying to find that out, but that reminds
me. Helen wanted me to find some documents that Randolph might have hidden in Henley House."

Rose snorted, "Hidden up there in that mess? Not much chance for finding them in that case."

"You've known the family for years. Any idea what they'd be?"

"No idea at all. What's the matter? You didn't like the coffee, hon?"

"I already had too much today. Do you think the documents would be connected with the property?"

"Can't imagine. Old Mr. Henley kept on top of all his legal stuff. Not likely there'd be documents floating around. But if they are, maybe the police will find them. They're taking it all seriously. A blonde detective talked to me already. I told them pretty much what I told you. Of course, they were in a bit more of a hurry."

"That reminds me, I'd better get going. Dogs to walk and feed. Thanks so much for all this information. It helped me understand these people a bit more. I wish I'd known more about Miss Henley."

"If you come back again for a visit, I can show you some pictures of those girls. My, they were lovely."

"Thanks. I will come back, and when I do I'll rig up a gadget to catch your mail, so it doesn't fall on the floor."

"I'd appreciate that. Here, I'm going to put you in my book. Hand me it, hon. It's on the table in front of you." I passed her a little address book with a happy spaniel on the front of it and waited until she'd written in my phone number and address. "You never know," she said.

I said, "Don't bother walking me to the door. I'll be okay."

"Are you joking? I don't leave my door unlocked these days, hon. People are getting murdered in this neighborhood, and I'm not planning to leave this world before my time. So you're going to drop in again sometime?" Rose trailed behind me all the way to the front door, her breath rasping.

"Sure I will, Rose. And you know what? I'll bring my

grubbies by and I'll help you clear out your second floor if you'd like. We can do it bit by bit over time. I can haul stuff down, and you can decide what to do with it."

"Well, that's just sweet of you, hon. I look forward to that. Now, I need my nap," she wheezed, "but when you come back, remind me to tell you about Crawford, the other cousin. They all grew up together."

"Who? Crawford?" I said, but the yellow metal door closed and the lock clicked.

# 7

By the next day I took stock of my situation. My major client was in the morgue. My dogs were sleeping. My phone was bombarded by crank calls. Jack was checking out point-of-sale systems for his cycle shop. Sally had taken the kids to the pediatrician. Margaret was doing whatever lawyers do. And I was just plain stuck.

I reminded myself that an important tactic is to keep busy when you get bogged down. Have some pleasant little projects to take your mind off your problems and reinforce your serenity. I made a new set of color-coordinated files for my office and paid my bills. I had already put my spice shelf in alphabetical order and stocked up on the toilet tissue, paper towels, and candles on sale at Hannaford's. I arranged them neatly in the lovely little storage closet I have next to my bedroom. I shook Truffle and Sweet Marie awake and took them for a much longer walk than they wanted. Then I went back to being stuck.

So much for theory. I could not take my mind off Miss Henley's death and the documents I'd been paid to find.

Were they connected to her death? If I could find them, would that point to a culprit? I could hardly complete the project. For starters, the site was off limits, surrounded by police tape. But I didn't feel comfortable about keeping the money. It wasn't a legal issue. More of a niggling moral quibble. It was a large enough sum that I felt I had to earn it.

For reasons that seemed solid at that particular moment, I decided to visit Olivia Henley Simonett. Maybe she could shed some light on the documents.

But first I hit Kristee's Kandees.

———❦———

The front entrance to Stone Wall Farm was flanked by twin pillars. The two-story white building sprawled across a broad lawn. At the far end of the long grassy expanse a fringe of woods framed the area. In the distance, a range of misty Catskills loomed. Pretty spot. But if it was a farm, I was an astronaut.

I admired the immaculately trimmed grass, with not a stray leaf in sight. There might not have been any wood smoke, but you could sure smell money in the air. I pulled into the visitors' parking lot and slid the Miata into an empty spot. It was half the size of the shiny black Lexus SUV parked on one side and the aged blue Cadillac on the other. In the row of parked vehicles opposite mine, a new bright green Echo and a red Jeep made a cheerful statement next to a brown utility van and the large wheelchair-accessible van with Stone Wall Farm's name and logo tastefully displayed in black letters on the glossy white surface. The only vehicle out of place was an ancient, badly rusted Toyota Supra.

I couldn't imagine what it cost to keep a loved one in a place like Stone Wall Farm, but like Rose, I'd never be able to manage it. Inside the building, the grand foyer smelled of wax and fresh flowers. Soothing toile wallpaper and immaculate wainscoting warmed the entrance. A bird of paradise flower arrangement in a heavy black vase perched dramatically on a demilune table. Behind it, a vast mirror, framed in gold leaf, magnified the works.

*Ka-ching.*

Handrails had been mounted along the walls, but they were painted to match the wainscoting and blended in. I approved of everything I'd seen so far in my visit to Stone Wall Farm. Next my eye was drawn to the broad curved staircase with the polished mahogany banister, sweeping gracefully to the second floor. The corridor above was set off against the dark wood railing. A very appealing picture. Probably not so different from Henley House at the height of its glory. In fact, except for the cutting-edge safety and security details—coded-card system, fire detectors and monitors—Olivia Henley Simonett probably felt right at home here. Of course, she would have to use one of the two elevators set off to the side of the staircase.

A polished reception area with more fresh flowers lay straight ahead of me. I walked past the formal sitting room to the right. I stopped to observe. Two white-haired women with walkers sat chatting on one of several chintz sofas. Behind them a girl of about twenty with purple spiky hair stared out the window. She wore a uniform that matched her hair, and was holding her fingers in a way that smokers do when they need a fix and can't get outside.

A painfully thin man with lank dark hair sat hunched over in a motorized wheelchair in high-gloss red. He couldn't have been more than twenty-nine, his poor bony shoulders making dents in his T-shirt. He faced a large baroque cage with a pair of small parrots. He was quite obviously upset. I couldn't make out what he was trying to say, but his agitation was growing. His legs jerked.

One of the women on the sofa turned toward the girl with the purple hair and whispered to her.

"Pretty boy," the green parrot said seductively.

The blue and yellow one tried its luck with, "Treat time?"

The girl at the window turned, walked to the young man, and gently pushed his hair back. "You got your hair in your eyes again, dude. You're going to need to get a do like me, Gabriel," she said. "And a bit of gel."

His answer was unintelligible to me.

"You're welcome," she said, patting his shoulder. "All part of the service."

"Thank you," said one parrot.

"Snack?" said the other one.

"May I help you?" a voice said.

I whirled, expecting a third parrot, perhaps pink. A bird-like woman smiled at me. I recognized that particular smile. It was the type you reserve for prospective clients. I should know. I have my own prospective-client smile. I took a lesson from this woman and reminded myself to let my smile reach all the way to my eyes.

I did my best to smile back. I'd felt apprehensive coming to Stone Wall Farm, but now I was relieved. The place was immaculate, well run, organized—qualities I love.

I asked for Olivia Simonett. The birdlike woman gave a small flutter and said, "Oh, I don't think . . . I mean, well . . ."

"It won't take long," I said confidently. "I just want to say hello to Olivia. I brought her some chocolates."

"She's been very . . . perhaps you shouldn't . . . so distressing."

A bell rang sharply on the desk, and the woman nearly took flight. The bell rang again, and she fluttered down a short hallway to a doorway marked "Executive Director." A tall woman with smart silver hair stood in the door watching me. From where I stood I could feel her ice blue eyes assess me, before she turned away.

I shuffled my feet for a moment and then gazed up the long, curved polished wood staircase. I thought I saw a movement. I squinted. Sure enough, I spotted shoulder-length white waves and a flowing flowered garment. Olivia was making her slow way along the upper hallway, with the help of a walker and the sturdy dark-haired attendant, whose glasses still had a definite tilt. I moved without thinking.

They had just entered a suite when I caught up. The door stood open, revealing a vast and lovely room, full of light and chintz and flowers. A talk show played on the television set.

The attendant whirled and gasped, "Who are you?"

"A friend of the family."

"Oh. Well, I suppose that's all right. Marilyn hasn't been herself."

Marilyn? Was I in the wrong spot?

I stared at the elderly woman who had just slumped into an oversized velvet recliner. She wore a flowered silk dressing gown in soft shades of pink, silver, and fuchsia. Her pink hair ribbon was tied neatly. Despite her unfocused eyes and the white hair, there was no mistaking that splendid Henley nose and eyebrows. This was Olivia Henley Simonett.

"Olivia," she snapped at the attendant before snatching up a handful of tissues and blowing her nose. She turned to me and said sadly, "My name is Olivia."

"Yes, of course. I know that. And I am Charlotte, Olivia. I brought you some truffles."

The attendant flushed a deep and unbecoming red.

"Olivia, Olivia," she muttered. "Lord help me. I had another patient named Marilyn, and I guess I am getting old and making mistakes. I am so sorry, Olivia, honey."

Olivia giggled. "You *are* getting old. You sure are. You are a real mess. I know your name, Francie Primetto. You should know mine."

The nurse flushed deeper. "That's embarrassing. I'm new here with Olivia. We've had a complicated staff shuffle, and

I'm just used to the night shift. Everyone's asleep in the night."

Her patient said, "Now you're on the day shift, Francie. So you have to be nice to me. You have to remember my name."

The nurse's broad face broke into a smile. "I sure will be. You're a lovely lady, Olivia."

"I am." Olivia shone her smile at me. "And you are lovely too. Helen used to bring me chocolates. She was always wonderful."

"I'm sure she was," I said.

"Can I have them? The chocolates? I've been good. Haven't I, Francie? Very, very good."

I hesitated a bit. Were there rules here? No chocolates before lunch?

"I have been good," she said. "All day."

To hell with the rules if there were any. I don't approve of rules governing chocolate anyway. "I brought them for you," I said, passing over the small gold-wrapped package.

"Those are my favorites. Helen brings those." She pointed to an empty box in the wastepaper basket. "But these are good too."

Did I see a sparkle of mischief in those startlingly blue eyes? They gave her quite a youthful look. Perhaps living in a place like Stone Wall Farm, where every physical need is taken care of, keeps you young in some ways. Of course, I was sure Olivia Henley Simonett, if she'd had any choice, would have chosen to live a normal life outside this perfect prison. Even as we stood there, the ribbon seemed to come undone.

If Helen Henley had lived to be a hundred she would never have let her hair tumble around her shoulders in long, bedraggled white waves. The staff of Stone Wall Farm would have been on their toes. Keep that ribbon tied, you slackers. Or else.

I don't know what made me say, "Your ribbon is coming

loose. Can I fix it for you?" Olivia Simonett was so fragile and childlike; it made me want to protect her. I could understand Benjamin's reaction more now that I'd met her.

"All right. Helen used to do that for me." Her wavering smile flickered then faded. "But something happened to Helen. What happened to Helen, Francie? Did she die?"

The nurse reacted. "Oh honey, we're not supposed to get you upset."

As the blue eyes filled with tears, Olivia's voice soared in panic. "Did Helen drown?"

Francie caught her breath.

"Did she? You have to tell me." If Olivia's wailing got any louder, they'd hear it downstairs.

"No. She didn't, Olivia," I said. "She didn't drown."

"That's good. Drowning is the worst. I don't want to think about it. I can't. I just can't."

"No, honey, don't think about it," Francie said.

"But she died though. Didn't she? Helen died."

How many times would Olivia have to be told this? Would it be just as painful every time?

"Yes, Olivia," Francie said. "She did."

Olivia unwrapped the chocolate box and flipped off the lid. "That's sad about Helen. Very sad."

"I'm so sorry," I said.

Olivia widened her bright, innocent eyes. "Why are people always dying?"

"There, there, Olivia," Francie said. "Don't worry about it, honey."

"Randy too. Randy died. Silly Randy. Randy never brought me a present. I thought maybe I wouldn't get any more chocolates."

As I searched for words that wouldn't make the situation worse, she reached for a truffle. "Oh goody. I like the white ones best. There are three in here."

So much for the sad end of Miss Helen Henley.

I said, "Olivia, do you think your silly cousin Randy would have hidden some papers from Helen?"

"Randy was naughty. He liked to make Helen mad."

"Did he? What would he do?"

"Tricks, bad tricks. I don't remember."

"Did he ever talk to you about any papers?"

She frowned. "No. I don't think so. Randy liked paper. Lots of it. Helen said too much. She was very, very mad at Randy. But she never got mad at me. She liked me. I'm the pretty one." The hand shot out toward the chocolate box.

The nurse said, "Oh Olivia, honey, save some chocolate for later. What about your lunch?"

"I don't want lunch."

"But don't you want to go down to the dining room with the other ladies? Everyone will be there."

Olivia shook her head. "I don't like those ladies. I want to stay here. I just want chocolates. I want to watch my television."

"Honey, you'll have to wait."

Olivia showed her Henley side in a little flash of temper. "You are not the boss. I am the boss. And I want *all* the chocolates."

Francie dropped her hand and shrugged. "All right, but the doctor will give you a hard time and it won't be my fault. You know you're not supposed to have much caffeine. You know it . . ."

"Don't like this doctor. Let's get a different one."

It seemed like time for me to leave. Olivia was a frail, spoiled elderly child. She was far too damaged to offer useful insights on what Randolph might have hidden.

Olivia didn't lift her eyes from the chocolate box as I said good-bye.

Outside in the hall, Francie thanked me for coming. "She sometimes forgets her manners. Can't be helped in her condition. I'm glad you came. And not just for that poor lady in there," she said with a soft laugh. "I needed the break too. It's been a long week."

"That must be very hard on you," I said.

"Well, she is really upset about her cousin, even though her behavior doesn't necessarily show it. She's quite depressed. I can't even get her to go downstairs to socialize at all."

"You said a long week. Surely you can't work straight through."

"Not usually, but since last week, she's had terrible dreams in the nights. They've had to increase her sleeping drugs, so someone has to be here."

I leaned in and whispered, "You mean since Helen, um . . ."

Francie whispered back, "Even before that, although it sure didn't help. Olivia gets the best of care. She's got the money to buy it, and she's willed most of it to this place, so you can just imagine they make darn sure she's happy. I got double time and a half since I started with her, so I don't mind the daybed. Top quality, like everything else here. Mind you, I'm getting a bit too old for this, but I couldn't say no. My husband's out of work, so the money is a godsend. And I can't say I begrudge her that fortune." Francie's plump, tired face fell. "Imagine losing your husband and children that way. I'm glad to have my old guy even if he is useless. I shouldn't joke. Olivia's lost all her relatives over time. No money can ever replace that."

"No."

"It makes you grateful for whatever you have. Every relative."

That reminded me. I stuck my head back in the door. Olivia peered at me, mischievously. Chocolate streaked her chin.

"Olivia," I said, smiling, "do you remember Crawford?"

The smile slipped, replaced by shock.

"Your cousin Crawford. You all grew up together. Do

you know where he is? Do you know what happened to him?"

Olivia Henley Simonett flung the chocolate box at the television set. She threw back her head and howled.

———+▸+———

As I settled in on the sofa that evening with Truffle and Sweet Marie, we were joined by Jack, who had managed to score a jumbo package of M&Ms and a week's supply of tiny green dog treats.

"Come on," he said, "snap out of it. How bad can it be?"

I muttered, "It can be craptacular. First, I got all these calls from nutbars pretending to be clients, and then I had that disaster with Olivia. When am I going to learn not to be so impulsive?"

"Never, I hope," Jack said.

"You're biased. You think there's a chance I might say yes to one more dog. But this is serious. I wish I had kept my mouth shut."

"What kind of an aspiration is that? You want to be boring? Speaking of boring, how come you haven't ripped open that package of M&Ms yet? Let's go wild and eat the red ones first."

"When I left, Olivia was still shrieking. The entire staff converged on the scene. Even her dozy attendant was really ticked off with me. She said it would take them two days to get her settled down again."

"How could you know that would happen?" Jack said.

"Maybe I should have used my brains. Found out more about her before I asked upsetting questions."

"My guess is the outburst had nothing to do with you. This woman is brain damaged and drugged and quite removed from reality."

"I feel terrible. The problem is there's this one other cousin that no one's been talking about, and it occurred to me he might be the only person who'd gain from Miss

Henley's death. I simply asked if she remembered this Crawford. That's what set her off."

"My point exactly. Normal people don't start screaming when they hear the name of a relative, dead or alive. Olivia obviously needs some help."

"And don't *you* go suggesting that what she needs is a rescued dog," I said.

"Go ahead and laugh, lady, but there's a huge body of evidence proving that residents in seniors' homes and rehabilitation centers recover faster and improve their cognitive abilities when they have access to pets. So there. Mock that."

I thought about the parrots and the young man in the wheelchair. However, I hated to agree with Jack, in case I found myself the temporary owner of the dog in question.

"My own cognitive abilities allow me to anticipate what you're up to and say no way."

"Don't get hissy. Let's talk about it some other time."

"Remember the topic at hand. I can't go back to Stone Wall Farm and ask any more questions."

"I'm thinking that's a positive. And here's a little challenge for you, Charlotte."

I snapped, "What?"

"Miss Henley is dead. Let it go."

"But I feel guilty about the money."

"What money?"

"She gave me an advance. Didn't I tell you that? I put it in the bank that same night. But I didn't really earn it."

"What was it? Some kind of retainer?"

"Yes."

"What's your problem? The money's yours. Legally. And ethically. You held up your end of the bargain. Trust your neighborhood philosopher on that."

"If I can find those papers, then I'll feel better."

"Miss Henley no longer cares about the papers or whatever they are. Anyway, you don't have access to the house."

"Maybe that's true. But those documents were important to Miss Henley. They may also be important to Olivia Simonett."

Jack slapped the side of his head. "Call me crazy, but didn't you just burn that bridge? So, if you got the guilties, you can return the money to the estate or you could donate it to a worthwhile charity, say . . ."

"An animal rescue foundation?"

"Why not? So far, you're just stirring up trouble. That way you could have a clear conscience."

"I don't know what it's going to take to clear my conscience."

Jack said, "Oh I get it. You feel bummed out because you didn't respond to Miss Henley's totally absurd and manipulative demand that you meet her in the middle of the night."

"If I had just gone out to meet her instead of sitting here eating chocolates, she'd probably be alive now. So excuse me, I think I have a right to be upset. So let me deal with it in my own way. Hang on a sec."

Jack said, "Don't answer the phone, Charlotte. It will just be another crank pretending to be a client. Just chill out."

I picked up the phone and said, "Charlotte Adams here of Organized for Success. First let me tell you what I have to say about Miss Henley: not a single word. None whatsoever. And that's final."

"This is Inez Vanclief."

"I'm sorry, I—"

"I am the executive director of Stone Wall Farm."

"Oh."

"I understand you created quite an uproar here today."

"Well, yes, and I'm sorry about that. I didn't mean to. I was just trying to find out about—"

"Mrs. Simonett has been extremely agitated since your visit. Her attendant tells me you bullied her, as well as brought in unhealthy snacks and encouraged her to miss out on lunch with the other residents. This is a sick, fragile, elderly woman. We have a responsibility to our residents here and we take it seriously. Stone Wall Farm is a private facility on private property. This call is to make sure you understand you will no longer be welcome here."

"What?"

"Do I make myself clear? Your presence will not be tolerated."

"But I may be able to help Olivia. I was working for her cousin, Helen Henley, when she died and—"

"Good-bye, Miss Adams."

# 8

I arrived at Sally's carrying a stack of flat-packed boxes and plastic bags with safety scissors, glue, and fat new tubes of finger paints. There was already a truckload of craft supplies at Sally's, including lots of stuff I'd brought, but the chances of finding any of it were slim. The kids followed me as I stumbled through the chaos in the foyer and into the living room.

"Can I wear your shoes, Charlotte?"

"Where are the doggies?"

"What's in the bag?"

"It's a project," I said.

The idea of a project was greeted by squeals. The two kids jumped up and down on the white leather sofa in excitement. "A project! A project!"

The baby flung a cracker.

Suddenly Madison plunked herself down. "What's a project?"

"We're going to do a special craft," I said.

Sally leaned against the door, arms folded, smiling.

"We're going to make a treasure chest for each season," I said. "We'll paint them and decorate them."

"Yay!" Dallas screamed.

"What's a season?" Madison said, frowning.

"Better start from the beginning," Sally said. "I'll clear the coffee table for painting."

I stared at her. The ultrachic glass-topped coffee table sat on a pale silk rug. It was all part of the trendy furniture Sally and Benjamin had bought when they were in stylish-young-couple mode. That was before Dallas, Madison, and baby Savannah arrived. Now Tonka toys and Barbies and Barney had been introduced into the mix.

"Let's not wreck the living room."

"Why not? It's already wrecked, and the table's the perfect height for finger painting."

Perfect for finger paints? So not.

"Kitchen table," I said.

Sally narrowed her eyes. "Coffee table."

"No arguments."

"Remember democracy? My kids, my house."

"My project, my rules," I shot back. "For this afternoon, democracy's dead."

The kids painted and decorated intently while Sally and I helped. In between, I filled her in on Olivia Simonett's story and what had happened at Stone Wall Farm.

"Sheesh. That's a sad story." Sally reached over and stroked the hair of her two little artists. Dallas ignored her. Madison pushed her hand away.

She said, "My kids are my life. I can't even imagine it. How would you go on without them? She must have wanted to die herself."

"I'm not sure she ever fully understood what happened."

"Maybe that's good." Sally shivered. "So what's the story on this Crawford? Why did his name set her off?"

"I don't know. But I plan to find out."

"On the other hand, why don't you simply forget it? The

Henley situation seems to be bad luck and bad business."

"I wish I could forget it."

An hour later, Sally's kitchen brought to mind a bad acid trip, not that I would know, and the first treasure chest, *Spring*, was complete. The box was now brilliant blue with green strips of grass, birds, and flowers. Baby Savannah had tossed on some cereal. The kids had finished painting a large spiky-rayed sun and cutting it out, with Sally's help. We glued it on as the final touch. The sun appeared to be snarling, but you can't win 'em all.

The *Spring* treasure chest was a hit.

"Next time I come over we'll do *Summer*," I said. "And wait until you see what we're going to do with them."

"What?" Both kids stared at me with wide eyes.

"They're treasure chests. We'll use them for treasures. You pick some toys you want to put away to be your treasures next spring."

All three kids started to wail as I left, reminding me I still had a lot to learn.

"Sorry," I said to Sally as I peeled their small hands from my legs. "I have to find out about this Crawford. I'll be back for the next stage of the project."

Sally leaned against the door frame, and for the first time I noticed the deep blue circles under her eyes. She said, "Maybe you should just forget this whole crazy situation, including Crawford, whoever he is, if he's anyone."

"I can't."

"Isn't that just like Hellfire to keep making trouble even after she's dead? Let it go, Charlotte."

"You know, sweetie," I said, opening the door and preparing to make a break for it, "that's so not going to happen."

My next stop was Rose Skipowski's house on North Elm. I'd brought along a nifty little bribe, my gym bag—which I keep stocked with jeans and T-shirts for grubby work, plus a couple pairs of old sneakers—and a fresh package of dust masks. I sniffed the wood smoke in the air and waited. The fat grey cat trotted down the hill to join the party.

"I'll be damned, hon. You did come back." Rose was resplendent in an acid green jogging suit and her electric white running shoes.

"Well sure." A tantalizing scent of fresh baking drifted out the door.

"And there's that miserable cat again. Don't let it in."

"It's obviously not starving." I shooed the cat away from the door.

"I think Helen fed it after Randy died. Now it's seeking a new slave. I suppose I should call the ASPCA about it. But it seems cruel, when someone in the neighborhood is feeding it. Here, scoot in before it gets past you."

"I know a person who can find a home for it," I said.

"That would be a big weight off my mind."

Inside the door, I bent and picked up the day's mail on the floor. "I brought you a little gadget to solve your mail problem." I produced a trim basket with suction cups that fastened to the metal door under the mail slot. "This will catch your mail and flyers, and you won't have to bend down to the floor."

A loud meow sounded through the mail slot.

"I'll brew up some coffee. Come in and have a cup."

I closed the door behind me and followed her slow progress into the living room. I remembered Rose's lousy coffee just in time. "Thanks, but I'm trying to cut down."

"I should too, but I'm still hooked. You'll have some peanut butter cookies though? Fresh made. They're even better than the sugar cookies, if I do say so myself. Won more than one ribbon with this recipe. You're just a slip of a girl. Don't have to worry about calories."

"Peanut butter cookies for sure. Let me help."

Rose shuffled off to the kitchen. "I have a bit of trouble

breathing. But I'm not a basket case, you know. I can take care of myself. Now what else can I get you?"

I waved my gym bag. "I brought some gear to help you sort out upstairs, anytime you want."

"You know something, hon? I'm not up to that today. Just join me for a snack."

"No problem. I'll leave the bag here though, and I can pop in when I have a bit of time and you are up to it. How's that sound?"

"Sounds good to me."

"Where can I stash it?"

"Right in that closet, hon."

I placed the gym bag on the floor of Rose's hall closet and made myself comfortable in the living room.

I called out, "Okay, now. I hope this is not going to upset you too, but I really need to know about Crawford Henley."

"What do you mean?" she said, returning with a plate that had enough cookies for a football team.

"I got into hot water at Stone Wall Farm when I asked Olivia about him."

Rose set the cookies on the retro coffee table. "You went to see Olivia?"

"I took her some truffles. I wanted to talk about Randolph Henley and Helen. She was fine with all that. But the question about Crawford set her off. She flipped. I got a call from the executive director. I'm not even allowed back on the property."

"That's peculiar. Don't worry, hon. Olivia might flip, but old Rose is not about to. Poor Crawford. Make yourself comfortable and I'll start at the beginning. Eat your cookies."

No arguments from me.

She settled into her orange armchair. The acid green of the jogging suit made a stunning contrast. "To begin with, hon, Crawford wasn't the least bit like the rest of them. I remember him as a teenager. If there was a tree, he had to climb it. If there was a pond, he had to swim in it. If there was a squirrel, he had to smack it with a slingshot. He was a real boy. That was a pretty stifling household, and Crawford wasn't the type to be stifled."

"Go on," I mumbled through a mouthful of cookie.

"He grew up to be the same kind of man, full of adventure. Went off hiking in the Himalayas, went prospecting for gold in Alaska, and even spent some time in the Brazilian rain forest. You getting the idea?"

"Did he ever settle down?"

"Didn't have to. He had just enough inherited money to live life on his own terms."

"So he never came back to Woodbridge?"

Rose shook her head. "Never say never. Last time I saw him was at the funeral for Olivia's husband and babies. Don't think he showed up again after that. He thought the world of Olivia, but he used to butt heads with Helen, and he'd tell anyone who'd listen that poor Randy was a waste of space."

"Did he get along with his grandfather?"

Rose snorted. "Well, I guess not. That was where the real fireworks came in. Old Mr. Henley used to ride him pretty hard. Crawford always took it in his stride. Then there was some strife about a girl. There were lots of girls, of course. He was so good-looking, with that white blond hair and those blazing blue eyes. A real heartbreaker. But Crawford fell hard for this one girl. Father was a bricklayer upstate aways. As if that mattered. The old man didn't think she was good enough. He wanted each of his grandchildren to make the kind of marriage that Olivia made."

"Money attracts money."

"Exactly."

"So it didn't work out with this girl?"

"I heard the grandfather tried to pay off her family. Then all hell broke loose when Crawford found out that the old man planned to mess up his engagement. Crawford shot off his mouth, and old Mr. Henley said he was going to cut him out of his will. There was some kind of trust fund for the cousins. I don't know whether he cut Crawford out or not. Crawford left town, and he never set foot in Woodbridge again."

"It's just that Olivia got so agitated when I mentioned his name. I wonder if he might gain from Miss Henley's death."

Rose blinked at me. "Not likely. I'm pretty sure he's dead, hon."

"Dead?"

"That's what I heard anyway. I mean, not officially. The family never had a funeral for him that I knew of."

"Oh. But I thought . . . when you said, ask me about Crawford . . ."

"That was silly of me. I was just talking. Glad to have someone here. Wanted you to come back. I didn't realize it would cause trouble with that sweet, sad soul, Olivia."

"It's entirely my fault, Rose. I have a habit of looking before I leap. But, so after Crawford died, would the money have gone to the other cousins?"

"Helen and Randy got the benefits while they were alive, although I don't think it was any great amount. Grandfather Henley didn't believe in giving anyone a free ride. They had to earn their own money too, or marry it. Olivia married it. Helen earned it. She couldn't have lived high on the hog on her teacher's salary or pension, but with that trust fund, she had a good life. She was always able to buy a new car every year, dress beautifully, and travel to Europe. She had enough to buy whatever she wanted."

"But what about Olivia?" I said before snagging another irresistible cookie.

"Olivia was rolling in it. She was the sole heir to the Simonetts. Her husband was the last of that line. The Henleys were paupers next to them. So Olivia, the poor lamb, could buy and sell Woodbridge a couple of times over. Trust me, that place, Stone Wall Farm, costs the earth. Then on top of it, she's got all those private nurses. Even so, she probably doesn't even make a noticeable dent in her interest every year."

"Mpph," I said with my mouth full.

"But to be fair to Olivia, she's never been mean with it. Always gives generously to others. Her whole estate will go to good causes. That's nice."

"I heard a big chunk is going to Stone Wall Farm. Apparently there's some kind of foundation."

"I guess I'm out of the loop lately," Rose said. "But no reason that place shouldn't get something, especially if it meant that needy people could get in."

I carefully didn't glance around at the spare, worn possessions of Rose and her seventies time warp. I knew she wasn't thinking about herself, but in my mind I couldn't help making a comparison with Olivia's luxurious life.

Maybe Rose read my mind. "Never mind that, hon. I wouldn't have traded my life for Helen's or Randy's. Not even Crawford's globe-trotting adventures. And especially poor Olivia. You see, I had love in mine. I had someone I cared about and who cared about me. A kind, good person. And I had him for a long time. That's more than any of the Henleys could ever have said."

—◆—

Every time I walked through the door, my phone was ringing. Although I'd pretty well given up on any of these calls turning into business, I answered to hear the anxious voice of a woman who needed five years of paperwork sorted so she could find her passport and go on her honeymoon to Paris. I slotted her in for an assessment the next morning. Five messages waited on my voice mail. The most intriguing one had to do with an out-of-control collection of dolls. That presented a striking image.

Speaking of out of control, my collection of miniature dachshunds fit that bill. I discarded the crank messages and recorded the numbers of the would-be clients, noted the problems, and turned my attention to Truffle and Sweet Marie. I grabbed their leashes and headed out with them into the fading afternoon light. They repaid me by barking at people with hats, small children, and all items with wheels. I hustled along, heading for the next block where we are usually alone to attend to nature's call. Truffle and Sweet Marie scampered happily, apparently pleased that two adorable children wearing cute little hats had run screaming from them. Ah yes, my little cream puffs were happy to be outside making trouble.

I was stooping to scoop when I noticed a young woman sitting on the grass. She was slumped over, leaning against a tree, her head in her hands. Her jeans had to be wet from the damp grass. Her grey hoodie didn't seem nearly warm enough for this chilly evening.

Not your problem, Charlotte, I told myself firmly. You do not have to rescue everyone. In fact, you do not have to rescue anyone. You just have to get that doggy doo into this bag. That's your task. Take care of it and walk on by. If you are bothered by people's problems, make a donation to an appropriate charity.

Really, I hate it when I get into that self-talk mode.

And it so rarely works.

As Truffle and Sweet Marie continued their walk, I watched the girl out of the corner of my eye. Not many people have hair that shade of purple. Noticeable even at dusk. Truffle and Sweet Marie spotted her too and barked like they each weighed ninety pounds instead of ten.

"Settle down, guys," I said, pretending not to stare.

It took a minute before I realized it was the young woman from Stone Wall Farm. I brightened. That meant she wasn't homeless or destitute, probably not desperate in any

way. Maybe her favorite sitcom had been canceled. Or her
boyfriend hadn't called. Or she'd found a zit. Whatever the
tragedy, it had no connection to me.

Truffle and Sweet Marie thought it had to do with them
though. They broke away from me and zoomed straight for
her, barking their pointy little heads off. She glanced up in
time to see two small torpedoes shooting her way.

I caught up breathlessly, bleating apologies. "They're
all bark," I said. "They hardly ever bite. Ha, ha. Here, let
me get my mitts on them before they . . ."

Of course, they were already jumping all over her.
Maybe she'd had liver for lunch.

"Never mind," she sniffed. "They're cute."

I was close enough now to see the tear tracks. Sweet
Marie licked her cheeks.

"Are you okay?" I asked.

"Not really," she said.

"Can I help?" Damn.

She managed a crooked smile. "I doubt it. Not unless
you can get me my job back."

"You lost your job? That's rough."

"Not your problem."

"Sorry to intrude. My name's Charlotte. Charlotte
Adams. I saw you when I was visiting Olivia Simonett yesterday," I said. "So I sort of felt that I knew you."

"That's why you seem familiar. I'm Lilith Carisse. And
that's where I was working. Until today."

"You worked for Stone Wall Farm?"

"Not directly. I was on private duty for Gabriel. He was
my patient. I'm a nurse's aide. I was his regular caregiver."

"Gabriel. Right. The young man in the wheelchair?"

"Now I'm out on my butt with no good reason. I don't
even know what happened. It makes me really crazy." She
sniffed and wiped her eyes on her sleeve. "I'd like to kill
her."

Truffle chose that moment to snuggle in.

The girl stroked his fur and rubbed her face against him. "These dogs feel just like velvet."

I said, "Um, kill who?"

"Inez. The boss there."

"Ah. Tall? Silver hair? Eyes straight from the freezer? I think I know how you feel."

"I doubt it. What's going to happen to Gabriel now? Who's going to make the effort to understand him? Who's going to take him for walks and talk baseball scores with him? Who's going to fix his hair? Who's going to make sure he knows what's happening on the indie music scene?"

Sweet Marie snuggled in to offer comfort. The girl held on to both dogs.

In my opinion, Gabriel had really lost big-time.

"What happened?" I asked.

"I have no idea."

"They just fired you right out of the blue?"

"Yeah. I thought the job was going well. I've been working real hard with him. Gabriel wasn't nearly as depressed as he used to be. His speech was even improving. Most of the time he was sleeping better. Then all of a sudden, boom, I'm out on my butt. No notice. No nothing. Inez fired me on behalf of the family. She had the authority. I really care about Gabriel, and now he's going to slip back, for sure. Although I hope I'm wrong."

"If it's any consolation, I had a problem there too. Inez Vanclief basically told me she'd take legal action if I went back. I was pretty stunned."

"Huh. What did you do?"

"I brought some chocolate truffles to Olivia Simonett."

Lilith let a chuckle slip. "Oh yeah, Olivia. She can't get enough chocolate."

"I asked her a question and I guess it got her upset. I have no idea why."

"Did you say yesterday? Right. Oh yeah, she was screeching her head off for a while. Did Icy Inez ask what happened?"

"No."

The girl gently set the dogs on the ground. She jumped to her feet and brushed off the seat of her jeans. "You think they'd want to know what set her off. That poor Olivia's like a volcano lately."

"I think it has to do with her cousin's death."

"She's not that stable at the best of times. Brain damage. Not as bad as Gabe, but bad enough."

"I asked her about another cousin and that's all it took. I didn't intend any harm."

"I know it's superstitious to say, but maybe it's the full moon. Or winter's coming. Gabriel has been so agitated this past couple of days too. The usual tactics weren't enough to soothe him."

"All I know is, Olivia just got hysterical. Her caregiver was standing next to me. She blamed it all on me."

"Francie? She's not the sharpest knife in the drawer. She gets everything wrong. She had a couple of shifts with Gabriel before she got switched to Olivia. Never even got his name right. It always took me days to get him back to normal."

"She seems kind enough."

"She's freakin' useless. People like Gabriel and Olivia need attention. Someone to talk to them, help them to use their brains, make them laugh, treat them like human beings. They need to live lives, not just spend time cooped up with someone who's no better than a sleepy . . . zookeeper."

"I guess the main idea is to keep Olivia happy and alive."

"Happy, yes. Alive, I'm not so sure."

"What do you mean?"

"What do you think? Olivia's an unpredictable, high-maintenance patient. Even though she pays through the nose, they have to work their buns off to keep her quiet and content. And she's got a huge personal fortune that she's supposed to be leaving a major chunk of to the Stone Wall Farm Foundation."

"I'd heard that."

"It will probably happen now that she doesn't have any relatives left to keep an eye on her."

"What do you mean?"

"That cousin, Helen, the one who was killed, she had a big argument with Inez about it. Called them gold-digging, money-grubbing thugs. I'm not kidding."

"Wow."

"Yeah, and she told Inez not to count on getting her filthy hands on the money. Loud enough for everyone to hear."

"And now Helen's dead."

"That's what I'm getting at."

"When did Inez and Helen have that argument?"

"Let me think. Last week. Tuesday? Maybe even Wednesday. One or the other, because those were the only days I was working. Does it matter?"

"It might. I'm sure you've heard that Helen died sometime last Wednesday night and the police think it was foul play."

Her jaw dropped. "Foul play?"

"You didn't know?"

"No one mentioned that at Stone Wall Farm. I've been so busy studying for my courses. I got exams coming up in December and I don't even turn on the TV."

"I wonder if the police know about this argument."

She shook her head. "I think Inez is a miserable cold fish, like she fired me without a blink. But it's just a job for her. It's not personal. And she wouldn't get the money herself anyhow. If you're suggesting that she might have killed . . . Are you?"

"Okay, it sounds crazy. But some very strange things have happened and I'm trying to understand what's going on. Now I'm worried about Olivia."

She shook her purple head. "The poor lady's so damaged. She's like a great big old doll that likes to misbehave for attention. She's a bit spoiled if you haven't noticed. But I don't think Inez would hurt Olivia. Nobody at Stone Wall Farm would."

I did my best to gather up Truffle and Sweet Marie, who had developed a major crush on Lilith. "I'd better get home. I have plenty of work to do."

"Thanks for talking to me. It's pretty cool for a stranger to care a bit."

I smiled at her. "You'll be fine, Lilith."

Her purple hair stood straight up and defiant. "Yeah, I can always get another job and continue my courses. But who the hell's going to care for Gabriel?"

While she worried about that, I'd be worrying whether she was right about Inez Vanclief.

*Save last minute panic:*
*stock up on chocolates or other small luxuries for*
*hostess gifts.*

# 9

Jack wore his best little-boy grin. He held out the extra-large box of pizza from El Greco.

"It followed me home," he said. "Can we eat it?"

Well, Truffle and Sweet Marie sure thought we could.

Jack headed straight for my kitchen without waiting for an answer. I noticed he had a bottle of wine precariously cradled in his arm.

"I know you prefer the nutritional properties of the all-chocolate evening meal," he called back over his shoulder. "But real food won't kill you for once."

I knew real food wouldn't kill me. I had a freezer full of the stuff: broccoli, cauliflower, crunchy green beans, corn, okra, and spinach. That's all fine until a pizza prances through your front door. The veggies were already frozen. They'd keep.

"I got extra anchovies, because I know you love them. They'll be good for your brain. You just relax. I'll do *every-thing*," Jack said, meaning he'd cut the pizza wedges.

Truffle and Sweet Marie joined him in the kitchen. I

stayed on the sofa with no intention of moving. "Do I hear the crash of crockery?"

"I know it's fancy, but you're worth it. Maybe we should even use napkins."

"What a catch you turned out to be," I said. "I hope word doesn't get out to the single female community. You'll be chased through town by women in white dresses and veils. Watch out for any that say, 'Tick, tick, tick.'"

"How about some wine?" Jack said. "Your choice: red or red?"

"I'll go with the red."

"Your wish is my et cetera."

As we made ourselves comfortable in the living room, I had to ask, "What exactly is it we're celebrating?"

"We're just having dinner together. But I suppose we could celebrate. What did you have in mind?"

"Maybe how lucky we are."

Jack raised his glass. "To lucky us."

I raised mine.

He said, "I'm glad you're feeling cheerful again, Charlotte. You've been pretty glum since, well . . ."

"That was before I saw firsthand how much worse off some people are."

Jack nodded. "We're warm and dry with plenty to eat—in fact, way too many anchovies. We have cuddly creatures and a choice of wine, within limits."

"And we don't need to rely on caregivers. We're not in pain. Our minds are working more or less clearly."

"Speak for yourself," Jack said, refilling the glasses.

"We haven't just been fired."

"Whoa. Back up, lady. I must have missed a chapter."

"I guess I didn't tell you about Lilith. She was working at Stone Wall Farm, caring for a wheelchair-bound man. She got the axe for no reason."

"How do you know it was for no reason?"

"Personal experience. I might have had my doubts, except remember how I was treated."

"Right. But you don't really know why this Lilith lost her job. Maybe she didn't take good care of her patient."

I thought back to Lilith's face as she talked to Gabriel. The gentle way she'd pushed the hair from his eyes. How she'd listened to him, found the meaning in his garbled words. And smiled like she meant it.

"She really cares about Gabriel. She's probably the only person in Stone Wall Farm who does."

"Did you say Gabriel? Huh. I wonder if that was Gabe Young."

"Who's Gabe Young?"

"Don't you remember? Tall, dark-haired kid. Very intense. He was a year behind us at St. Jude's."

I shook my head.

"He lived over in the Forest Glen area on one of those eternal crescents."

"I think I remember him, vaguely. I don't have any recollection of the accident. I must have been on tour with my mother."

"And you weren't into basketball anyway. I knew Gabe from the team," Jack said. "He was amazing. He would have ended up with a sports scholarship, no question about it. He was working hard to make sure it happened. Then his car got hit by a trucker who'd been on the road for twenty-six hours. Two other kids died, and Gabe was in a coma for a long time. I didn't even realize he was still alive."

"Maybe it's the same guy. Except, if his family has enough money to keep him in Stone Wall Farm with private care, he wouldn't have needed a scholarship."

Jack said, "I think that money came from the lawsuit over his injuries. Serious money in that settlement with the trucking company. You going to eat the rest of that pizza?

No, not you, Truffle. You've had enough. Oh all right, just one more anchovy. So Gabe Young is at Stone Wall Farm."

"Go ahead, Jack. Take the last three pieces. I have an idea about how you can earn them."

"What do you mean earn them? I brought this pizza and that wine you're swilling."

"Please don't introduce the word 'swill' into the conversation." I smiled and slipped an anchovy each to Truffle and Sweet Marie.

Jack sniffed his glass. "What are you getting at? There's nothing the matter with this. It was on special. Two for one. What?"

"It's definitely time for you to pay a visit to Gabriel Young at Stone Wall Farm."

"Sounds like a plan. I should go check up and see how he is doing. Maybe tomorrow."

"Definitely tomorrow."

———————

Kristee smothered a yawn as I pushed open the door to Kristee's Kandees at ten the next morning. The bell jingled, and she straightened up and attempted a smile.

"Well, Charlotte Adams. Twice in one week. You plan on gaining more weight?"

What did she mean *more* weight? I made a mental note to find another chocolate shop with a more congenial owner, even if I had to drive to Poughkeepsie.

"Just stocking up on gifts," I said evenly.

She yawned again. "Excuse me, Charlotte. I'm just bushed lately. Can't wait to get to bed, but that'll be past midnight. What can I get you today?"

She did have circles under her eyes. And a bit of icing sugar in her hair. It drew attention to the fact her roots were showing, I was pleased to note.

"I'll start with your black and white fudge," I said. "A dozen pieces."

"Fresh out of it, I'm afraid. I can't keep up with demand."

"People love that stuff."

"Lucky for me. But Thanksgiving's coming and people are stocking up for that. Then Christmas will be right behind it. Another six weeks of this. That's why I'm so tired. I've been up half the night catching up."

"All right. I'll have a couple of gift packs of your special truffles, dark, white and milk chocolate. So business must be going well."

"Yes and no. Some people don't want to come uptown after that shooting on the road last week. How dumb is that? So I have to run around delivering orders to my good customers. I am putting a ton of mileage on my van. I don't know how much longer I can keep that up. I charge 'em for delivery but it takes my time."

Kristee reached for her tongs and began to pick up the chocolates and pop them into the open boxes. She might be mean and petty, but I loved to see the reverent way she handled each piece. Kristee stood for quality. "Not just that, but I've had a couple of setbacks. The memorial reception just about cleaned me out."

"That's good news, isn't it?"

"Yes and no. Good for cash flow. But I have to have stock for my other customers if I want to hang onto them."

My mind had begun to race. An organizational problem. The type I like to sink my teeth into. "You said a couple of setbacks. What else happened?"

"I had this dumb prank call last week. It cost me half a day's business." She snapped the tops on the boxes with a bit more emphasis than necessary.

"You're kidding. How?"

"They said my mom was taken to the hospital. So I'm here by myself, and I had to close up and race all the way up to Troy. It was hours before I figured out Ma wasn't in the hospital at all. I found her home watching her stupid afternoon soaps. She won't answer the phone when they're on. How nuts is that? What a horrible day that was."

"I've been getting crank calls too, but that's horrible. Who would play such a rotten trick?"

"You got me there. Could have been worse. At least my mom was okay. That's all I need is another funeral to deal with at this time of year."

I guess I stood there with my mouth hanging open. Kristee interpreted it to mean that I was drooling over the fudge.

"I'll get it for you in a second. Yeah, that prank call set me right back. Ah heck, I messed up that bow. I'm still that upset I guess." She tossed the botched bow into the wastebasket and started again. This time she got it right.

I said, "I'm glad your mom wasn't really in the hospital, but you have to wonder who would think that was funny."

Kristee shrugged. "I'd blame it on the competition, but I really don't have any. The homemade fudge and dessert business is not exactly on the radar of any corporation."

"I guess you need some extra help to get you over the hump."

"You volunteering?" Kristee smirked.

"Not me. I've got a new business to run," I said with a weak grin.

"No man in your life, right? I heard your fiancé left you high and dry."

I didn't rise to the bait. How could I have forgotten how bitchy Kristee was? How could someone with that kind of tongue make confections that were fit for the gods?

"I have plenty to do. And *lots and lots* of friends," I said. Kristee yawned again.

I said, "But you should be able to find someone to help you."

"I don't let anybody but me make the product." She gestured toward the back from where the smell of chocolate was wafting seductively. "Just need someone to work the counter with the public. But who wants to be on call for a couple of weeks during the busy season? Anyone who works here has to be nice with people and flexible and really reliable. The kids prefer to work at the mall. They like the fashions."

"I might know the perfect person. Just to get you over the hump."

Kristee handed me the boxes and the bill. "The problem is, Charlotte, *I'm* really fussy."

"I know someone who needs a job in the short term but is also studying. She'd probably be happy to get some hours. But don't let me make you feel pressured."

"That's real nice of you, Charlotte. If you want a job done right, you do it yourself. I've had real bad luck with part-timers here."

"You know your business," I said as I paid for my candy and pocketed my change.

"I feel mean about it, but I've been fooled before," Kristee called out just as I opened the door to leave.

"It's all right," I said. "I'm pretty sure she's found a better job anyway."

As I headed for the Miata, I reminded myself that I am not responsible for everyone's well-being. I don't have to solve everyone's problems. And that was just as well because I figured Lilith might have just had a real close call.

— ◈ —

My cell phone was ringing as I got into the car. I hoped it wasn't a client rescheduling. Luckily, it was just Jack.

"You want the good news or the bad news?"

"Bad news. Get it over with."

"Okay. Guess who else won't be allowed back to Stone Wall Farm?"

"I have a client meeting in ten minutes, Jack. And I'm not there yet. No guessing games, please."

"Me. I am now persona non grata at a nursing home. Me. The nice guy who went out to check up on an old school friend. Does this make sense in any way?"

"Oh crap. What happened?"

"I biked out to Stone Wall Farm this morning. It was Gabe Young all right. And he was glad to see me."

"Did you ask him about Lilith?"

"Yup. Worked it into the conversation. Took awhile. You gotta really concentrate with Gabe. And there were some parrots that kept interrupting. Anyway, you were right. I'd say he's pretty broken up over that girl."

"Did he make a fuss? Is that why you can't go back?"

"A bit. You can't really understand what he's saying. It must take awhile to get used to it. He had some kind of an attendant, but she couldn't figure out what he was talking about. All of a sudden this ice queen shows up breathing frozen mist and my ass is so out of there."

"That's Inez Vanclief. She's a bit scary."

"More than a bit. She threw me out."

"But she must have told you why."

"Yep. She said that I was a disruptive influence. And not to come back if I didn't want legal action."

"Welcome to the club. I'm worried about what's going on there. Did you catch sight of Olivia?"

"Just a brief glimpse. She was walking on the second level when I went in, but I got booted out before I could find a way to see her."

"What's going on out there? It's all so weird."

---

My new client clearly had a problem. I could sum it up in four words: her husband, his toys.

She was a sweet lady in her midfifties with a tight copper perm, a bandage on her knee, and a two-story, immaculate home that smelled of furniture polish and potpourri. She bit her lip and clasped her hands together as she led me to the site of the problem.

"My, my," I said, as the garage door swung up.

"Like I told you," she said, "I just can't stand it anymore."

"Is it always like this?" I stared into the interior. Two huge motorcycles, an all-terrain vehicle, and a motorboat. A ride-on mower, a machine to blow leaves, and another one to blow snow. A few extra motors and lots of cans of 10W-40 stood around to give the place ambiance. Three tall, shiny red toolboxes, the type with wheels, looked on proudly. As did a lot of stuff I couldn't identify.

"Sometimes it's worse."

"And your laundry equipment is on the far side of all these vehicles?" I stood on my tiptoes but could barely see the washer and dryer.

Tears formed in her eyes. "He puts things on top of them. Greasy tools, gears."

I gasped, "Not machine parts."

She had a catch in her voice. "It's always been bad, but it's been getting worse this past couple of years. We finally have a bit of money, and we bought this lovely house. He has the kind of toys he's always wanted. Now he wants to enlarge the garage. Because he has his eye on a vintage Harley. I'm worried. I'll have to use the Laundromat soon."

I closed the door to the garage firmly and said, "Let's head back to the kitchen."

"But don't you need to check out what's in there? See how much stuff he's got? Otherwise how are we going to organize the space so that I can get my laundry done without bruising my knees and banging my head?"

"We'll make our plan over another cup of your very good coffee."

The kitchen was homey, neat, and smelled of the apple cake we'd shared when I arrived. I'd eaten it because you never know when there might be a shortage. And I'm very polite.

"Maybe your husband should just take over the laundry," I said. "That might solve your problem. Lots of men do laundry."

She frowned in surprise. "He wouldn't. Never. And if he did, I wouldn't like that."

"Do you enjoy doing laundry?" I said as she poured the coffee.

"Really, I do. I used to love it. Sorting, selecting water temperatures, softeners. Making clothes nice and clean again. I never thought it was drudgery. Now . . ." She sat down and massaged the bandage on her knee. "I get so far behind. I've started to put it off. It's become a nightmare."

"I'm not surprised. But you know what? You don't have an organizational problem. You've got a turf war."

"Oh."

"First, you obviously have a comfortable life, enough money to buy vehicles and a really nice, big house. So why are you doing your laundry in the dark back corner of the garage? Think about that. Second, why compete with your husband and his toys for space when you have a perfect spot in your house?"

She said, "I do? Where?"

I stood up and pointed to the bright mudroom that led to the backyard. "Lots of room here for your washer and dryer. You can have a few drying racks, cupboards over the machines for your products, and you'll have plenty of room for an ironing board and all that. You can whip your washing outside on a clothesline, if that's fun for you."

"But that would be a renovation. It would be really expensive. I thought you'd help me sort out the garage."

"That stuff in your garage isn't badly organized. It's big. It's bulky. It's in the way. It takes up a lot of space and keeps you from your machines, but it seems to be quite orderly. Is it causing your husband any problems?"

"No. He can get at what he wants."

"That's it. It's not your stuff. It's someone else's. You can't really solve that, can you?"

She shook her head sadly. "You're right. I feel like I'm stopped everywhere I go. Nothing I do around here matters a bit. He has no idea what's involved in getting his stupid clothes clean, and you wouldn't believe how mucky his stuff gets. Lately, I've been thinking of packing up and moving. I have fantasies about divorcing him from a distance. Isn't that awful? He's not a bad person; he's just turned into a big middle-aged kid. I'm probably way too upset over that garage. It's not like laundry's the most important aspect of my life. I've got friends and my part-time job and my two choirs."

"It's important to you. That's what counts. And think about my suggestion. You've got the appliances. Your sink's on the wall right behind it. Your plumbing will be a piece of cake. It won't be expensive. I can do a plan for you and help you pick out some nice shelving at the building center and your problem will be solved. No more dark spaces, no more bruised ankles. No disputes over who owns the space."

"I don't think he'll go for it."

"You might want to give a lawyer a call and find out the average legal costs for a divorce for someone in your circumstances. You'll have to pay for the advice, but it will be worth it. Then subtract the potential cost of this little reno and decide. I think you'll find you're way ahead."

A sly little smile was playing on the corner of her mouth. "I don't really want a divorce. And I sure don't want the big goof doing the laundry. I just want my space. I don't know why I didn't think of using that mudroom myself."

"All's fair in love and turf war."

———

That had gone well. I was on time and under budget as they say. I'd calculated two hours for the appointment and was out of there in less than thirty minutes. My client had a bit of homework to do: make a list of features she'd like to install in her new laundry-utility area and figure out if her old appliances would stand the transition. I was off to comb through building-supply stores, catalogs, and Web sites to see what could make her life a bit easier. We'd get together with the results. I was humming as I hopped into the Miata.

On the way home, I whizzed by a solitary figure peddling like hell on a battered blue bicycle. I couldn't miss the purple hair.

I pulled over and waited.

As Lilith passed by, I called out to her. She slowed and leapt from her bike. I would have ended up in intensive care if I'd attempted that maneuver. I wondered if Jack could have pulled it off.

Lilith grinned. "I'm in a better mood today. Not feeling sorry for myself. I sold my old Toyota Supra, so I know I can keep going until I find a job. I won't have to drop out of my night classes and leave Woodbridge."

"Great," I said. "You seem very comfortable on that bicycle. I'd break my neck if I tried to dismount that way."

"Two years as a bike courier in the city. It's like being in the Cirque du Soleil," Lilith said. "You develop techniques and nerve."

"And a certain artistry too."

"I suppose. But I really like to work with people. That's why I'm studying. I want to be in special education. I think the right teacher can make a big difference. I'm learning a lot about the way the brain works and all that."

"You'll be great at it."

"Thanks. I just have to find a way to keep a roof over my head until I can finish my course. Thanks, Charlotte, for being so nice. I have to go. I've got a batch of résumés to drop off."

I watched her purple head disappear around a corner. Lilith would be fine. But I felt a real sadness for Gabriel Young and what he'd lost.

# 10

Who knows why I turned left instead of right after talking to
Lilith. I didn't take long to realize that I'd blundered into Forest Glen and had lost my bearings in the endless tree-lined
crescents. Jack had mentioned that Gabriel Young grew up in
this neighborhood. But of course, Jack was checking out a
possible storefront for his retail dream, so he didn't answer
his cell when I tried to call. I cruised slowly through the crescents, not sure what I was searching for. All the houses were
similar: large split-levels or two-stories on treed half-acre
lots. Some had the family name hanging on little signs, but
most didn't. I didn't spot any Youngs. I'd just decided that
this was a waste of time, when I drove by a white Cape Cod
nicely situated on a well-kept lawn. A long ramp had been
added to the front. I noticed the battered basketball hoop attached over the black garage door and felt a lump in my
throat. Leaves danced across the lawn, and a woman walked
briskly from the side of the house brandishing a rake. I pulled
the Miata over and parked. In my mind, all people who rake
leaves are basically decent.

I stepped out of the car and approached her.

She had Gabriel's wide dark eyes and prominent cheekbones. Her salt-and-pepper hair was cut short. She wasn't the type for makeup. As I got closer I could see the lines on her face, as if each one had been scratched on by her son's tragedy.

She stopped raking and stood watching me, with an unwelcoming scowl. "I'm not planning to sell it. Thank you."

I blinked. "Oh. The house. I'm not house hunting. It's a beautiful property though."

"Sorry. I thought you were another real estate agent. Seems like every day there's a different one hanging around."

"Are you Mrs. Young?"

She nodded and frowned again.

"I'm Charlotte Adams. I was hoping to find you. It's about your son, Gabriel."

The rake tumbled to the ground. "Gabe! Did something happen?"

"As far as I know, he's fine. But I'm not so sure what's going on at Stone Wall Farm. That's why I wanted to speak to you."

"Stone Wall Farm has been a wonderful place for Gabe. He's been making such great progress lately." Leaves swirled merrily around her. Her smile lit up her face, erasing the wrinkles.

I said, "I think some of that might have to do with Lilith Carisse, his caregiver."

The smile slipped. "Oh. Lilith."

"I have been trying to help Lilith find another job, but before I recommend her, I need to know why she was fired."

"I'm not so sure I should tell you. There are . . . issues."

"So I hear. But I have seen her with Gabriel, and she seemed to be so caring, so tuned into him."

"Poor Gabe is very fragile emotionally. He doesn't need to be distressed."

"Lilith caused him distress? Really?"

"She was talking about going back to school full-time. Gabe would become very worked up every time she mentioned it. Apparently Gabriel's outbursts upset the other residents. Mrs. Vanclief asked us to take action on it."

"It's hard to believe that Lilith would upset him."

"She's quite young. She probably had no idea of the impact of her casual conversation. I wasn't sure it was the right choice, but Mrs. Vanclief insisted I sever the contact now before Gabe's behavior got worse."

"So would there be any reason not to recommend her for a job?"

Her eyes met mine, then slid away. "I'm not sure I treated Lilith fairly. I know she truly cares about Gabe. Perhaps I should have given her a chance to tell her side of the story."

"Thank you. I appreciate this."

"Charlotte Adams, you said. I know your name from somewhere. Where would I have seen you?"

"I have no idea." It seemed very unlikely that anyone at Stone Wall Farm would have told her about me. They didn't even know I'd noticed Gabriel.

She pointed her finger at me. "Of course. I saw you on the news. You're the woman who found the body in that awful old house. Hellfire Henley."

I don't know what shocked me more: that people in Woodbridge would be thinking of me as the woman who found a body or the loathing in Mrs. Young's voice when she said "Hellfire Henley."

"Yes," I said. "It was a tragedy."

Mrs. Young's face contorted. "I don't think it was any kind of tragedy. That ghastly woman. She tormented Gabe in school. When she started to come to Stone Wall Farm to see her cousin, he got practically hysterical. His emotions are so unstable. In a way, he's stuck at the adolescent boy stage and she really set him back. Lilith helped a lot, but it was very difficult for him and for me."

"Miss Henley tormented Gabe? But the poor guy's in a wheelchair."

"I mean she tormented him at St. Jude's. He wanted a scholarship so badly, because his father had one, you know. My husband was able to go to Cornell, even though his family could never afford it. Gabriel wanted to show his father he could do it too. That awful woman would taunt him. Fail him by one mark. Give him detentions so that he'd miss a practice. Make some horrible remark just before he'd take a test. Even in his damaged state, he hasn't forgotten that. And the wicked creature always made a point of seeking him out to speak to him every week when she visited Stone Wall Farm. She'd put her hand on his shoulder. Whisper something to him. The vile old hyena." She bent to pick up the rake. She held it like a weapon. "I had to make a point of getting him out of there every Wednesday afternoon. Now we don't have to worry about that. Maybe I shouldn't say it, but I'm happy she's dead and I hope she suffered. Whoever did it would have had a good reason."

I stood there with my mouth hanging open, trying not to imagine Gabe's mother taking aim at Miss Henley's head with that rake. As she stared at me, I finally got a grip. "It must have been a terrible situation for you. Did you ever tell Inez Vanclief?"

"Of course I did. Couldn't get anywhere. Olivia Simonett is leaving tons of money to the foundation. I'm sure you've heard that already. Olivia just loved having her cousin's attention. I also heard that Hellfire was opposed to the bequest. So let's put it this way: the administrator wouldn't rock the boat with either one of those women."

"What about your husband?"

"He died last year. Heart attack. But he wouldn't have been any help. He liked old Hellfire. She never tormented *him*. He was a fighter. She preferred to find the ones with a weakness, probe it, make them squirm. I tried to explain to him, but he always just thought that Gabe just needed to show some spine."

"Oh boy, that's bad.

She nodded. "I don't know why I'm confiding in you. My husband would have had a fit if I'd blabbed about our personal business." She gave a small laugh. "But now I can be as indiscreet as I want."

"There's more to it. I've been told not to visit Olivia. In fact, I'm not allowed on the Stone Wall Farm premises. And my friend Jack Reilly, who used to play basketball with Gabriel, has been refused permission to visit him. I wondered if the decision to tell Jack to stay away came from you."

"A friend visiting? That would have been very nice for Gabe."

"I believe it was nice for both of them."

"But, perhaps this Jack got Gabriel upset? I told you his emotions could be triggered so easily."

"I doubt it. But let's say, for argument, that's what happened. Would you expect the Stone Wall Farm staff to let you make the decision about who could visit?"

Her gaze had strayed to the driveway and the old basketball hoop over the garage door. I wondered if she was seeing her son as he had been fifteen years earlier, shooting hoops. Happy and with his life ahead of him. A scholarship, a career, someday a wife and children.

She said in a distant voice, "Of course. Gabe was in a coma for so long. Friends . . . fall away, you know? People don't know how to deal with what remains. No one comes anymore. He's lonely. That's why I got the parrots for him."

"He seemed to love those birds."

She nodded absently. "He did, but the last few days, he won't go near them. Perhaps he's depressed. He really needs a friend."

He had one, I thought. Lilith. No wonder he's depressed.

※

I had plenty to think about after I left Forest Glen. Gabriel's mother had hated Miss Henley. She didn't even bother to keep her raw emotion hidden. Even though Miss Henley was dead, she wasn't quite dead enough for Mrs. Young. And it was easy to understand how she felt. How many other people nursed the same kind of rage?

I was still pondering that as I whipped back uptown to hit Ciao! Ciao! while they were serving lunch. The tiny café was buzzing as usual with conversation and laughter. I chose a rustic roll with prosciutto, Asiago cheese, arugula, and red peppers, and a bottle of San Pellegrino sparking mineral water. I squeezed through the crowd into the last remaining seat at the little counter in the corner. It was a sandwich worth remembering and a lunch I should have shared with a friendly face, but I wasn't in the mood for chat and I worked my way through the sandwich without savoring it. I was stuck on that idea that many people had wanted Miss Henley dead. Former students for sure, their parents too, apparently. And what about some of the teachers she'd worked with? The ones at the memorial sure hadn't been overcome with sorrow at her passing.

Besides feeling guilty, I had another good reason to try and figure out who might have wanted Miss Henley dead. I knew Pepper wouldn't jeopardize her career just to give me grief and she was a detective on the fast track. But I was equally sure that she wouldn't mind a bit if I got dragged through the doo-doo in the course of her investigation. I had to stay a step ahead of her and offer up some credible suspects. So far I was batting zero. But I had an idea.

I planned to spend my afternoon checking out laundry-room equipment, shelves, storage, and new gizmos to make my client's life easier. Plus I wanted to find some special little trinket for Rose since she kept filling me with cookies and information. I headed across the street from Ciao! Ciao! to the gift store, Mystic Mabel's Magic Tables. I paced up and down the aisles ogling an array of wonderful objects. Thanksgiving decorations, polka-dot martini glasses, even a whimsical erotic cookbook. Neat stuff but none of it quite right for Rose, so I kept hunting. I knew the owner, Mrs. Neufield, as a teacher who spent thirty years at St. Jude's until her abrupt departure at the end of my senior year. I had seen her at the memorial, but I hadn't had a chance to talk there. I decided today was a good time to pump her for information about teachers, parents, and students who might have hated Miss Henley. Too bad Mabel Neufield was the kind of person who had never whispered a negative word about anyone, probably in her life. I should have remembered that.

"Oh dear, Helen was a strong character, for sure," she said, wringing her hands. "But she played by the rules. Who knows? Perhaps her students are all better because of her."

Your nose is getting longer, I wanted to say.

"That may be true," I said, with just a tiny bit of emphasis on the "may." "Did she have any enemies on the staff? Someone who might have reason to . . ."

A bead of sweat sprang up on Mrs. Neufield's downy upper lip. "Charlotte, dear, I know this is hard on you, especially finding her like, um . . . but really, I think it will turn out to have been a terrible accident."

"Uh-huh, maybe," I said. "But then again, probably not."

Her eyes didn't meet mine, not even a little bit. In fact, they kept drifting to the far corner of the store. I glanced there and she gave a nervous little jerk.

"The other teachers respected her. I imagine some of them might have liked her. I can't think of a person who would wish her harm. I mean that kind of harm. Anyway, we've all been retired for years."

Well, that was so much horse dropping. Mrs. Neufield

was either unwilling or unable to speak the truth. Whatever. I kept my thoughts to myself and smiled. I picked a small orange plate that said "SIMPLY THE BEST" in white letters. It would go with Rose's décor and certainly summed up her cookies.

While Mrs. Neufield wrapped the plate for me, I moseyed around the shop a bit more and checked out the corner she'd glanced at. A collection of small framed paintings of vegetables were displayed artfully. The veggies beamed out, bold and adventurous, even mischievous. Why was I not surprised to see them signed with a dashing "SK"? The hand of Mr. Kanalakis at work unless I missed my guess. I lifted one off the shelf and peered behind it. Sure enough, "Spiros Kanalakis, RR 2, Oxbridge, NY," and a telephone number were written on the back. I copied down the number and returned, smiling, to the cash register.

I left with the gift-wrapped plate and a new plan. Not everyone was as nice as Mrs. Neufield. Not by a long shot.

The rest of the afternoon passed in a blur of cutting-edge laundry technology: front-loading washers that saved water, flat drying systems for delicates, flexible wall storage, collapsible drying racks to save power, fashionable detergent containers, lightweight ironing boards, baskets, baskets, and, yippee, more baskets. Plus a surprising encounter with a $350 iron. By the time I exited my last stop, I had come up with some easy options to give my client a premium laundry room at a penny-pinching price. I just loved that. I figured she would too.

I was smiling when I eased into my driveway. A red Jeep pulled in behind me, taking me by surprise. A man stepped out. I stayed in the driver's seat and clicked down the door lock. I guess I still have some of the old habits of living in the city. I unlocked it as soon as I saw who it was.

Dominic Lo Bello. I rolled down the car window. The wind ruffled his hair. His smile lit up the late afternoon.

"You're a hard girl to track down," he said. "I've been

checking out every ice-cream cooler in town. But no you anywhere."

Be still my foolish knees. "I've been busy."

"Maybe hiding. But one of your friends ratted you out."

"Ah." Sally. Hopeless romantic, unrepentant match-maker. Watcher of biological clocks. And way out of line as usual.

He grinned. "I ran into her downtown and we had a chat. I told her I wanted to ask you for a coffee."

"And she told you where I live?"

"She made me give references, if that eases your mind. And she checked them out first. You can call her and ask her."

"I will."

"So how about it? You want to get together for a cap-puccino? There's a new fair-trade coffee shop with a nice view by the river."

"Jumpin' Java. I know it."

"Does tomorrow work?"

"Tomorrow would be fine." I barely managed to keep from squirming with joy. References. What a riot.

"Three sound about right?"

"Sure."

He waved as he headed off in the Jeep.

I was very, very happy that he hadn't heard my heart beating.

Jack was waiting as I walked through the door. He had his cycling gear on, ready to head out onto the rainy, slick roads, a perfect target for any distracted driver.

"What did that guy want?"

"Um, you're not going out on a night like this, are you? It's really dark and slick."

Jack had his own agenda. "I don't like the look of him. Kind of unsavory."

"Hmm. You are wearing black clothes and a cap at night. How unsavory is that?"

"Very funny. I have all these reflective stripes. No one

can miss me. I'm heading uptown to check out what I think is going to be the perfect retail location. What do you really know about this total stranger who mysteriously popped into your life?"

"Not a lot. But he appears to have enough sense not to ride around on a bike in the dark. And he comes with references. Can we say that about you?"

From the top of the stairs came a racket. Apparently Truffle and Sweet Marie weren't impressed.

"That reminds me," Jack said. "That other dog is still available. Maybe you should rethink your decision. You know, in case you need protection."

But I was a big girl. Not at all afraid of a cup of coffee with a man with shy-woodland-creature eyes.

———————

Wednesday is always catch-up night for me. Truffle and Sweet Marie love catch-up night. Perhaps because I start by cleaning out the fridge. Of course, this week all it contained were three kinds of Dijon mustard and a curling slice of pizza from El Greco, heavy on the anchovies. I put on my new Black Eyed Peas CD and picked up my basket of cleaning supplies. I dusted, vacuumed, and generally slicked up the apartment to the music. I tossed the covers of the doggie beds into my washing machine and hand washed two sweaters and my lingerie. I made another attempt to find out where the dogs might have hidden my lucky pen, and then put an extra coat of waterproofing on my winter boots. I checked my seasonal to-do list and moved my winter coat from the back of the closet, along with my basket of wooly socks, gloves, and scarves. I paid my bills and straightened up my business files. I made my obligatory weekly call to my mother and left my usual meaningless weekly message. I didn't mention the murder. I'm not completely out of my mind.

Finally, I updated my current list and wrote "Lilith—job

help?" on it. I added "Crawford? Olivia? Mrs. Young? St. Jude teachers—Mr. Kanalakis!"

I actually get goose bumps whenever I finish my weekly cleaning ritual. I can't really share this feeling with any of my friends because they tend to get a bit irritable any time I talk about catch-up night. Especially Sally.

Never mind. I raided the freezer and made a crisp and tangy shrimp stir-fry and settled in for an evening of relaxing with my two favorite cuddlers. They appreciate my systems. The missing pen was just an oversight, I was sure.

On the downside, I had plenty of time to think about Dominic Lo Bello. I reminded myself, the trouble with letting your knees melt is that you might need those knees someday. Say, to stand up for yourself.

I turned my mind from Dominic to Mr. Kanalakis and used my cell phone to call the number I'd copied down from behind the vegetable painting. I borrowed the name of my mother's main character in her detective series and booked an appointment for the next day.

At nine o'clock when I heard Jack arriving home, I called out, "Come on up. I have your favorite chocolate."

"Mr. Kanalakis? You're kidding," Jack said when I had sidetracked him with chocolate and filled him in on my plan. "Holy crap. You're going to track him down?"

"I already have."

"And what? You're thinking of going to see him?"

"Not thinking. Planning."

"Not by yourself, you're not," Jack said.

"That's the whole idea, Jack. Have another truffle."

———

Thursday dawned, mild and sunny, probably because I'd hauled out my winter clothing the night before. Never mind. I woke up early with plenty of time to give the dogs the kind of long walk they refuse as soon as it's the slightest bit wet or cold.

Later as Truffle and Sweet Marie slipped back to bed, I savored my first morning coffee and planned. I had the can't-find-her-passport-to-go-on-her-honeymoon client scheduled for nine and the out-of-control dolls for eleven. I was meeting Dominic at three. I planned to pop in to see Rose in between. The rest of my list had lovely tasks on it, including "sketch laundry room solutions" and "read up on doll storage." And some not so lovely: "buy food." For some reason I didn't feel much like heading to the grocery store. I was sketching up a few tentative concepts for the laundry-room client when the doll client called and muttered an excuse for canceling. Perhaps the dolls had pulled the plug on the project. The minute I hung up, the missing-passport client called to say she'd found it and didn't need anything organized.

All right. Roll with the punches. I used the time to plan a drive in the country.

—※—

A tempting aroma wafted gently around my nose when Rose opened the door. I couldn't believe my luck.

I breathed in deeply and said, "You made Toll House cookies?"

"Why, hon? You don't like 'em?"

Like them? I love Toll House cookies more than is normal for a functioning adult. Maybe because my mother never made them. Of course, she never made any cookies, as I may have mentioned. In fact, I'm not certain we had a working oven. Never mind. I'm trying to stay in the now, as they say.

"Sure I do," I said with restraint. "And I have something that will go nicely with them." I handed over the gift-wrapped package containing the pretty plate.

Rose said, "Aw, hon. You didn't have to do that." But I could tell she was pleased. Her cheeks still had a pink tinge long after we settled into the living room. The tinge went well with the robin's egg blue jogging suit. The suit itself was a jolt to the retina, especially against the orange background of Rose's chair. Sometime after her second cup of coffee and my fourth Toll House cookie and tall glass of water, Rose said, "You know, hon, you don't need to bring me presents."

"I thought that plate would go well with your living room. And with your cookies."

"Listen, hon, I'm stuck here on this street with no one around, and I'm not much good at getting out with this claptrap oxygen tank on. I have a bad addiction to baking, and here you are showing up, happy to chat. I should be buying you presents." She raised an eyebrow.

I said, "In my defense, it was just this one gift, one time."

"And it's beautiful and I love it. But I want you to feel free to drop in anytime and help me eat my cookies. No gifts required. So now that the politics are out of the way, what can I do for you, hon?"

"Talk to me about Henleys, of course."

"Don't you think you should try to put that whole Henley problem behind you?"

"I still feel guilty because I cashed Miss Henley's check."

"Well then, give it away. Maybe the food bank. Or the historical society. You could even ask Olivia if she'd like it to go to a certain charity. She used to support the Children's Hospital."

"I'm not allowed back in to see Olivia, remember? She was so upset when I asked her about Crawford that they had an awful time with her."

Rose frowned. "I still don't understand that. Olivia always had her little tantrums, even when she was a kid. Pitch a fit and then get over it. Sounds like that's what happened here. Although I have no idea how Crawford's name could set her off. Maybe it just hit her that she must be the only cousin left. And she's old and fragile too. You want another cookie? I made a double batch."

"So you don't think Crawford ever upset or hurt her."

"No, I don't. He thought the world of her. End of story. Come on, just one more won't hurt you. They're only cookies, you know."

I took the cookie. Information doesn't come cheap.

I said, "When I asked her about him, she was shocked. No act, no time lag. Her face changed, as if she'd been slapped."

"I still think it must have another explanation. Someone she saw passing by in the hallway at that moment, perhaps. An image on the television."

"If you say so."

"What puzzles me," Rose said, "is why Stone Wall Farm would take that attitude. They must know that it's good for their residents to get visitors."

"Well, that's the sad bit. It's not just Olivia. There's Gabriel Young too."

"I've got lots of time and plenty of cookies, so tell your story, beginning to end. Don't be springing surprises on me. Who's Gabriel?"

By the time I finished, Rose had a faraway look in her eyes.

"It sure seems wrong," she said. "I used to be able to visit Olivia every now and then when my husband was alive. Now that stupid old car of his just sits in the back of the house, rusting. It really burns me."

I nodded. My mouth was full.

Rose said, "Oh well, what can you do? People die. You know, I've been feeling bad that I missed out on that memorial service. It's only right that I go by and see my old friend Olivia. Bring her a little treat and talk about old times. Maybe tote along some of the old photos that I have of the family. Yes. That's just what I'll do."

"I would really appreciate it, Rose. But how will you get there? You can't be seen with me. Or Jack. They wouldn't let you through the door."

"I can always take a cab."

"Forget the cab. That will cost you a fortune to get out there. I know someone who can probably take you. You'll like her too. I'm pretty sure she'll go for your cookies. I'll let you know as soon as I clear it with her."

"Have it your way." Rose shrugged. "Something wrong with that last cookie on your plate, hon? You think it's gonna kill ya?"

# 11

Finding Mr. Kanalakis was like taking a trip back in time in more ways than one. After a lot of false turns, Jack and I finally bumped along the dirt track to a log cabin in a clearing. The cabin could have been straight from a history book except for the dusty Ford van parked near the front door. Mr. Kanalakis emerged from the cabin as we got out of the car and blinked in the bright light. He'd been fresh out of university with a master's in fine arts and the ink barely dry on his teaching diploma the semester he'd taught us art at St. Jude's. We'd never seen anyone like him. Not just because he'd been a hunk, which he had been. But also because he was the size of a truck, with more enthusiasm and fun than the rest of the staff squared. He'd boom with laughter and the light fixtures would shake. Keeping order hadn't been any kind of problem, not with those hamlike hands. We'd called him Hercules. "Herc! Herc! Herc!" had been a favorite refrain. The kids had loved him, while he lasted. Which was less than six months.

Now his ponytail was greying and his hairline had crept back a couple of inches. He must have been carrying an extra sixty pounds. But his wicked black eyes hadn't changed. This was still a man to command attention.

"Looks like you got me," he said. He still had that hint of the South about him; I never could put my finger on his origins.

I had trouble making eye contact. "I needed to talk to you. I didn't know how you'd feel about that if you knew it was me."

He shrugged one massive shrug and headed into the log cabin. Jack and I followed him. Jack was trying not to sniff the air too obviously. Me too. Turpentine, for sure. But perhaps an underlay of cannabis, unless I was mistaken. The walls were covered with dark brooding canvases, oozing menace and testosterone. I found my eyes drawn to them. Each had at least one dramatic slash of red.

Jack seemed riveted by the interior of the cabin. "Hand-hewn logs?" he said.

"Yep." Mr. Kanalakis didn't offer us any hospitality, not coffee, not cookies, not hash brownies.

"You heat by wood?" Jack said.

"Heat pump and passive solar for electricity. I'm off grid here. Produce more than I need."

"Wow," Jack said.

I just hoped it didn't mean that Jack now needed an off-grid, passive-solar bike shop in an upscale part of Wood-bridge, because that was going to take some effort.

I said, "I just want you to know that I've always been sorry for my part in what happened."

"You were just kids."

"I wanted to tell the principal it wasn't true. Pepper was with me that afternoon, but her father would have beaten her black-and-blue if he found out she'd played hooky."

"Yep. He'd sure done that enough times."

"She was so frightened."

He nodded. "I figured it out. I knew you gals didn't start that trash talk. It was Old Hellfire wanting to get rid of me. She knew her way around a nasty rumor."

"You still blame Miss Henley for starting that story about you and Pepper?"

"Everyone else believed she did," Jack interrupted. "You're the only one who ever gave her the benefit of the doubt, Charlotte. And I want to say none of the kids believed it, sir."

"I just couldn't accept that she could start such a terrible lie deliberately. I told myself she misunderstood," I babbled.

"Yep, well, don't worry about it. Getting fired was the best thing that ever happened to me," Mr. Kanalakis said, staring down at me. "In terms of my art."

"I'm sure it was." I glanced around the log cabin at the paintings. Unlike his frisky vegetables paintings at Mystic Mabel's, these paintings were large, dark, menacing. Each one more unfathomable than the last. I noticed the signature on these was "Kanalakis." He wouldn't want any serious collectors to catch that he did quick commercial stuff for gift shops.

"If it weren't for that tall tale, I'd still be a third-rate art teacher dealing with a bunch of horny adolescents at St. Jude's. The old bitch did me a favor really. And I made sure she knew it every time I ran into her." Mr. Kanalakis folded his massive arms and leaned back against his kitchen sink, which was pretty much the only place that didn't have a canvas in the way.

"You did? Did you see her often?"

"Not if I could help it. Even the thrill of telling her how well I was doing wasn't worth the aggravation of seeing the poisonous old hag."

This is what I needed. Someone who didn't hold back.

"So can you think of anyone else on the staff who might have hated her?"

He blinked. "You mean, besides me?"

"Well, ah, yes. I mean, is there anyone else you can think of?"

"Do you think I murdered her?"

"Not at all. I just—"

"Because I didn't."

"Of course not. I don't mean to—"

"She did get me fired midterm from my first teaching job. She was the one who accused me of making out with a student. And she made sure that I'd never get another job teaching in another school in the state, if not the country. She lied and schemed and plotted. I'm lucky I didn't get arrested. And an innocent girl was lucky she didn't get the shit beat out of her by her thuggish cop of a father."

This conversation couldn't be good for his blood pressure if the color of his face was anything to go by.

I broke in, "You did say that getting fired worked for you."

"Sure, it did. But I still hated her and I absolutely would have enjoyed killing her. I often imagined how I could do it. Something dramatic, something painful, something artistically right for her. Maybe involving a hot mangle or a silver smelter or an iron maiden. I just never got the opportunity."

I said, "Hm."

"Oh well," Jack said.

Mr. Kanalakis sighed. "Just disappointing, that's all."

"For sure," Jack said.

"Do you think she suffered?" Mr. Kanalakis added wistfully.

"Definitely," I said. "Are you in touch with any of your former colleagues from St. Jude's?"

"Nope. They wouldn't come near me afterward. I was like a leper. They would all have been scared shitless of what would happen if Old Hellfire found out they had any contact with me."

"I suppose I'm wasting your time. I just wondered if

you had any idea of who else might have wanted to kill her."

"Who didn't? That's my point."

"Well, I didn't," I said.

"I'm surprised. I imagine most of your friends did."

Jack said, "Hold on."

"And your little friend Pepper sure had reason to."

Jack said, "Whoa, easy there."

Mr. Kanalakis grinned and said, "Why should you care about all of this? The witch is dead."

"Maybe I feel guilty because I didn't meet her the night she died."

"You've got to be kidding." He threw back his head and roared. He had some serious fillings. "Guilty? For all I know the historical society bumped her off to get the property, or the mailman did it because she bitched about the service. The point is the world is better off without her and there's no need to feel guilty about it. Rejoice!"

I let him spew it all out before I returned to my theme. "What about the people she used to teach with?"

"And if some poor, beleaguered, tortured, timid soul finally snapped because she'd been pushed to the limit for years, what, you think I'd turn her in?" He appeared to have second thoughts about this statement while the words were leaping from his mouth.

"You mean like Mrs. Neufield?" I said.

He slammed his hand down on the counter. Dishes rattled on the shelves. "Leave her out of this."

Was it my imagination or had his olive skin turned pale?

"Mrs. Neufield?" Jack said.

Mr. Kanalakis scowled in my direction.

Jack blurted out, "Sweet little Mrs. Neufield? Are you kidding, Charlotte? I can't even imagine that."

I said, "Neither can I, actually." Although now that we'd said it out loud, I began to wonder. Had Mrs. Neufield been pushed beyond endurance?

Mr. Kanalakis said, "I have to get back to work. Got some ground to cover before my upcoming show."

I said, "And I'm going to be late for an appointment."

"Me too. Places to go, people to see," Jack said with a last longing glance at the log cabin. "Thanks."

———

By the time we hit Woodbridge, Jack and I had had a couple of heated discussions about Mr. K., Mrs. Neufield, and Pepper. We stopped bickering only as I dropped him off at home.

"Do you want me to see the space too?" I said.

"Maybe another time," Jack said. "You'd just want to organize it."

Rats to that. I burned rubber all the way to Sally's and forgot about my planned trip to Hannaford's. All this investigating was playing hell with my to-do lists.

Sally's front door was unlocked. I buzzed into the kitchen with a proposition. Sally and the kids had just finished a late lunch. Plates were scattered here and there on the kids' table and the counter. But for once the three kids were playing quietly, and Sally was perched on the granite breakfast counter in her kitchen reading *Today's Parent*. I pulled up the stool beside her.

"What smells fantastic?"

"Grilled cheese sandwiches. They're all the rage in this classy joint. I wonder if they'll catch on with the rest of the world."

"I missed lunch," I said wistfully. "I didn't get to the grocery store yet."

"Huh. And you call yourself a professional organizer. You want a grilled cheese sandwich?"

"Too much trouble. You've finished already."

Sally said, "Don't be a doofus. I can make those suckers in my sleep. How come you missed lunch?"

"Because Jack and I went to visit Mr. Kanalakis."

"No way."

"Way."

Sally punched her fist in the air and yelled, "Herc! Herc! Herc!" She stopped. "I saw him at the memorial reception, but I didn't get a chance to talk to him."

"Seems he's making it as an artist instead of an art teacher."

"Really. Why did you go see him anyway?"

"He must have hated Miss Henley and the St. Jude's administration. I figured he'd be willing to talk about the staff."

"Was he?"

"Not really. I got the impression that he was protecting Mrs. Neufield. Jack is mad at me for even suggesting it."

"Well, she left in a hell of a hurry too. Miss Henley had it in for her for sticking up for Mr. K."

"Yeah. I know. And Mr. K. didn't mean to draw attention to her. I'm sure of that. He turned pale when I mentioned her name."

Sally opened the fridge. "You know what? Mrs. Neufield would never manage to get the best of Miss Henley."

"But in a heated confrontation. All that resentment and hatred for years spilling out. Bang on the head, with one of those wooden beams. And that's it. Good-bye blight of my life."

Out came the cheese and the bread and butter.

"No. Mrs. Neufield wouldn't stand a chance. No matter how angry she was. Perhaps if she had a gun, but even then, Hellfire could make hamburger out of her. Have you forgotten how cagey she was?"

"That's what Jack said. Sort of."

"Sorry, Charlotte, but Jack's right. First of all, what would she even be doing there at Henley House?"

"I haven't worked out all the details yet."

"Well, I don't buy it. Maybe Mr. K. was just trying to distract suspicion from himself." Sally is one of those women who can whip up a sandwich, or even a meal, and not lose her train of thought.

"No. I hope you're right. I don't want it to be Mrs. Neufield. Or Mr. K. for that matter."

"How would you feel about it if it was Pepper?"

"Be serious."

"If anyone had the motivation, she did. Her life was really hell. Mrs. Neufield and Mr. K. were able to get away from it, but Pepper was stuck there until she graduated."

"Pepper wouldn't be pushing for a homicide investigation if she did it. She'd settle for accidental death."

"Not really her decision, is it? Doesn't it depend on the pathology report?"

"Come on, Sally, even if she hates me and you're furious with her, Pepper didn't kill Miss Henley. We both know that. It's more likely it was someone from Stone Wall Farm. They're the ones who stand to gain. I heard that Miss Henley wanted Olivia to change her will. And oddly enough, now she's dead. Very convenient. Jack and I try to talk to Olivia and we get the boot. I think Olivia is in a dangerous position there. That Vanclief woman is cold and calculating. There are millions of dollars riding on one fragile old woman's will."

"Poor Olivia. Benjamin gets really upset about her. She used to be his patient and he was really fond of her. He thinks they keep her way overmedicated and that they encouraged her to get another doctor who would do whatever they said. I bet it's to make sure she keeps them in her will. Benjamin says there's not a single thing he can do. People are entitled to change doctors, and they have qualified medical staff attached to the Farm."

"Maybe we can do something."

"Like what?" Sally popped the sandwich into the toaster oven and I filled her in on my proposition.

I said, "My friend Rose Skipowski is going to visit Olivia and see if she can figure what's going on out there.

And also see if there's any clue about why she got so upset about Crawford. She's going to bring some old pictures for Olivia, I think."

"Sounds promising."

"The problem is I'm not allowed on the property and neither is Jack. She can't get out there by herself. So I thought, if you drove her out and took her back, then I would take care of the kids. We'll work on the next set of toy storage boxes. Want to do that?"

"Do you think you'd be all right here on your own? With the kids?"

I bristled. "Of course I would." I did not think, oh how hard can it be.

Sally said, "Okay, sounds like a plan. Let's do it."

"Nobody would recognize you at Stone Wall Farm, right?"

"As far as I know. It's not like I accompany Benjamin in his practice." Sally handed me a knife and a fork and a glass of milk. Life was improving.

"Tomorrow morning? Around ten thirty?"

"You're on," Sally said, popping the grilled cheese sandwich onto a plate with an expert flip of her spatula. She slid the plate across the counter toward me. "I'm overdue for an adventure."

"Good. I'll let Rose know. Here's her phone number in case you have to cancel. And I'll give her yours."

"And speaking of adventures, did you ever hear from Woodbridge's only eligible bachelor?"

"I'm having coffee with him today. That's all, Sally. Just coffee. A small jolt of caffeine. I don't even know the man, so please don't push it. And don't get started on my biological clock."

She grinned. "Tick, tick, tick."

*Cut up fresh veggies and freeze them for a quick stir-fry on nights you don't feel like cooking anything elaborate but are running low on chocolate.*

# 12

I dashed home to walk Truffle and Sweet Marie, and we set a new record for speed walking around the block. For some reason, I needed another shower. I changed clothes three times before heading out again. The sun had vanished and the November wind was sharp, so I settled on my red boots, leather jacket, and a bit more lip gloss than usual. It had nothing to do with anything.

Certainly not the coffee date. Well, it wasn't really even a date. Just a coffee with someone I hardly knew and probably would never see again. Anyway, I had a bit too much going on in my life already to think much about him. That was my story and I was sticking to it.

By the time I got to Jumpin' Java it was eight minutes after three. I was mortified. I pride myself for being on time, even for unpleasant meetings. Which this wouldn't be.

Jumpin' Java was packed, even midafternoon on a weekday. It was the newest of the hot places in Woodbridge, finished in espresso-colored wood and leather, and softly lit. Every table was occupied by some young entrepreneur, artist, or academic. But there was no sign of Dominic Lo Bello. He wasn't there. Oh crap. Serves you right, I told myself firmly. That's what you get for being late. People just leave.

"Charlotte," a voice behind me said.

I whirled. A bit too dramatically for Jumpin' Java perhaps. Every eye in the place was on us now.

"Did you just get here?" I asked, with just the slightest implication that perhaps he hadn't been on time for our whatever it was.

"Been here awhile," he said. "Just topping off the parking meter."

"Oh. Sorry I'm late."

"You're not really late."

"It's not like me to be late. I had a small emergency. Not serious." No way was I going to tell him the emergency had consisted of indecision about the pencil skirt or my new dark indigo jeans with the red boots. The jeans had won.

"Can I help?"

"Oh no. No. No. Everything's fine."

He raised his hands in surrender. "Would a cappuccino improve the situation?"

"It would." I glanced around. Oops. We were obviously objects of fascination to everyone there. I lowered my voice. "I can't talk about it."

"Right," he whispered, pointing to a table I'd thought was occupied. His black leather jacket hung on the chair and his camera case claimed the table.

"Have a seat. I'll be right back."

I sat down and told myself to get a grip. And regain my sense of humor. Sheesh. As I turned, I spotted Lilith leaving Jumpin' Java. Even her purple tips drooped. She was clutching a number of brown envelopes, résumés most likely. She loped across the road, and I gasped as she narrowly missed being struck by a car. She kept walking.

"Nice boots," Dominic said, arriving with a cappuccino for me and an espresso for himself. "Hey, what's wrong?"

"See that girl? She got fired from Stone Wall Farm. She might have to drop out of her part-time college classes if she doesn't get a job. She's already sold her old car to keep a roof over her head. She's getting around on her old bicycle. She seems so desperate. Maybe I should go after her and see if . . ." I stopped and wondered, where was her bike?

Dominic put the cups down. The cappuccino was just the way I love it. Lovely, frothy foam, with a light elegant dusting of chocolate. He slipped into the chair, rested his elbows on the table, and leaned forward. Up close, I could see the small strands of silver in his hair. He was older than I'd thought originally. Was that bad or good? Or did it matter at all? Whatever. It sure took my mind off Lilith.

He said, "Do you have a job for her?"

"Not right at this minute. I would have had plenty for her to do if the Henley House project had gone through. But not now."

"Do you know why she got fired?"

"Yes. It was quite unfair." I tried not to stare into those dark brown eyes. I didn't want to drown.

"You're sure?"

"Oh yes. I had a problem with Mrs. Vanclief. I'm not allowed to go back there either. Nor is my friend, Jack. It makes me wonder what those people are up to."

"Let me guess: you plan to find out, right?" he said, giving the laugh lines another outing.

Lilith had totally vanished from view by this time. "Mmm. Yes, and it's a long, distressing story. So, let's just enjoy this for now. Tell me about your photography business."

"Not much to tell. I do have a lucrative contract to do some promotional stuff for those fiends at Stone Wall Farm Foundation."

"Ah, the very outfit I was just trashing."

He grinned. "No skin off my back. It's just a contract to take some photographs. I think they plan to expand because they're willing to put some money into a glossy prospectus and brochures. An updated image for their annual report, that kind of PR stuff."

"Who do you deal with?"

"Mrs. Vanclief. Inez. You know her?"

I made a face. "The ice queen. Sorry for dissing your client. Again."

"Hey, it's just business. I haven't made any friends out there. Anyway, I have a few other plans while I'm in the area."

"Really. Like what?" I said, relieved that he wasn't ticked off about Stone Wall Farm.

"Well, it's very beautiful country around here. As long as I'm in the area, I think I can put together a pretty decent coffee-table book of historic sites in the Hudson River Valley. You have mountains, river, woods, and all that wonderful mist."

"You like that, do you?"

"Love it."

I decided not to mention that I hated what it did to my hair.

Dominic was warming to his topic. "There are such great old buildings; some of this stuff is a couple hundred years old. I found city houses and tumbledown farms and even old fences that make great shots. It might not pan out, but I'm doing my best to pull an interesting project together."

"I thought I saw you near Henley House the other day."

"Probably. I've been there half a dozen times. That's such an amazing house," he said. "So atmospheric. It sits up on that hill and broods. It's one of my favorite shots. I've been trying to capture it at different times of the day and even at night."

"Huh."

"I guess you don't share my enthusiasm for it. I can certainly understand, considering what happened to you there. And I'll take what I can get," he said.

"So you knew I found Miss Henley's body?"

"Hard not to know that. Every time I turn on the TV, I see your face or that blonde police detective."

"That's Pepper. She hates me," I blurted.

"Hates you? The cop? Why?"

"Long story and very personal. She'd love to pin this murder on me."

"What? How could anybody suspect you of such a horrible crime?"

"Let's change the subject."

We moved on to photography and why it obsessed him. About organizing and how much I loved it. About small dogs, which I think are necessary, and cats, which he preferred.

"Although, I am willing to be open-minded about the dogs," he said when we could no longer justify hogging two chairs in the popular spot.

"That's very generous of you," I said with a smile.

He shrugged into his jacket. "Feel like a walk along the river? It gets dark so early now, I like to get outside when I can."

"Thanks," I said. "But I have to get to the library. A bit of Henley research."

"Sure. But I would like to see you again sometime. If that's okay."

Oh yes, it was.

---

"Dish," Sally shrieked. "I want to hear every detail."

"There are no details. It was just coffee with a very nice man." I held the cell phone away from my ear.

"Don't blow this opportunity. Remember your biological clock is ticking."

"Bye now."

"This guy's a keeper, Charlotte. Give him a chance."

"I'm on my way to the library to check out Crawford Henley. Talk to you later."

Of all the items that were bugging me, Crawford Henley was at the top of the list. Frankly, it would have been great to find out that Crawford Henley was alive and angling for the Henley estate. He would have made an excellent suspect, even though he'd have to be well into his seventies. That would have taken the heat off Mr. Kanalakis and Mrs. Neufield, which would be good, and Inez Vanclief and whoever she was working with. Oh right, and me.

I spun the Miata into the library parking lot. A large dark and dusty van was taking up two of the last three spaces. I hate that. I briefly thought about leaving a note on the windshield. But I was in a hurry and scurried through the door seeking my favorite librarian, Ramona.

As usual the library was teeming with people. Most of them stared at me or gave each other elbows in the ribs and meaningful nods in my direction. I kept my nose in the air and aimed straight for the Woodbridge Room.

The Woodbridge Room is a wonderful full-scale replica, built in the style of the nineteenth century, glass doors on the dark oak cabinets. That's where you go if you need to ferret out any aspect of the town history. I figured between the oral-history collection and the archives, I'd find out what I needed to about the mysterious cousin.

I spotted Ramona's silver brush cut. Apparently, she'd been waiting for just such a question. "What a relief!" she said, her complicated silver earrings swaying with enthusiasm. "If I'd had to pull out one more city directory, I would have absolutely screamed. You want info on the Henleys? We're up to our patooties in Henleys here. Mr.

Henley endowed our local library collection. What do you want? Letters, photos, papers? I wouldn't be surprised if we had their toenail clippings. Oh, it's all right, Charlotte. I was just kidding. We should be able to hunt down this particular Henley. What's his name again? Crawford?"

"Thanks," I said.

"So what have you done so far? I won't want to waste time repeating steps," she said.

"Talked to people and searched Google. I found a few Crawford Henleys, but they're not the one I need."

She nodded. "Often nothing does the trick like old-fashioned paper. Hang on." She plopped down the first boxes of clipping files. "These will keep you out of trouble while I head off to storage to double-check for some other stuff."

"I don't think I can even get through this today," I said. But she was gone. Happy, happy.

I was happy, happy too. I love libraries. Not for the silence, because libraries are always humming with activity. I love them because they are all about organization. Getting the right stuff together, neatly, accessible, easy to find, easy to use. Yum.

The clippings were in acid-free boxes. I was very pleased about that. I worked my way through papers from the early fifties. Plenty about old Mr. Henley and his business dealings, plus formal parties, engagements, births, and deaths.

My hand stopped over one clipping that announced Olivia Henley's wedding to John Clinton Simonett. Olivia's face shone out at me. The photographer must have enjoyed setting up that scene. She gazed over her shoulder at the camera, a seductive smile on her lovely face. The angle would have been designed to draw attention away from the Henley nose. It was hard for me to reconcile the straggly white hair I'd seen on Olivia recently with the elegant swirl that topped her head in the photo. Diamonds twinkled on her ears.

The bride was willowy and golden, the groom darkly handsome. All that money and all those good genes. Six bridesmaids flashed identical debutante smiles. One plain, solid young girl stared straight at the camera without smiling. From the expression on her face, she wanted to seriously discipline the whole lot of them. Give them a good clip on the ears perhaps. Miss Helen Henley, no question about it.

Two young men lounged in the front of the bridal party. One was glancing away, awkwardly. The other confronted the camera, challenging and mischievous. They had to be Randolph and Crawford. But which was which? I put my money on the taller, fairer version being Crawford, unafraid of the camera or the world.

I lost track of time, I was so deep in concentration, flipping through the remains of these Henley lives. I opened the next acid-free box. I heard a soft cough behind me.

"Sorry, Charlotte, did you miss the announcement? It's time to pack up. This is our early closing night," Ramona said.

"Early closing?" My mind was still back in the file.

She shrugged. "Budget cuts. Staff hours have been reduced."

"But I was just getting warmed up."

"We'll be back tomorrow."

I can't wait that long, I thought.

At the moment she flicked off the lights in the Woodbridge Room, a light must have gone on over my head. "Ramona," I said, "do you have a contact at the historical society?"

"Sure. There are quite a few people involved, but some of them are a bit dithery. I'd say your best bet is Mr. Simon Quarrington, Professor Quarrington to be more correct."

"Do I have time to get his address?" I said, as the rest of the library lights started to go off.

"We're supposed to get everyone out, but hold on one second and I'll get it for you."

"I appreciate it," I said as I followed Ramona back to her desk.

"Well, I know you must be under a lot of strain after what's happened. I sure would be, with all that media attention and everyone in Woodbridge watching your every move. I hope you find whatever you need." Ramona flipped quickly through her Rolodex, scribbled an address on a piece of scrap paper, and handed it to me.

I glanced back longingly at the boxes of clippings. Ramona pointed firmly toward the front door.

She'd given me a new worry. Really, was *everyone* in Woodbridge watching my every move?

———

Where had the day gone? I still hadn't been to Hannaford's and I was running out of time. I dashed into the Delhi Deli and grabbed enough vegetarian pakuras and somosas to keep me alive. I added a few onion badjis and creamy dip to my basket. There was plenty for Jack too, just in case he showed up at dinnertime.

Truffle and Sweet Marie were waiting for me with their legs crossed. I called Rose from my cell as I walked them.

"That's terrific, hon," she said when I told her Sally would pick her up the next morning at ten thirty. I passed on Sally's number too.

"Let her know if you're not feeling up for it," I said.

"I hate being such a burden to people," Rose said. "Wish I'd learned to drive. Bet I'd be a lot freer now, instead of staring out the window, moping over that useless hunk of rusting steel."

"Is it still running?"

"My neighbor takes it out every now and then for me. He had it out about two weeks ago, but of course, now he and his wife are gone to Florida."

"I could start it up for you from time to time."

"Thanks, hon. The keys are right here, anytime."

"I'll take you for a spin in it soon. Now about Stone Wall Farm. Sally's happy to be part of the adventure. She loves to talk too. Relax and enjoy it. Let me know what happens with Olivia. Gotta run. I'm being pulled in all directions here." An idea started to take root in my brain as soon as I hung up. I thought it just might work. But first, I would need to figure out how to contact Lilith.

---

"Jumpin' Java? You told me you were just there today," Jack said. "And I can make you coffee at home after we eat. Do you have any food?"

"I need to pick up something at the coffee shop. There's never any parking in that area this time of night, so I was hoping you'd circle the block with the car. I don't want to argue with you about it, so you don't have to come. However, there might be some pakuras and samosas from the Delhi Deli in it if you do."

Jack said, "Any onion badjis?"

"Possibly."

"I'm in. I can show you the retail spot I've chosen for my bicycle shop while we're out."

Inside Jumpin' Java, the scent of French roast was haunting, and the young hip crowd was making noise and demanding new variations on the dozens of variations already offered. I figured that stress on the baristas would work in my favor.

"Excuse me," I said to the black-clad girl at the counter. "My friend dropped her résumé off here this afternoon and now she's worried she put the wrong paper in it. Her name's—"

"Applications are over there," the whippet-thin barista said, brushing back her hair from her eyes with one hand and pointing with the other.

"Well, I . . . thanks."

Huh. So much for privacy. I found Lilith's envelope easily. I opened it and peered inside just long enough to memorize her address and cell phone number. I nodded and waved good-bye to the barista. I don't think I registered on her retina. Too many picky caffeine experts to deal with.

Back in the Mazda, I wrote Lilith's address and phone number in my address book before I could forget them.

"Coffee at home now?" Jack said.

"Chocolate would be even better. Right after we make a quick stop at this address."

Jack glanced at the address I'd written, and five minutes later we pulled up in front of Lilith's apartment building. No one answered even though I rang the bell for several minutes.

Jack raised his eyebrows as I returned.

"She's serious about getting a job. I imagine she's out searching now," I said. "She really needs at least part-time work to stay in school. I think I can help. I left her a note."

"You can't bail out everyone, Charlotte," Jack said.

"I like to help people."

"I know you do, and it's good for the people who get helped. Not sure how great it is for you. Okay, turn here and slow down. You can see the space I've picked for the shop."

"Hmm," I said, staring into a large, gloomy empty unit. "It's a bit off the beaten track, isn't it?"

"Not too trendy here, for sure. But cycle shops are destinations. If you want to drop five thousand on a high-end Italian number, you're willing to go a half mile out of your way to see what's available. It's a large space and it's a good price. So I've signed the lease. And . . ." He stopped and turned to peer out the rear window of the Miata.

"What?"

"It's okay. I thought someone was following us, that's all."

I whirled around. "Oh crap. Did you get a good look at him?"

"No clue, but it's all right. He turned down that street."

———————

When we got home, Jack busied himself with some esoteric business involving inventory of high-end pedals. Truffle and Sweet Marie busied themselves by sleeping. I tried calling Sally, but her line was busy. Professor Quarrington's answering machine picked up on the first ring. A mellifluous voice asked me to leave a message. I didn't.

Lilith didn't answer when I gave her a buzz. What to do? The house was still in good order from the night before, if you didn't count the empty fridge. I refused to turn on the television, in case I spotted my own guilty face again. I flipped through my favorite magazines but couldn't concentrate. Even the calls from pretend clients trying to get the dope on Miss Henley had tapered off. I could have called my mother, but I'm not crazy.

It seemed like it had been a long, long day, but some of my to-do list remained undone, so I decided to tackle that, just to keep busy. I called my laundry-room client.

"I have a design done up for the perfect laundry room in your mudroom," I chirped when she answered. "And some nice options for shelving and storage. When would you like me to drop by?"

"It doesn't matter."

"Okay. Well, I could be there in—"

"No. I mean it doesn't matter because I can't do it."

"You've changed your mind?"

"It's been changed for me. My husband won't agree to it." I was sure I heard a catch in her voice.

"Sorry to hear that."

"I'll pay you for your consultation of course."

I bit my tongue before I could say, "Oh don't worry.

There's no charge for that." Not charging is the best and fastest way to fail.

"I'll drop off the sketches and the catalogs. I've suggested some fixtures," I said. "You never know."

"He's out tonight. I suppose you could drop them by. What harm could it do?"

———

It had been a beautiful day, but it was not a beautiful night. The skies opened as I left the house. Lucky for me I keep an umbrella in the car. The roads turned slick with puddles and patches of sodden leaves. Even so, I decided to kill two birds with one stone and drive by Professor Quarrington's home on my way to the client's house. Maybe the head of the historical society was just screening his calls. Maybe a knock on the door was in order. I double-checked the address that Ramona had given me and mapped out a route that took me past his home.

I slowed as I drove down the lovely old street he lived on. I peered through the windshield trying to see some of the numbers through the gloomy night. I thought I must be getting close when someone leaned on their horn behind me. What was that about? Even if I was crawling along, there was no one coming the other way, so why didn't he just pass me?

Good riddance, I thought when a dark van shot by. As I watched with my mouth open, the van made a U-turn and headed straight for me, high beams shining in my eyes, blinding me. I gripped the steering wheel and made a sharp turn to avoid being hit head-on. The Miata shot off the road and bounced onto the sidewalk. A white picket fence loomed straight at me. I heard my car hit the fence and the fence hit the ground and my chin hit the steering wheel. I staggered out of the stalled car. I watched slack jawed as the van rocketed off, splashing dark water in its wake. It vanished around the corner before I could even identify the make. I turned back to the Miata, which was resting on a section of downed fence, and tripped over a stray picket, tumbling to my knees. I felt the stiletto heel of my beautiful red boot snap off.

What was going on?

As I stood unsteadily, dazed and rubbing my chin, the porch light flicked on at the nearest house. A bald man with an oversized umbrella came out and walked toward me. He seemed deep in thought, pipe in mouth, head lowered. He raised a pair of spectacular eyebrows at the sight of the Miata, partly on the lawn, partly on the sidewalk. He bent down and examined the picket fence. He straightened up again and gave his shiny bald head a perplexed scratch before he noticed me and transferred the stare in my direction.

He said, "By any chance would that be your vehicle on my front lawn, miss?"

"Someone ran me off the road," I said with a definite wobble in my voice.

"Excuse me, but did you say someone ran you off the road?"

"Yes. A dark van. He turned and came right at me." My hands were shaking and so was I.

"For heaven's sake. How dreadful."

"I'm sorry," I said.

"Sorry? Never mind sorry. Are you injured?"

"I hit my chin on the wheel."

"Head injuries. Quite dangerous. Don't want anything to happen to the brain. Shall I call for an ambulance?"

"I feel bad about your fence. I love picket fences." I tried to keep my voice steady. I didn't want him to think I was on the verge of tears. Even if I was.

He said, "You love picket fences? Really. Well, I've never been very attached to that one. I much prefer a lovely stonework wall. Or a bit of wrought iron filigree, but there's no accounting for taste. Lucky for you, I haven't got either one or you would have been badly injured. Now see here, young lady, you're trembling. You'd better come in and have a glass of juice or a tumbler of brandy."

"No, thank you. You're very kind. I'll leave my information so we can settle up for the fence. I don't know if the insurance will pay for it."

He bent and picked up my broken boot heel. He raised his spectacularly expressive eyebrows and said, "Shouldn't we call the police?"

"The police?"

"Yes, the police. I believe you just told me that someone tried to run you off the road."

"I don't think I want the police. My head is really spinning. Perhaps I just imagined it."

He glanced back at his ruined fence. "Imagined it?"

"No, I suppose it really happened. But it's just so hard to believe."

He shrugged. "There are lots of insane people out on the road. But you are definitely shaking."

"And I'm not sure where I put my umbrella," I said idiotically.

"Really? You have to watch out for shock, you know. In you go." He took my arm and led me, half limping, half hopping, up the stairs and through the shiny black front door into the house, before I could even admire the brass knocker.

"I must get to my client's before her husband gets home."

"Brandy first, police second. I'm afraid your client is way down the list."

To tell the truth, I felt very reassured that this professorly type was taking care of me. My knees were knocking, my chin had started to throb, and I felt as though I was only one degree from being an ice cube.

Of course, he was bald and that helped. I have always liked bald men. My mother's third husband was bald, and I have fond memories of him. So, for whatever the reason,

I found myself in a warm, traditional, inviting foyer with white wainscoting and soft light. I sniffed just a hint of pipe smoke.

He led me into what must have been the living room. I collapsed into a wingback chair with a faded burgundy stripe. The room was warm; a fire burned in the fireplace. Deep built-in bookcases flanked the fireplace. Unless I was mistaken, the books were double lined on the shelves. Good use of space, even though it might make them hard to find. In addition, books tumbled here and there in piles around the room. Volumes were stacked in between the lovely antique chests and the comfortable old chairs. More books lurked under the coffee table. Five or six lay open on top. I must have interrupted a project.

My hands were still shaky when he returned with a brandy snifter. I clutched it while he stepped out the front door and returned in about thirty seconds.

"Drink up. And I'll call the police unless you'd prefer to. And there's one less problem to worry yourself over," he said. "As far as I can tell, that damn fence is salvageable. Came down in one piece. I suppose I'm stuck with it."

"I'll come over with my friend tomorrow and put your fence back up," I said. "If there's any damage, I'll pay for it. I shouldn't be nosy, but are you working on a big project?" I pointed to the open books on the coffee table.

"Always working on a project. Historical society stuff. Great fun. Keeps me out of trouble now that I'm retired from the university. By the way, in the confusion, I quite forgot to introduce myself. I am Simon Quarrington."

"Very nice to meet you," I said.

He cleared his throat. Kindly. "I don't believe I quite got yours."

"Oh. I forgot."

Alarm flooded his face. "You forgot your name? We really must call for help."

"I forgot to introduce myself. I'm Charlotte Adams.

And normally I make a bit more sense." I stared with dismay at my muddy knees and broken boot.

He showed no reaction to my name. I figured he wasn't the TV-watching type. Good.

"Well, Charlotte Adams, you've had a nasty scare. I believe this is exactly the sort of circumstance under which one does call the police."

"I don't even know if I can explain it and make sense," I said. If this was the one person in Woodbridge who didn't know, I preferred not to fill him in on the situation with Miss Henley and Pepper.

"Your choice, I suppose. But I do believe they have to be informed about accidents."

"You said the fence was all right, and there doesn't seem to be any damage to my car. And I really have to get to see my client."

"Actually I don't think you should drive anywhere. And heavens, you've worked your way through that brandy too. Is there anyone we can call?"

"I might just walk home."

He held up his hand. "Not a good idea. And since you've knocked over my fence and refused my offers to call the police, the least you could do is indulge me in this, Charlotte Adams."

I said, "I can call my friend Jack. He'll bike over."

"Did you say bike over? Oh dear. On a night like this? I'd take you home myself, but I'm not allowed to drive anymore. Meddling doctors, you know."

Jack's on my speed dial, naturally. I took out my cell and pressed "1." As it rang, I said, "Please don't worry about me. It's strange but I was trying to locate your house. I wanted to speak to you and I couldn't reach you on the phone."

"Speak to me?" The spectacular eyebrows rose higher. "Whatever for?"

"Why doesn't he pick up? Sorry. Yes, I wanted to talk about the Henley family," I said.

"Oh well, yes. Lots to talk about there," he said, giving the eyebrows a waggle.

"I'll have to leave a message for Jack and then we can . . ." At that point, my eyes rolled back in my head and I slid onto the faded blue carpet.

*Keep an ongoing list for grocery and cleaning items,
and schedule a regular time for shopping.
That way you'll never run out.*

# 13

"On the bright side," Sally was saying to someone I couldn't see, "some of those EMS guys are probably ready to settle down."

I opened my eyes. Jack's baby blues stared down at me. Sally leaned over his shoulder. A pair of flamboyant eyebrows appeared over her shoulder.

Not surprisingly, I said, "What?"

"You lost consciousness, my dear girl," said a voice I dimly associated with the eyebrows.

"But how . . . ?"

"I finished the message to your friend and these two turned up. Bit of luck, really, the timing of the message beep, I mean. Not the car on the lawn."

"Too weird," Jack said.

At that point a nurse stuck her head into the room and said, "Doctor's here. Patient only, please."

Much later, after a very boring series of neurological tests, the doctor set me free, with some painkillers and a lecture about driving. Sally drove me home. We dropped off the professor on the way. Jack retrieved the Miata from the lawn and followed us.

Jack accompanied me up the stairs to my apartment and offered to walk the dogs. I sat, still stunned, on the sofa, as he hooked up their leashes. He glanced over at me and said, "Did you recognize the van?"

"No. There must be a thousand dark vans in Woodbridge. Everyone seems to have one."

"But this particular one was aiming for you. Do you think that this whole Henley mess might be getting just a little bit dangerous?"

———

My to-do list was crammed:

+ *Find job for Lilith.*
+ *Babysit kids for Sally during Stone Wall Farm trip.*
+ *Locate obit for Crawford Henley.*
+ *Laundry client—apology*
+ *Red boots?*
+ *Buy food.*

Perhaps I should have added "Get head to stop throbbing" and "Have chin amputated."

I wobbled into the kitchen and put on the coffee, before walking the dogs. The fresh air didn't help. I dragged myself up the stairs toward the coffeepot and watched Truffle and Sweet Marie scamper back to bed. I winced as I took the first sip. My jaw hurt when I opened my mouth. I'd found that out the hard way while brushing my teeth. That was too bad. I had a lot of talking to do.

I finished the coffee and picked up the phone. After nine. Okay to call someone.

"Is this Lilith?" I said, wincing with every word.

"Mumph?" A very sleepy voice.

"Are you all right?"

"Who *is* this?"

"It's Charlotte. Charlotte Adams. We met at Stone Wall Farm. And later in the park. I'm . . ." Ouch.

"Oh right. How did you get my number?"

"I was a bit worried. I saw you downtown and you seemed so—"

"Freaked out?"

"I was going to say 'despondent.' "

"That's me, all right. Someone stole my bike."

"Oh no."

"Oh yes. Now I'm up the creek."

"I hope you don't mind me mentioning it, but someone I know might be needing some occasional help. I know you're a certified caregiver, but I thought, just temporarily, it might help to get some extra cash until you find a new job in your chosen field."

"Who?"

"A friend of mine. She's an older lady on a home oxygen program and can't really get around, although she has a perfectly good car in the backyard. If you were willing, I thought I'd pass your name to her."

"What kind of car?"

"I don't know, actually. It's under a tarp. An old one."

"Doesn't matter," Lilith said. "I don't even know why I asked. Sure, give her my name. I could work in a few drives, even when I find a new position. Sometimes older people just need someone to drop in. They need to talk and maybe just reach stuff on high shelves."

"If business picks up, I'll have occasional jobs," I said. "Sorting and packing for clients. It's occasional and intense."

She snickered. "I hope none of your clients are like Miss Henley. And, before you answer that, yeah, you can call me. Thanks."

"And before I forget, would you know if Olivia Simonett ever had a visit from her cousin, Crawford? That's who I was asking her about when she pitched that fit."

"Crawford? Randolph used to come in. He was an old weird dude, but Olivia loved his visits. And then Miss Henley, of course, used to bring her chocolates and then sit there with a face like a lemon. That's it."

"But no cousin Crawford."

"I wasn't there all that long. The person who would have known was Wynona. She took care of Olivia for years. Olivia was a lot better off with Wynona than with that ditz Francie."

"Wynona. Any idea where I could reach her?"

"What do you mean, reach her?"

"To ask her about Crawford."

"She can't answer."

"Perhaps if I ask her very, very discreetly."

Lilith snorted. "I doubt that since she's very, very dead."

"Dead?"

"She was killed in that uptown shooting. How could you not know that?"

⸻

"Oh my God," Sally gasped, clutching the baby. "Shot? Do you think it's connected?" We were whispering in the dining room so the children wouldn't hear any talk of random shooting. Even though the dining room was blanketed in toys, the kids were in the kitchen. So far the latest box-decorating project was keeping them quiet. The theme was Thanksgiving. I'd picked up some paper turkeys and pilgrim's hats at the Dollar Do! on the way over. Dallas and Madison were gluing with glee.

"Of course it's connected, Sally. First Olivia's caregiver is killed and then Miss Henley. It's obvious someone is trying to—"

I was cut off by a bloodcurdling scream coming from the kitchen. Sally poked her head around the corner and said, "Don't glue your sister's hair, angel."

She whipped back again. "Trying to what?"

Further screams erupted from the kitchen, each fresh shriek bringing goose bumps to my arms.

"Keep people away from Olivia," I shouted over the wails.

Sally said, "I told you so. Right from the beginning, taking on Hellfire as a client was a mistake."

"That shooting did not happen because I took on Miss Henley as a client." I headed toward the kitchen. To hell with chain of command. Someone was being murdered if the shrieks were any indication.

Sally yelled, "Oh no, her hair."

Oh crap. Who knew you could cut hair with safety scissors?

"It will grow back," I said, bending to cuddle Madison. "Better than ever. You wait."

Sally held a fistful of blonde curls in one hand and shook her finger at her son with the other. He was wailing too. That was wise under the circumstances.

It crossed my mind there might be more to this motherhood business than I had imagined. I was beginning to find the prospect terrifying. Perhaps I should trade my biological clock for a wake-up call.

"So," I said in my softest voice, "Olivia is the one in the Henley family with the big bucks."

Sally nodded.

"And the two people closest to Olivia have been killed: Wynona Banks and Miss Henley."

"Code name Hellfire," Sally whispered.

"It could be connected to this cousin Crawford or—"

"I thought we were worried about the people at Stone Wall Farm."

"We are. But maybe this Crawford is lurking around and plans to pressure her to change her will."

"I bet the Stone Wall Farm people took out a hit on Miss Henley and Wynona to get at Olivia's money."

"Took out a hit? You watch too many movies. This is Woodbridge, Sally. We don't hire hit men to knock off our teachers."

"Maybe we do if we have a hundred million reasons." We stared at each other over the heads of the sobbing children. Sally hissed, "Okay, Rose and I will see what we can find out."

"I hope Rose can get in. They're cutting Olivia off from everyone."

Sally said, "You distract the ankle biters. I'll sneak out now."

A note to those with ticking clocks: you can only distract small children with piggybacks for so long. Eventually, not even making milk shakes in the blender or having bubble baths will calm them down. Sooner or later, you hit the wall.

Sally left at nine forty-five. At ten fifteen I called Jack. "I'm at Sally's. Get the hell over here. Now."

Sally was back by eleven thirty and not one second too soon. Jack was lying on the living room floor. Dallas was riding him like a horse. That had been fun for the first fifteen minutes. I had been trying to show Madison how to organize the can cupboard, but that venture hadn't gone all that well. Baby Savannah had finished flinging her applesauce at the humans in the house and was killing time by banging pot covers on the kitchen floor. I had forgotten to turn off the water in the sink.

"Thank God you're back," I wailed at Sally.

"What's that in your hair?" Sally said.

"Applesauce. Jack has strawberry yogurt in his."

Sally glanced around her former designer kitchen. "Well, I'm glad you're getting us organized."

Jack limped in from the dining room and squeaked, "Save me."

"What happened, Sally?" I asked.

"Oh boy," Sally said. "It was—"

The bang came from the front hall. We all jumped. The glass rattled in the cupboard doors.

The kids shrieked, "Daddy, Daddy!"

Benjamin seemed more grizzly than teddy as he lumbered through the door. "Sally, what the hell have you . . . ?"

Jack managed to break his fall.

Oh crap. "Sorry about the applesauce, Benjamin. I guess I must have missed that bit."

Benjamin picked himself up and thundered, "What the hell have you done to that poor old woman, Sally?"

Sally said, "Bye, Charlotte. Bye, Jack. See you later."

—❧—

Jack and I headed straight for North Elm Street. As we walked up the stairs to Rose's place, I said, "I'd rather be single all my life than marry a cute little person who turns into a savage beast over a teaspoon of applesauce."

"That goes double for me," Jack said, rubbing his back.

"You still have a bit of strawberry yogurt in your hair. I suppose it's a look."

"Never mind that. I feel lucky to be alive."

"What happened to you, hon?" Rose said when she opened the yellow door. "You're kind of . . ."

"Long story," I said.

"Is this your young man?" she batted her pale eyelashes in Jack's direction.

"No. He's my . . . Jack."

Jack brightened. "Do I smell chocolate chip cookies?" He didn't appear to notice Rose's neon yellow jogging suit with the black contrasting piping or her blue hair or her oxygen equipment. Jack has a one-track mind and we're not talking sex.

"Still in the oven. To tell you the truth, I was so upset by that visit to Olivia, I headed right into the kitchen when your friend dropped me off."

"That's why we're here," I said.

"Will they be ready soon?" Jack said.

"You better come in. I'm still a bit shaky. And I'm awfully sorry to let you down, hon. But the visit didn't quite turn out right."

"What happened?"

"We didn't even get up the stairs. Olivia caught sight of us and started howling and swinging her arms like a wild woman and shouting, 'Get out! Get out!' Then she just collapsed. It set that poor lad in the wheelchair off too. A woman—that executive director you talked about, I guess—came running out of her office and started barking orders. Even the parrots were screaming."

"Wow," Jack said. It sounded like he was sorry he'd missed it.

"So you didn't even get to ask her about Crawford?"

"That's what I'm telling you, hon. She was walking in the corridor with her helper and she spotted us downstairs and all hell broke loose. The staff came running and Sally and I were out of there like last week's garbage."

"But you were always friendly with Olivia, right?"

"I've known her for more than seventy years, not close but real congenial. I can tell you, I'm shaken up over this."

"Sally didn't even know her."

"Olivia's going downhill fast. Sure she's been upset by Randy and then Helen, but she's getting on in years, like me. Past a certain age, you have to get used to people dying."

Jack said, "Maybe she just reacts badly to guests."

I said, "But she was fine with me, until I mentioned Crawford."

Rose said, "I don't know why she'd pitch a fit over Crawford. I told you he was her favorite. If he wanted her millions, all he'd have to do is ask and she'd give him the world on a plate. But Crawford was never all that interested in money. Otherwise he might have knuckled under to the old man. Instead, he walked away from the Henleys. I don't think it was Crawford's name that got her going when you were there."

"Possibly I misinterpreted the whole incident."

Jack said, "But it could make sense if they are really trying to separate Olivia from anyone who cares about her. Maybe they know about this Crawford guy. Maybe they're aware that he might stand to inherit. They wouldn't want her making contact. Maybe they've told her stuff about him. Scared her a bit."

I gasped, "That would be awful."

Jack shrugged.

Rose said, "If they cut her off from everyone she knows, she'll just sicken and die. And nobody would think twice about it, at her age."

I shivered. "It's horrible. We have to intervene. I'll get in touch with Margaret Tang. She'll have some advice about reaching Olivia."

Rose said, "But I don't like that place. It seems to have been taken over by completely new people. I never saw any of them before. I wished I'd caught sight of Wynona. We should get in touch with her."

Uh-oh. "Um, about Wynona, Rose."

"You've seen her?"

"Wynona's dead."

"Dead? She can't be dead. She's not even sixty!"

"She was shot, last week. That drive-by shooting uptown."

Rose paled and slumped in her chair. "Must have been while I was in the hospital. I missed out on everything."

I said, "I'm sorry I just blurted it out like that."

Jack said, "And someone ran Charlotte right off the road last night. See that big honking bruise starting up on her chin. That's got to be connected."

Rose lifted her own chin. "I think we should go to the police."

"That's part of the problem. Inez Vanclief has been

threatening to call the police on us," I said. "Maybe she already has. We need a bit more to bolster our case, or else they might suspect us of trying to get at Olivia. As soon as I get the last bit of information about Crawford, we'll approach them."

Rose nodded. "But we can't wait long. What if something bad happens to Olivia?"

"I think if we have some solid information for them, it will help."

Jack sniffed. "Hey, there's a buzzer ringing. Does that mean those cookies are done?"

———

I left a message at Margaret Tang's office before I headed out. I drove down Long March Road with my boots in the passenger seat. I took my damaged boot and heel to First Rate Shoe Repairs, one of the few spots in Woodbridge without an alliterative name. I held my breath as the elderly stooped shoemaker turned the boot over in his hand and gazed sadly from it to the heel, the way a doctor might regard a patient who had short hours to live. After a while, I cleared my throat.

He blinked as if he had forgotten I was there.

"What do you think?" I said, still holding the perfect mate.

He nodded and turned the boot over a few more times. He stroked the buttery soft leather.

"Nice. Very gude quality."

No kidding. I'd just paid the bill for them, so I knew that.

"Can you fix it?" I said after a longish pause.

"Mebbe," he said.

"Great!"

"Have to be efter Christmas. To do a gude job."

"Christmas? But it's not even Thanksgiving."

"I got a bicklog here." He pointed toward a back room

where a mountain of sad boots and shoes towered. "Everyone wants shoes fix right away."

I could understand that. I wanted my boots fixed right away. I said, smiling, "It will be hard to wait that long. I really, really need those boots. It's winter."

He peered over the counter to see what I had on my feet. Boots, of course. Last year's black suede, still pretty yet practical.

I said, "Well, the red ones are special."

He shrugged.

"And they're way better in the snow."

He gave a skeptical glance at the stiletto heel and grumbled, "Maybe New Year's."

"I'll be back." I grabbed my boot, backed out of the shop, popped the boot and the heel into the back of the Miata, and made tracks for the library.

———

Don't ask me why I was so hung up on Crawford Henley. I just couldn't let go. Anyway, Ramona had probably worked hard and I didn't have the heart to pull the plug.

"Good news," said Ramona, snazzy in a denim skirt and knee-high indigo suede boots with flat heels. All Ramona's outfits were blue and drew attention to her eyes.

"I could use some," I said.

"I guess so. What happened to your chin? You look a bit, um, pugnacious perhaps."

"You should see the other guy."

"Ha. I've loved that joke all my life. So, back to business. I found an item that suggests he died about twenty years back. I'm searching for an obit, but it's been one interruption here after another all week. Must be the full moon."

"You're sure he died?"

"Nope. Not sure. Just found a couple of articles that you might want to read. One in particular. Always good to have confirmation. Could be a mistake. Or a different Crawford Henley."

"Listen," I started to say.

The door to the administration office opened and a frazzled man stuck his head out. He crooked his little finger.

Ramona turned to me and rolled her eyes. Her silver earrings swung. "I'm needed by the committee of the bemused. Don't worry. I'll keep at it."

"One more question," I said. But her denim backside and indigo boots had already vanished behind the paneled door.

---

The front door opened. My client glared out at me.

"Oh, it's you," she said.

"I hope you got my message last night. I mean about the accident."

"Yeah. Your chin's kind of swollen. Might as well come in out of the rain although I don't want to waste your time."

I stared around at the front entrance. On my first visit, it had been immaculate. Now a man's suit jacket lay on the floor. A pair of boots was upended. Newspapers were stacked haphazardly. I tried not to stare at them. They reminded me of Miss Henley's horrible death.

"If it's a bad time," I said.

"No worse than any other time," she said.

"I brought by those catalogs and preliminary sketches for you. Like I said, I thought you might want to keep them in case you decide to go ahead with the project in future."

"You may as well come in."

I stepped in and followed her to the kitchen. A pile of dishes sat on the counter. A red and mushy lump was concealed on a plate. I found it hard to believe a home could go downhill so fast. It had been only a few days since my first visit.

"Don't mind the mess," she said with a sly smile.

"Oh," I said, "it seems fine."

"Get real. It looks like shit on a stick. You need a lot more practice if you are going to be a good liar, lady."

Sometimes it's a terrible burden being a polite person.

"I'm on strike. Imagine the state of it by the end of the week," she snorted. "I can hardly wait."

"Ah."

"Just take those shirts on that chair and toss 'em on the floor," she said. "I'd like to have a peek at this impossible dream. Oh here, let me do it."

I noticed she planted her heel right on one of the shirt collars as she studied the sketches I had made.

She said, "Very nice. Very, very nice. I would have loved that. Sure would have. Not that it matters anymore."

Her tone seemed different. Possibly even dangerous.

I left the sketches and departed with a sense of impending disaster.

With three ex-stepfathers, a boatload of ex-step-boyfriends, and one ex-fiancé in my life, I am not so comfortable around marital disarray.

---

I picked up a message from Sally on my cell phone. That's what I get for turning off the phone when I'm with clients. Even the reluctant ones.

"Charlotte? You won't believe this, but that evil ice queen out there recognized me from a cocktail party. She's actually threatened to report Benjamin to the medical board all because I went to see Olivia."

My mouth hung open.

Sally continued, "Of course, Benjamin did nothing wrong and neither have I. And neither have you. But he's furious. He's told me not to make contact with Olivia. And to let you do your own investigating. No doctor wants complaints lodged against him, but even so, I sure wish I'd picked a man with a bit more fight in him."

—◆—

I was headed for Hannaford's. My cell phone trilled and I pulled the Miata over to answer. Normally, I would just let it go to message, but normal was before. Every phone call could be about a life-or-death situation. Or it could just be Jack with an update on his cycle shop. I was hoping it was Margaret Tang returning my call.

"Hi. It's Dominic. I've just been wondering what professional organizers eat for dinner."

"It all depends. Food usually. Why, what do freelance photographers eat for dinner?"

"Those poor fools, they don't even know where to eat, let alone what. They need guidance. Especially the ones who are not from this neck of the woods."

"Really? Well, if I were offering advice to someone new, I'd say you can't beat the Jubilation Café."

"Sounds uplifting."

"The food sure is."

"How about I buy you dinner?"

I didn't hesitate long. "On the other hand, maybe I should buy yours to show my gratitude."

"But I haven't helped you."

"Not yet."

"Tell you what, this one's on me. You can show your gratitude the next time."

"Deal."

Damn. I forgot about my swollen chin.

# 14

It's not like me to try on every article in my closet and then fling each rejected outfit in a heap on the bed. But every outfit was wrong. The colors too bright, the blacks too black. Clothing I loved seemed too short, too long, too boring. Truffle and Sweet Marie were happy to curl up on each discarded outfit and wait until the next one came along.

What was wrong with me? My closet is organized by season, color, and type of clothing. I have a fully planned wardrobe that can get me from a meeting to a nightclub with a shuffle of a camisole and a flick of a chandelier earring. I have invested time and money in being ready for any occasion with a minimum of effort and a maximum of effect. Any occasion but this dinner apparently.

Forty-five minutes later, I finally settled for my pencil skirt, a lace-edged camisole in champagne silk, a fitted cotton velvet jacket in black. I'd been saving that for something special. I added my black wedge boots with the frisky little bow on the back. I would normally wear large fishnet stockings with those. But I wasn't sure that would send the right message. What message did I want to send? I turned my thoughts to jewelry. On the fourth try, I settled on double hoop earrings and a chunky bead necklace. Too much? Too little? Too late? And who was at the door?

"What's wrong with your legs?" Jack said, frowning slightly at the large fishnets.

"This isn't a good time. And what are you talking about? You're wearing biking shorts in the middle of winter."

"Why isn't it a good time?" he asked as Truffle and Sweet Marie leapt around him, wanting to be picked up.

"It just isn't."

"No problem. I'm just checking to see if you've given any thought to that dog yet."

"Yes. And the answer is still no. I'm getting dressed, Jack."

"But you are dressed."

"I might have to change. See you later."

"Hey, I'll check in later this evening in case you've had second thoughts. Where are you going anyway?"

"Out to dinner."

"Hey, great. Maybe I'll come along."

"Uh, no."

"Why not?"

"Because it's like a . . ."

"Like a what?" Jack said. "A diet?"

Good question. I took a deep breath. "No. Like a date."

"A date?"

"Is that so surprising?"

"Well, I mean . . ."

"What do you mean, well I mean? Is there some reason I wouldn't be able to get a date? If there is I'd like to know what it is."

"No need to yell. Sorry. No reason. Just that I didn't know you knew anybody to have a date with. How come you didn't tell me?"

"It just happened. It's not important. I don't have to tell you everything. And even if it's not important, you can't come along."

"Okay. What happened in your bedroom? There's stuff all over the place."

I reminded myself that it was time to get a decorative screen or divider so that my bedroom would not be visible from the hallway.

"Just having fun with the dogs," I said. "Time to go, Jack. I'll talk to you later."

"Sure thing. Who's your date with?"

"Dominic Lo Bello."

"That photographer guy?"

"Yes."

"Huh."

I hate that. "Don't you pull that 'huh' stuff on me."

Jack shrugged. "How can you just drop the investigation to go gallivanting around with some guy you hardly know?"

"Gallivanting? You sound like your own grandmother. And for your information, if things work out, it will advance the investigation."

Jack said, "There's something about him. Something untrustworthy. Maybe it's the way he dresses. Maybe it's those shifty eyes. I wonder if he has a criminal record. Anyway, don't worry about the stockings; they sort of draw the eye away from your chin."

"Whatever," I said in a suitably huffy way.

<hr>

I stepped back in after a quick walk with the dogs to find the message light flashing.

"Miss Adams? This is Simon Quarrington. I do hope you are doing better after your ordeal last night. It has occurred to me that you wanted to ask me something and that's why you paid me a visit originally. Something to do with the Henleys, I believe you said before you lost consciousness. I will be most happy to answer your questions, and I will make a point of picking up the phone should it ring. I certainly don't do that for just anybody."

Well, obviously my luck was about to change. I checked my watch. No time to call before dinner.

---

The Jubilation Café earns its name. There's a sense of exhilaration about the place, maybe because the food is so damn good. Nothing breaded and fried has ever been served there.

I chose the citrus-glazed salmon with risotto and asparagus. Dominic had the free-range chicken stuffed with walnuts and blue cheese, and a barley and porcini mushroom casserole. I had to pass on the wine since it wouldn't go too well with the painkillers for the jaw. Dominic said he could do without any too. The sympathy vote, he claimed. Since he wasn't staring at my chin, I had to assume that my artistic application of makeup had done the trick. Of course, the expensive and dim lighting didn't hurt either.

"So," I said when the last bite of risotto had disappeared, "are you finding lots of material for your book?"

He grinned. "You have the most unbelievable architecture in this town. And in the surrounding areas too."

"Yes. I'm glad I moved back here from the city. Too bad you missed the fall colors."

"Might have to come back for those. Or just stay around."

I felt like a teenager when I heard this, despite the elegant and adult ambience of the Jubilation.

He said, "You haven't told me what I can do for you yet."

"It will sound a bit strange."

He leaned forward and grinned. "Try me."

"I think I told you I'm not permitted to visit Stone Wall Farm."

He raised an eyebrow. "You did."

"I am really worried about one of the residents. Olivia Henley Simonett."

"Sounds familiar," he said.

"You were at Miss Helen Henley's funeral. You must have seen her. She did a little . . ."

"Wave and dance at the front of the church?" He chuckled.

"That's her."

"I know who she is. Poor old lady. I felt sorry for her. What are you worried about?"

Words poured out of me like coins from a lucky slot machine. "It's probably crazy, but she's supposed to be the last of the Henleys. Helen Henley was murdered and the other cousin died not long ago. And Olivia's absolutely loaded. Massive chunk of change. The rumor's out that she's leaving her money to the Stone Wall Farm Foundation."

He shrugged. "That's a good thing, no? It's a place that cares for damaged people who need special care. Seems like an excellent place to leave a massive chunk of change if you have it to leave."

"Normally, I'd agree. But the staff seem to be trying to keep Olivia away from people. I've been tossed out. Do I look dangerous? Or difficult?"

He glanced at my chin. "Maybe a little bit."

"I told you about my friend, Jack, being thrown out. Now Olivia's former neighbor, Rose Skipowski, got the boot too. And Sally caught hell from her husband, Benjamin, about going out there. Benjamin's a doctor and your Mrs. Vanclief threatened to report him to some medical authority."

"For the record, she's not *my* Mrs. Vanclief. I don't actually have my own Mrs. Vanclief. And I'm glad."

"Sorry, I got carried away. This is the same administrator who told Benjamin that Olivia didn't want him as her doctor anymore."

"Hmm. Old people can be difficult. And if you don't mind me saying so, this Olivia Simonett sure didn't act normal at that funeral. But in a place like that, the staff has to make sure the clients aren't upset."

"Hear me out. The last thing is that Olivia's longtime caregiver has been murdered."

His fork clattered. "Did you say murdered?"

"I did. Shot. Right in her car. Uptown, not all that far from here. Can you believe that?"

Dominic frowned and rubbed his own perfect chin. He said, "That random shooting? I thought that was a case of someone being in the wrong place at the wrong time."

"Wrong place for her."

"What do you want me to do?"

"Just try and see if Olivia's all right. Maybe they have her drugged or something. She could easily have a fall if she's overmedicated. There has to be some reason why they're doing this."

A small smile played at the edges of his very nice mouth.

"Do I sound crazy?" I said.

"Maybe a little bit paranoid. But on you that's kind of cute."

I felt a ridiculous blush starting around my waist and rushing upward. "I don't want to jeopardize your contract with them. But I'm very worried. I already found one dead person this month. That's not paranoia."

He nodded. "I shouldn't have said that."

"And I shouldn't have even asked you to do this. Now it sounds presumptuous even to my own ears."

"I can understand why you're worried. Sorry about the paranoia joke. But your reaction might be just the shock of finding that body. That kind of stress plays hell with your emotions. I know I went right off the rails after my wife died. But I'll do what I can to check things out."

"You might not get near Olivia. But where there's money, there's talk. She's been there a long time, and people love to gossip and speculate. You could pick up something useful."

"I'll find a way to talk to Mrs. Simonett herself."

I felt such a ridiculous rush of relief, all I could do was grin like a fool.

He said, "I'm a photographer. My job involves getting close to people, even if they don't want that. Anyway, maybe she'd like to have a photograph taken."

"Wonderful idea. She's on the second floor. You can see the door to her suite from the entrance."

"Suite? You mean she has more than one room?"

"Living room and bedroom, bathroom, with space for her attendant."

He said, "I suppose I shouldn't be surprised. The place has a Cordon Bleu–trained chef and an amazing wine cellar. Why wouldn't the residents have suites?"

I agreed. "Stone Wall Farm really is a fabulous place. Except they may be in the business of murder."

——*——

When Dominic and I arrived at my house, Jack followed us, uninvited, up the stairs to my apartment. We were going to have one hell of a serious talk about boundaries the minute we were alone.

"Glad to meet you," Jack said, grabbing Dominic's hand with a grip that looked more like a wrestling move than a handshake.

"What are you doing here?" I mouthed.

Jack beamed. "You're just in time to join us to walk the dogs. They may be small but they can sure poop up a storm."

My neck felt very strange. Were my veins popping? I'd had one date in the past year. Was that too much to ask?

One solitary miserable date without Jack dropping by to talk about dog poop?

"Charlotte's thinking about getting another dog," Jack added, with a tired chuckle. "Don't know if I can handle the workload."

"What are you talking about?" I said, perhaps a bit sharply.

Dominic's eyes widened.

Jack bellowed, "Here Truffle! Here Sweet Marie!"

Two small torpedoes arrived on the scene, stopped in their tracks, and took an instant dislike to the latest competition for my affection.

"Thanks a whole hell of a lot," I snapped at Jack after Dominic had left.

"Cut your losses, Charlotte. He didn't put up much of a fight. How much work do you really think he has to do tonight? Didn't you say he was a freelance photographer?"

"Oh shut up, Jack. He wasn't in a *fight*. He was on a date. A date with a weird ending."

"It's not my fault the dogs were misbehaving. And don't get hissy. I'm just saying," Jack said.

<hr>

Saturday my jaw seemed to be turning greenish. There are worse things I suppose, but I couldn't imagine what they might be. Anyway, the green chin line went well with the black cloud over my head.

There was no point dwelling on my problems, though, because I had a full to-do list:

- *Let Rose know Lilith can drive her.*
- *Ask Lilith if someone had power of attorney for Olivia.*
- *Library re: Crawford*
- *Boots fixed—where?*

+ *Hannaford's for groceries*
+ *Call Mom.*

"Hello, Rose. This is—"

"How are you, hon?"

"Good news. I forgot to tell you yesterday. I found some-one who will be really happy to drive you places. In fact, it will help her out because she needs a bit of a break. So don't argue. You'll both benefit. And you'll get some use out of your husband's car."

"Let's hope it runs."

I chirped, "I have to go now, but we'll drop by soon."

I dialed again as soon as I hung up. "Lilith? Charlotte Adams here. I was hoping we could get together to visit my friend Rose. We talked about you driving her every now and then because . . . Lilith?

I thought I heard a faint snuffling noise.

"Are you all right?"

Lilith said, after a long pause, "I can't talk now. I'm having the crappiest week in my life."

"I can imagine. It can't be easy getting fired unfairly. But sometimes . . ."

"Listen, little Miss Sunshine. My freakin' building is on fire and I said I don't want to talk."

"But perhaps I can help. You remember my friend who needs the drives? Wait a minute. Did you say your building is . . . ?"

"Can you take a hint? For all I know, you're tied up with this somehow. I'll take care of myself. I've been doing it since I was fifteen. I survived the streets and I'll make it through this."

Survived the streets? "Lilith?"

Too late.

Five minutes later, I tried to turn the Miata onto Lilith's street, but as if the Saturday traffic wasn't bad enough, the fire department had the area closed off. In the distance I could see billowing smoke. I could smell the acrid stench even from two blocks away. I nosed the car into a makeshift parking spot and tried to proceed on foot, but a police officer was turning people back. "Sorry, miss," he said. "This street is off limits. We'd like to clear the area."

Poor Lilith. She'd been pretty upset, but I was sure I could do something for her. I didn't blame her for being angry. Or even for suspecting my motives. She'd been on the receiving end of quite a few kicks lately and she didn't have anyone to turn to. There must be something I could do for her.

But what? As I sat there racking my brain, another police officer came along and gestured to me to move my car.

———

I almost missed Ramona's call. I was busy ignoring Jack, who had made himself at home. Making himself at home included checking the amount of ice cream in the freezer. Jack was now flaked out on my sofa, surrounded by my dogs and gazing longingly at the fridge.

Jack said, "Aren't you going to get that phone?"

I snapped back to reality and snatched up the receiver.

"Good news," Ramona said. "I had a bit of quiet time here at information central and in addition to your articles, I was able to find the obit for one Crawford Lincoln Henley. I'm sorry about the interruption the last time you were in."

"Thanks for calling. Did you say obit?" I said.

"Believe it or not. Oops, can't talk long; the place is filling up."

"And we're sure it's the same Crawford Henley?"

"Says he was born in Woodbridge, New York, in 1934, son of James Washington Henley and Cecily Beryl Crawford. Died in San Diego on December 3, 1966. Survived by . . ."

"What?"

"Excuse me a second. Can I call you back? Now there's a line at the ref desk."

"But just tell me survived by whom?"

"Whom?" Jack said from the sofa. "Whom is very classy."

"Shh," I said. "I'm waiting for Ramona to come back on the line."

"We don't get a lot of whoms around here," Jack chortled. "Maybe you'll start a trend."

"You still there, Charlotte?" Ramona's voice came on the line.

"Yes. Crawford was survived by somebody, you said. Who was it?" I made a face at Jack.

"Got a serious outbreak of business questions here. I'm up to my patootie in patrons and they all think their questions are urgent. Five restless taxpayers standing in line. We're supposed give priority to people who actually come in over phone inquiries."

"But you called me," I said.

"I have to go. We close at three today. Why don't you pop in before then? I've made copies of the items for you."

"Just give me the name," I shouted.

Damn dial tone.

"Time for Vitamin IC," Jack said.

"Later. I'm heading over to the library to join the taxpayers in the line with my urgent question."

"Can't it wait until tomorrow?"

"No. It can't wait until tomorrow. The library's closed Sunday. You know that. Come on, Jack. We have to find out who's involved. If Crawford had heirs, then they'd have a stake in Olivia's estate. She's elderly and frail and absolutely loaded."

"But I thought she was leaving her money to Stone Wall Farm."

"We're just dealing with a rumor there. And even if she is, I'm guessing with her mental health being what it is, a good lawyer could challenge that 'of sound mind' stuff in favor of blood relatives."

"Huh."

"Hey, where's my other black boot?"

"Search me," Jack said. "They're not my style. Especially not if there's only one."

"Stop cracking jokes and help me find them."

"But the pooches just got comfortable."

"That would be the same pooches who stole the boot, I suppose." I headed into the bedroom and crawled under the bed. That's the hiding place of choice for plundered objects. No boot. I peeked behind the sofa. Nada. I called out to Jack, who wasn't being all that helpful. "The boot is not in the freezer. And answer the phone please!"

"It's Sally." A muffled shout from Jack.

"Tell her I'm going to the library to get Crawford's obituary." I tried the closet. I keep my shoes neatly arranged in clear shoe boxes. There was no boot on or behind the boxes. Hmm. I tried behind my dresser. Sometimes that was a good hiding place for my possessions. No boot. But I did find my missing telephone bill, slightly chewed, so that was worthwhile. I could hear the phone ringing in the distance, and Jack appeared in the door. "Margaret Tang," he said. "She said you've been trying to reach her."

"Oh crap. Tell her I'm going to the library. Explain that it's urgent. They're closing soon and I need to get that obit. I'll call her as soon as I get back."

Jack wandered away, giving the party line. He added an uncomplimentary phrase about my butt being visible from behind the dresser. Ingrate.

By the third call, when I was checking behind the clothes hamper, Jack no longer required guidance. He picked up and rattled off the party line. Library, obit, tonight. Butt behind dresser. Will call later.

"Who was that?"

"Rose."

"Really? I wonder why. I just spoke to her this morning. Do you think she's all right?"

Jack said, "She sounded fine."

"Mmm. She's not in the best of shape. Maybe I should have . . . well, as soon as I get back."

But Jack had gone off again, to answer the phone. Big surprise.

He stuck his head around the corner and snickered. "Todd Tyrell. Wanting an interview. I told him to try the library, you might be there. He found the idea of obits really interesting."

A vision of the next news item flashed through my head. "Maybe you shouldn't . . ."

But Jack was following the ring again. "You should get a portable for this room," he said.

"Put it back on call answer," I said before moving the bed away from the wall, just in case the boot was wedged there.

"I just did. And oh yeah, that guy you know called."

I'd been checking behind the Christmas decoration box and stuck my head out. "Can you be a tiny bit more specific, please?"

"You know, claims to be a photographer."

"Dominic?"

"Yeah."

"The same Dominic who was here last night and you know perfectly well what his name is?"

"I don't think that sentence is grammatically correct, Charlotte."

"What did he say?"

"Wanted to talk. I told him library and obit, butt behind dresser, the usual blah, blah, blah. You'd call tomorrow or the next day."

"Tomorrow? Or the next day? Did you get a telephone number for him?"

Jack brightened. "You don't have one?"

"No. Did he leave it?"

"He didn't. Sorry."

"Yeah. You look crushed. Can you check the caller ID?"

"Caller ID blocked. Gee that's too bad. Anyway, I told you I don't trust that guy. Why block your caller ID?"

I flopped down on my bed and felt a sharp point. I flipped back the throw and sure enough, the missing boot. Truffle and Sweet Marie managed to exude splendid innocence. The best I could do was deranged. I hoped that wasn't going to work against me at the library. What the hell did it matter? I dashed down the stairs and scrambled into the Miata.

—••—

I peeled up in front of the library and parked just as a crowd of people exited. I raced up the stairs and tugged on the door.

"Library's closed." An imperious grey-haired woman who had just left the building stared down her substantial nose at me.

"As you can plainly see on the 'Hours' sign," said another small plump woman with a tight, mean little mouth.

If these were the taxpayers in Ramona's line in the reference department, she had my sympathy. "I only need a minute. I need to speak to Ramona. It's a reference emergency."

"Aren't they all?" said a wild-haired woman with wool kneesocks, Birkenstocks, and a nasty smirk.

"I was in the middle of my information on the phone . . ."

"We had to leave, and we'd been standing in line for ages. You'll just have to come back Monday like the rest of us."

"Monday? I can't wait until Monday."

"I guess you'll just have to, won't you?" The smirk broadened, showing a couple of snaggly teeth.

"Young people. Very inconsiderate these days," the long-nosed woman said.

Her companion added, "That's right. They think they're more important than everyone else. For no reason that I can imagine. It's not like it's a matter of life and death."

"It is, actually," I said, raising my bruised chin.

"I doubt that. Now will you please stop blocking the stairway? I have things to do."

"And so do I," said the other woman.

"I am not blocking the stairway. There's plenty of room for you to pass." I peered beyond them, squinting at the door and hoping for a glimpse of Ramona.

"Really, some people will do anything to get their own way. Of course, the way you were raised, I suppose you're used to that."

I turned back and stared at them. "What are you talking about? I don't even know you."

"We certainly know who *you* are," the long-nosed woman said.

"Breeding tells," the smirker added.

"Breeding tells?" I echoed. "Tells what? Have I blundered into a Victorian novel?"

"I think you know. Like mother, like daughter."

All right. I'll be the first to admit that my mother had raised a lot of eyebrows in Woodbridge before she finally blew this pop stand. And sure, some of it had to do with other people's husbands. But I am not my mother. I live a sensible, ordered life. Clean, honest, toilet paper stockpiled. Serene. Well, except for the previous few days.

I stretched myself to my full height. "Excuse me?"

"I think you heard me the first time. Like mother, like daughter. Nothing but trouble."

For reasons I will never truly understand, that was the first and only time I have ever raised my middle finger to another human being. Really. Never before. Not even in the school yard. Not even on the interstate. Not even when I broke off my engagement. It is just so not my style.

At that moment I noticed a sudden explosion of light and spotted Todd Tyrell's super-white grin as he stood in front of his cameraman.

*Don't keep chocolate in the cupboard too long.*
*The fat rises to the surface, leaving a white coating.*
*Buy good-quality chocolate. Eat it often.*

# 15

In case you think no one in Woodbridge would be watching television late on a Saturday afternoon, you would be wrong. The phone shrilled on and on, as I slumped on the sofa letting it go to message while I chugalugged chocolate. Eventually I deleted a dozen crank calls from people with no life at all. But I had also missed a return from my returned call to Margaret Tang. She said to try her again tomorrow. Dominic had left a message saying he'd wondered if I'd be up for a movie and to get back to him by four o'clock if that sounded good. It sounded good all right, but it was now after five. I wanted to pull the wooly throw over my head and spend the rest of the night gnawing on the fringe.

I did pull myself together enough to hunt up Wynona Banks's number in the phone book. I tried the number in case someone in her family wanted to talk about Wynona and Olivia. I remembered vaguely that Wynona had been a single mother who raised five children. None of them lived at home apparently because the line had already been disconnected. I found four more Bankses in the book. The first three turned out to be no relation and the fourth simply didn't answer. I let it ring fifteen times to be sure.

Jack and the dogs were doing their best to cheer me up. Truffle and Sweet Marie used the time-honored ploy of chasing each other and barking, while Jack relied on his standby: tempting me with ice cream. He pointed out that although Tang's had been out of New York Super Fudge Chunk, he had stocked up on Chunky Monkey as a fallback plan. And he socked away a few Mars bars for insurance.

"Say the word," he said.

"No, I don't think so," I said.

He shook his head in astonishment. "Did you just say no to ice cream?"

"Yes."

"Okay, I'll get it."

"I meant yes, I did say no to ice cream."

"Get over it, Charlotte. Nothing's that bad."

"Something is even worse," I said.

"I thought it was kind of funny actually," Jack said, giving his middle fingers a workout.

"Not that," I said, running my tongue over my front teeth and flinching.

"What?"

"You know, I think I damaged my front teeth when I hit the steering wheel the other night."

Jack leaned in and squinted. "Huh," he said.

"Do you see a crack?"

"Maybe."

A tap at the door set the dogs in motion. Jack flicked on the television set just to ratchet up the commotion.

"I was worried sick. Why aren't you answering your phone?" Sally said breezing in. "Oh wow. There's Todd Tyrell!"

"Big whoop," I said. "What if my teeth break off? What then?"

Sally gazed at the television. "He is so gorgeous."

"He is?" Jack said.

I said, "Well, he thinks he is. What about my teeth?"

"I agree with him," Sally said.

"Yes, we know that. Brings the total believers to two," I said.

"That many?" Jack said. "Hard to imagine."

Fine, I thought. Forget the teeth. Obviously no sympathy here.

Sally shrieked, "And there you are, Charlotte! On the news flash!"

"We know, Sally. We've been watching. That's one of the reasons for the long faces," Jack said.

"Check out that digit." Sally bounced on the sofa, laughing and clapping like the kid she was not. "You go, Charlotte, girl! I have always wanted to do something like that."

Jack said, "Who hasn't?"

"I haven't. And I can't believe I did. I'm so embarrassed." I sank lower into the sofa cushions. I could always move back to the city and start over again.

Sally said, "Ooh, hey, a close-up! You look a bit . . ."

"Demented?" Jack said.

"Let me die now."

Jack leaned forward and speculated. "I wonder if that's the first recorded incident of reference rage."

"Very funny."

"It is," Sally said. "And very sulky too."

"So what if I am?" I said. "I feel awful. I haven't done a single thing on my to-do list today. Come on. What are you laughing at? Like Wynona Banks's family. How am I going to find them? I've tried every Banks in the book, but there's either no answer or they're not related."

"I still think that's a long shot," Jack said.

"Maybe she doesn't have a family," Sally said.

"I'm pretty sure she does. They're probably listed in the newspaper obituaries," I said, "but the library's closed. Not that I can ever go there again."

Sally said, "Benjamin always gets the paper. It goes right in the recycle bin because he's so busy, but I'll check."

"That's the first piece of good news I've had all day. Can we go over?"

"Puleeze, don't make me go home. He's been in a vile mood ever since I took Rose to the Farm. He's hardly talking to me, and I was so glad to get away."

"Why is he so upset? It seems like an extreme overreaction," I said. "You were trying to help. You didn't do anything wrong."

"Sneaky, yes. Wrong, no," Jack said.

"Tell that to Benjamin. He's still furious because that Vanclief iceberg phoned his office and said she would make a formal complaint to the medical board if there was another attempt by him or anyone in his family to contact Olivia."

Jack said, "That's outrageous. Benjamin hasn't even tried to contact her. Oh right. In the church when she collapsed."

"It's so obvious she's up to something."

Sally said, "But that won't make it easier for me. He's pretty steamed at me and at you too, Charlotte."

"Me? But—"

"He'll get over it. Anyway, I'd better get back. He'll be ever grouchier if he has to manage bath time for three kids on his own."

"I'm heading out too," Jack said. "Found a guy who does custom-shelving installations. I'm going to check him out."

"Custom shelving? That sounds like fun," I said, struggling up from the sofa too late. The front door slammed behind them.

Five minutes after they left I made a decision. I could spend the rest of the night staring at my front teeth in my magnifying makeup mirror and reliving my television cameo from hell, or I could do something useful without actually showing my green-chinned, tooth-endangered face around town.

In fact, I wondered what had taken me so long to think of it.

You couldn't grow up around my mother without learning that the big motives were greed, sex, revenge, jealousy, power, and ambition. You could also toss in love and the desire to protect a loved one.

I felt certain sex wasn't too likely this time. Ditto love. Greed made sense if you were thinking about Olivia, but not for Miss Henley's and Wynona Banks's murders. Unless, of course, they were killed because they stood in the way of Olivia and her millions. I made a header for each motive and started to list people I knew of who might fit on that list. Of course, there could have been thousands of others that I wasn't aware of, but I know enough to focus. I figured revenge was a strong possibility, although I couldn't figure out how Wynona would fit into that. Still people like Gabriel Young's mother, Mr. Kanalakis, Mrs. Neufield, even Pepper made that list. And who knew how many others. Still all that revenge related to Miss Henley. I couldn't imagine how it could relate to Wynona. And the more I thought about it, the more I believed the two were connected. I decided I'd get the biggest payoff from concentrating on greed. I listed the people and organizations that would benefit in some way from Miss Henley's death:

+ *Inez Vanclief from Stone Wall Farm Foundation – motive: to keep Miss Henley from influencing Olivia's will and to get Wynona out of the way*
+ *The Woodbridge Historical Society – inherited the Henley House and money to renovate*
+ *St. Jude's – a scholarship fund in Miss Henley's name. Doesn't really seem worth killing over*

+ *Other surviving Henley relatives – with Miss Henley out of the way, would stand to inherit Olivia's money. Who was Crawford Henley survived by?*

I'd already asked Dominic to see what he could find out about Inez Vanclief. Was there anything else I could do? I felt stopped on that one. I couldn't go out there, nor could anyone I knew. And all I had was speculation. That wouldn't get me anywhere with the police. With luck, Dominic would get a sense of things out there. There was always a chance I could gain some insights from Wynona Banks's family if I could track them down.

I'd given no thought to the historical society, except as a source of information about the Henleys. Perhaps I should consider the gentle and congenial Professor Quarrington in a different light.

As for St. Jude's, I couldn't imagine anyone killing over a scholarship fund that would benefit unknown students in the future. Neither the administrators nor the teachers would get anything out of it.

And, of course, I was stuck on the information about Crawford. Unless I could combine two things. I decided to return Professor Quarrington's call and ask what he might know about Crawford Henley's possible descendents. Maybe he'd let something slip about the darker motives of the historical society. Somehow, I doubted this. At the very least, he might have the paper with Wynona Banks's obituary.

⁂

Professor Quarrington opened his door and raised his eyebrows in welcome. "You certainly look much better than you did the last time I saw you."

I said, "It's very kind of you not to mention my colorful chin."

"Well, one gets to an age where the current styles are not always immediately understandable."

•

I laughed. "Something tells me blue and soon-to-be-green chins won't ever make the must-have list."

"I wasn't sure it was actually green, seems more purplish, but never mind. Come in, come in," he said. "I've managed to find that article you asked for on the phone. Quite a write-up about this Wynona Banks. Terrible tragedy."

"That's great. Does it list her family members?"

"Yes, five daughters. All different names. Married, I suppose."

"That explains why they're hard to find in the phone book."

"One of the reasons. As far as I can tell, only one of them lives here. The other four are scattered across the country."

I joined him in the blue room where the fire was burning merrily. Professor Quarrington busied himself getting water for me and a wee bit of brandy for himself. I sat and read the write-up. "May I keep this?" I said afterward.

"Of course. I made you a photocopy. Not completely in the dark ages here. Have a great little gadget. You said there was something else?"

"A couple of things really. The first is about Crawford Henley. Did you know him?"

"Not personally. He's supposed to have been rather . . . swashbuckling, really. Broke a few hearts and ruined more than a few reputations."

I laughed out loud, more because of the eyebrow activity than the comment. "That's what I hear."

"Of course, that was back in the fifties and early sixties when these things made a difference. By the time I moved here, he was long gone, but his legend lived."

"I wondered if the historical society had any information about his family. I'm trying to find out whether he had a wife and children."

"Well, he had cousins, of course. But I'm afraid I can't help you. I've had various bits and pieces about the Henleys, but they're mostly old photos of the house and the foundry.

A few of those family portraits, that sort of thing. Some objects, I suppose, which we will be able to put on display."

"Will you restore the Henley House?"

"We'll do our best. Helen left us some money as well, but, being Helen, there were terms. We're not to sell either her home or Henley House. That's just like her, not to make anything easy for anyone. It will be a costly project. I've been around to the Henley House this week. There's a lot of rot, roof is gone, verandah a death trap. I doubt if we have enough to cover the costs, even with the funds she left us." The eyebrows flickered. "We're happy to have both houses, of course, and Helen's own home is a little jewel. I wouldn't like to see them torn down or divided into apartments. Still, we'll have to get at the fund-raising. And it might not be that easy. She left provisos that her name be attached to both houses. A bit of ego."

I said, "Not that it's my business, but did you like her?"

"Actually, I admired Helen. She had spirit and mischief. It got out of hand from time to time, but I enjoyed sparring with her."

"I admired her too. Not the sparring part."

"The thing with Helen was you could never show any weakness. She'd go right for your jugular."

I nodded my agreement. "I've seen her in action."

"But back to this Crawford Henley of yours. The Woodbridge Library has a lot of information about the family. We worked with them to amass and organize it. We have a very cooperative arrangement. We contributed quite a few papers too. They'll find this Crawford for you."

"I got there too late."

The remarkable eyebrows ruffled in shock. "Too late? Has something happened to the library?"

I let that slip past, grateful that the professor hadn't seen the middle-finger incident on television. "I'm just impatient. I'll be there Monday as soon as it opens. I'll find out who survived him."

"The official ones anyway."

"What do you mean?"

Professor Quarrington harrumphed in embarrassment. "Well, you know," he said, "bit of a lad, this Crawford. Lots of ladies."

I nodded, waiting.

"Well, could have been some Henleys born on the wrong side of the blanket, as they say."

My green-tipped face must have fallen.

"Didn't mean to shock you, my dear."

"I'm not shocked. I'm horrified."

"Yes, well, of course. Moral standards and all that."

"No, I mean, if there are some illegitimate children, they wouldn't be Henleys."

"Most likely not."

"It's just worse and worse! The Henley heir could be anyone."

Professor Quarrington smiled sadly. "I suppose you're right. Anyone except the two of us."

————

Life is full of humiliations. Who doesn't know that? The ribbon of toilet paper trailing from your shoe as you reenter the board meeting, the brilliant glob of spinach on your teeth at the dinner party, or that magical zit that flares on your nose only during job interviews. They all let you know your place in the cosmos. But getting out of a police cruiser, for the second time in eleven days, and stumbling past a salivating crowd into the police station tops everything. I'd never seen a crowd there before, let alone had to push through one. I spotted the WINY logo among other media vans. I wondered if there was some high-profile event going on. A visiting politician? A ribbon cutting? Why would they have to pick that particular moment?

It wasn't until Todd Tyrell thrust a microphone toward me that I realized I was the main attraction. The TV guys were getting a close-up of the real me, no makeup, insufficient coffee, tousled hair. Apparently your civil rights in this country do not extend to being allowed to change out of your bunny slippers before being hauled off to the slammer.

The cameras panned downward.

Todd said, seriously, "Do you have anything to say to our viewers?"

I knew he was hoping I'd say yes. I shook my unstyled head. The officer nudged me forward, and I trudged up the stairs to the station. My knees wobbled. If I'd been thinking clearly, I might have asked myself exactly how Todd Tyrell knew I'd be taken in. As it was, I merely figured I was descending into hell. And that was before the interrogation room.

Inside the station, people swiveled to watch our progress. I felt dwarfed by the two lanky police officers who flanked me. Pepper marched ahead, her very special nose in the air, radiating triumph. Let me just point out, if you are feeling a bit down and dazed, worrying about being fingerprinted won't improve your mood. It just leads to you being stressed and slack jawed if they do take your mug shot. I can't imagine anyone not looking guilty by this point.

I sat fidgeting in the interrogation room for hours, although it seemed more like weeks. I reminded myself that I was just there for questionning. I hadn't actually been arrested. I had nothing to do but stare at the imaginary ink stains on my fingers. Normally, I try to take advantage of "downtime" to plan something, meditate, and think some useful thoughts. But of course, normally, my mind does not reflect the spin cycle on my washing machine. I tried recounting my blessings in life: a wonderful job, a town I thought I loved, a great apartment, good friends, and best of all, two terrific guard dogs. But every blessing had a downside. Who would hire me after my face had been all over every television screen in town in connection with a bird-flipping incident and a murder? How could I keep my apartment if I was in jail? Who would help Rose get a driver? Who would help Lilith find a job and a place to live? And worst of all, who would rescue Truffle and Sweet Marie if Mommy went to the big house?

I leaped to my feet when the door opened. For one crazy blink, I thought about making a run for freedom.

Not much chance of that.

When Pepper swept into the room, her makeup was fresh, every hair in place. She could have been a runway model in her cool blue suede jacket and top-stitched black skirt. Worse, she knew it and I knew she knew it and she knew I knew she knew it. Not even the small bandage on her ankle detracted. She didn't bother to keep that cool, amused sneer off her face. Whatever happened to the old-fashioned police detectives with their ratty raincoats and nicotine-stained fingers? The guys who could solve everything in an hour in someone's living room. They never needed to toss perfectly innocent people into interrogation rooms. They knew what they were doing.

The door swung open again and Margaret Tang entered. She gave Pepper and the other detective an enigmatic nod, and took the plastic seat next to me. Her eyes swept over me, from my hair to my pink, fluffy feet.

"Hi, Charlotte," she said as she snapped open her leather briefcase and pulled out a notebook and a Montblanc pen. "I got your message and five more from Jack."

Pepper's manicured index finger pressed the start button on the tape recorder. Pepper gave the background info, date, location, persons present. Her partner, whose name I hadn't quite heard, began with the questions. They seemed so harmless. All about who I was, what I did for a living, how did I know the victim. As far as I could tell, he was on my side. That was kind of sweet. After ten minutes or so, I was beginning to relax a bit. The police coffee tasted like iron filings, but it was reassuring to hold something in my hand.

Margaret left hers sitting there. Relaxing's not her thing.

Just when I was starting to feel optimistic, Pepper dropped her bomb. She produced an article in a plastic baggie. She dropped it on the table. She met my eyes.

"Is this your pen?" she said.

I peered over at it. "My lucky pen!"

Margaret turned her head toward me and gave me something very close to an expression. "Maybe not," she said.

I said, "It is! I got it for my sixteenth birthday. You remember that, Pepper You were there. You too, Margaret. I have been hunting everywhere for it. I thought my dogs hid it. Where did you find it?"

Margaret sighed.

Pepper said, "Can you account for why it would have been found under the body of Miss Helen Henley?"

I opened my mouth to speak.

Margaret said, "My client has no comment."

Pepper shot her a stare that could have melted the paint off a car.

I commented, "But I have no idea how it could get there. Did you really find it there? Perhaps I left it at Henley House. Maybe she picked it up. It's really hard to say. Can I have it back, please?"

"I don't think so." Pepper gave a low, throaty chuckle. That was the warm-up for three hours of very boring questions.

——◆——

"Good cop, bad cop," Margaret said by way of explanation when we finally emerged. "Watch out for that."

"Thank you so much for coming," I blubbered. "That was the longest day of my life. I wouldn't have survived without you. I thought I was going to be arrested."

"We were lucky to get you out of there this fast," Margaret said. "Pepper means business. She just doesn't have quite enough to lay charges yet."

"Yet?" I said.

"They have to hang this one on someone. The media's been all over it. All that beloved teacher bilge. The heat's on Pepper. She needs a collar. And there you are with your lucky pen underneath the unlucky victim. Oh yes, and she hates your guts."

"Do you think she will arrest me?"

"She'd need to make it stick. But if she can, she will."

I stared at Margaret, speechless, for once.

She said, "It's serious. If they do arrest you for this, you won't be getting bail."

The media vans were still circling when I scurried furtively from the station. I couldn't believe that they'd been there all along waiting for a glimpse. Was there no news at all anywhere else in Upstate New York?

Margaret hustled me past them and into her car. "No comment," she said, giving them a good shot at her outstretched palm. Unlike me, she didn't blink when the flashes went off.

# 16

Tomorrow is another day. Not such an original statement, but hard to argue with, and anyway, it's a motto that works for me. Get off to a good start, don't drag yourself down with toxic memories from the day before, remember the lessons learned, and get going. Sally says I make her want to throw up when I talk like that, but I can't help it. I'm an optimist.

Monday morning I had just finished walking the dogs and eating breakfast, when I heard a small snap, crackle, and possibly a pop in my mouth.

The bottom part of the tooth I had suspected of being cracked was now resting in the palm of my hand. I explored the jagged edge with my tongue.

"Cwap," I said. "Ith boken."

I did not check my messages; I did not turn on the radio or television. I did not approach my desk. I called my dentist and wailed.

I hurried through the marble foyer of the Woodbridge Medical-Dental Building. My dentist's office is across the hall from Benjamin's medical practice. I didn't really want to bump into Benjamin that morning. The dentist's new receptionist has the whitest teeth on the planet and she loves to flash them. She also has the blondest hair and the glamour "do" such hair deserves.

"Charlotte Adams! We were just talking about you." Her smile dimmed slightly as the words came out of her mouth. What's the policy about telling your clients you have seen them hustled into police stations and/or giving the finger to respectable citizens on the steps of the public library? Two pink spots appeared on her lovely cheeks.

"Well," she said, "how nice to see you. So soon after your last visit. What brings you in today?"

Her smile seemed glued-on by this point. Plus a small frown line creased her perfect brow.

She said, "You look a little . . ."

I frowned back. "A lil wha . . . ?"

"Oh nothing. I mean maybe a little out of breath. How can we help you today?"

"I haff bwoken hoof."

"What?"

"Bwoken hoof."

"Sorry?"

I opened my mouth and pointed.

"Oh gosh," she said. "I'll tell the doctor."

The dentist, you mean. "He knowth," I said, and I settled sulkily into the cappuccino leather seats in the office to wait.

She vanished behind the door, recently redecorated in a tasteful taupe. I was left alone, trying not to let my tongue explore the rough edges of the broken tooth. That had become like a full-time job. That tongue wanted that tooth. Now they both hurt.

I gazed around the office, trying to keep my mind off the throbbing. I'd been coming to this dental clinic since childhood. I'd been to this current dentist's father and my mother had been to his grandfather. They were old Woodbridge. I remembered the office of my childhood, full of oak and mysterious white enamel things and towers of *National Geographics*. I remembered the dentist's mustache and his twinkly blue eyes. I remembered getting a new toothbrush every visit and my horrified fascination with the very pink model of the freestanding gums with the full set of teeth.

The new dental generation was spiffy and stylish. Cavities might be in decline after all those toothbrush giveaways, but fresh business opportunities abounded. Hollywood smiles dazzled from every wall. Brochures for cosmetic dentistry grinned from the side tables.

I didn't feel much like smiling, and all those acres of teeth were making me twitch. I turned my gaze to the furnishings. Much more soothing. Business must be booming, if the solid wall of patient files was anything to go by.

Where was that receptionist? She'd been gone forever. I had visions of her draped seductively over the dentist's chair, gradually working her way up to mentioning my bwoken hoof. This dentist was one of the few truly eligible bachelors in town. Maybe *her* clock was ticking. I could have walked off with half the high-end furniture in the time she was gone if I'd been so inclined. Naturally, I simply sat there fidgeting.

Eventually she reappeared. Did I just imagine that she was straightening her blouse?

"The doctor will see you now."

I ignored the scowls from the patients who had arrived before me but would have to sit there longer. Minutes later I was in the chair with my mouth open. The one thing I hadn't liked about this guy's father was that he asked me complicated questions when my mouth was open. Junior had inherited that habit.

"Keep seeing you on television," he said with a merry

chuckle. "You sure do know how to keep in the news. Wish I could find a way to get on the tube like that. That would bring them in."

The assistant giggled.

I said something unintelligible.

Perhaps my inaudible answer encouraged him. We moved on from the weather, Thanksgiving, how was my mother, how was business, and other topics to the one I dreaded.

"Saw you at the funeral. Everyone in town was there. That was something, wasn't it? So many people turning up. Quite a celebration at the reception, wasn't it?" Blah, blah, blah?

Mmmph, mmmph, mmmph.

"Right. I wasn't sure about all that chocolate though. Ha, ha, ha."

I could have done with a fistful of chocolate right at that moment.

"Still, there you go, you can't beat the entertainment value. Of course, I've lost a patient, and that's always sad. She might have been hard on other people, but she took good care of herself. And her teeth."

I raised my eyebrows at him. It didn't stem the verbal tide.

"But she wasn't all that likeable, even if you didn't go to Catholic school. But I guess every family has to have one."

I made a sound indicating a question mark.

"Henleys have been coming to us going back to my great-great-grandfather. Gotta say I liked the others better. Randolph used to flirt with the girls, but he didn't smell too good so he never got lucky."

The assistant wrinkled her pretty nose.

"And Olivia Simonett is always so sweet to everyone. Sad to see her going downhill so fast. She gets excited about her new toothbrush, just like a little girl."

The assistant shuddered. "It must be hard to lose everyone in your family."

Maybe not everyone, I thought. Let's not count Crawford out until we know for sure.

He leaned over. "Now let's see what we can do about that tooth of yours."

I lay there for the duration, wondering if I'd ever get out of that chair. It was tied with the interrogation room for Most Miserable Place to Spend a Big Chunk of Time.

It seemed like hours before he finally said, "We've got you fixed up temporarily, but both those front teeth are going to need work. We'll get your appointments set up."

"Rlpph," I said. Which meant, "Let me out of here."

---

"You were provoked," Dominic said in a soothing voice. "That news reporter is a total jackass. And those women outside the library? What a bunch of pickled old prunes. And don't ask me what the Woodbridge cops were thinking. They must have leaked the information that you were being hauled in again. That was nothing short of abuse of power."

"Even so, I feel like a jerk," I said. Or something like that. My mouth was still frozen and it was interfering with my speech.

"Never mind. I'm calling to ask you to meet me for lunch. I really enjoyed our dinner and . . ."

I'd enjoyed our dinner too. "Lunth?"

"Yes, you know, that stuff people eat in the middle of the day."

"Not a good day for me." Meaning I was still drooling slightly from the freezing. Not my best look.

"I was thinking of Bruxelles. I've been smelling those fantastic Belgian waffles and maple syrup every time I walk by that place. I've had to start using the other side of the street so I can think straight when I'm setting up for photos."

I knew that waffle scent. It smelled good enough to bottle

as a new perfume line. But it was going to take every minute I had to get myself spiffed up to go into the library, possibly wearing a bag over my head. I needed that info on Crawford Henley from Ramona. Of course, I didn't want to miss out on seeing Dominic.

"Tomorrow?"

"I'm booked solid. I just had a cancellation for lunch," he said.

"That's too bad." I checked the mirror again to see if I could be rescued. Not a chance.

"Oh well, I have to do some retakes out at Stone Wall Farm. Inez Vanclief, the administrator, is asking for some stuff from a different perspective. Man, she's one demanding client. But while I'm there, without blowing my contract, I'll see if I can talk to your Mrs. Simonett."

"Do you think they'll let you?"

"I want to take some more shots of Henley House later this week, daylight and dusk. Maybe some from the inside. Or at least from the verandah. I'd like to juxtapose the surrounding properties, so I'll have to go onto the property itself. I'll tell them I need permission from her."

"Henley House has been willed to the Woodbridge Historical Society. They'd have to give you permission."

"You know that, but *I* don't. I don't live here, remember?" he said. "So I'll ask to see Olivia. She'll probably tell me the house isn't hers; I'll still get a chance to talk. I can be pretty charming when I put my mind to it."

I knew that. "Good luck."

"Keep your fingers crossed. I'll call you as soon as I get finished. And I have an idea. If I juggle my early evening appointment to the afternoon, we could have dinner together tonight, if you felt up to it."

"Sounds good. Waffles, mmmm." With the rest of the day to pull myself together, I might be less scary.

"I've picked up a couple more juicy jobs on this trip, so I'd like to celebrate. I'm not sure that waffles will do the trick. So what do you say we try O'Leary's? We can keep the waffles for some other time."

O'Leary's, contrary to the name, is the most upscale place in town. I would have been happy with waffles or even pizza and beer, but O'Leary's was a chance for a girl to dress up. I hadn't had many of those since I moved back.

"Mmm."

"Pick you up at eight?"

I felt a little tingle in my knees thinking about it. I could get out my little black dress and those new metallic strappy sandals I'd been saving for a very special occasion. I had a pair of chandelier earrings that would be just right. It would be dark enough to disguise the green chin, and with luck my dental work would hold up.

———

At four o'clock I felt together enough to drive to the library. I held my head high as I walked through the reference department.

"I need to speak to Ramona," I said to the librarian at the desk.

"Oh, you just missed her. She left early for a meeting."

Oh crap. "Did she leave anything for me? Charlotte Adams?"

"Of course, we all know who you are. I'll check."

Five minutes later, she shrugged apologetically. "I can't imagine where she put it. She's very organized and thoughtful. I know she felt awful about the other day when you got the short end of the stick because of *certain* pushy people. Anyway, I just can't find it. Sorry you've had to make an extra trip. It's some obituaries and an article, right? Well, at least it's not an emergency."

———

O'Leary's was everything I'd hoped: curved dark wood surfaces, starched white tablecloths, a menu to die for, and soft jazz in the background. My little black dress didn't let me down and my teeth didn't drop onto my entrée. My strappy sandals didn't even pinch my feet. How good was that?

Dominic was easily the most interesting man in the place. I could tell by the looks he drew from the other women. We had a corner table, with flickering candles and a waiter who knew when to hover and when not to.

Dominic raised his glass of pinot noir and clinked mine.

"End of a perfect day for you?" I said.

"Continues to be perfect," he said.

"How did it go at Stone Wall Farm? Did you get to see Olivia?"

The smile slipped. "I did."

"Didn't she give you permission for the photographs?"

"She did. Permission to take shots of her and of Henley House. Just in case there's some issue, I've already spoken to the representative of the historical society. They have no problem with it."

"Did something go wrong at Stone Wall Farm? Were the administrators hanging around listening to everything?"

He shook his head. "They pretty much were, but it wasn't a problem. Just that she's such a sad old lady. All that money but she never gets to go anywhere or do anything."

"Hmm," I said. "We don't know how lucky we are."

"I never want to live long enough to end up in a pretty prison like that. Never mind. The idea of the photo got her all excited."

"Were you pleased with them?"

"Couldn't do them today. She wanted to get her hair done first. She had her heart set on getting some special hairdresser. Doesn't matter to me. I'd like her to feel happy about it. Tomorrow's fine."

"That's nice," I said.

"It will give me a chance to probe a bit. I didn't want to come on too strong and blow it today."

"Right." I felt like screaming.

216          Mary Jane Maffini

He leaned forward and murmured, "This is our night. Let's forget about the Henleys and Stone Wall Farm and everything bad that's happened. We can get to know each other."

Three hours later, the restaurant staff had quietly set up for the next day, and Dominic and I knew quite a bit more about each other. Childhood secrets, memories, dreams, hopes for the future. I knew he was part of a big Italian family, fond of food, football, and fights. They were adjusting to having a photographer in their midst although it seemed just plain wrong to them.

He knew how I felt about my childhood too.

"Sounds like chaos," he said.

"Had its good points. I got to see the world."

He shook his head. "And your mother had four husbands?"

"So far. My dad was the first. He was French Canadian."

"Did you get along with him?"

"Never met him. Hubby number two is my earliest memory."

"Your dad didn't stay in touch?"

"I don't even know if he's still alive. But I guess I take after him. Maybe somewhere north of Quebec City there's a small, dark-haired guy with a color-coordinated wardrobe closet and a very neat kitchen."

He said, "My mom has a very neat kitchen."

"Great, pray that she never meets my mother."

"Funny, I was hoping she might."

"Maybe." I smiled.

He said, "No rush. We've got the rest of our lives. And there are lots of restaurants in Woodbridge."

Wow. Just listen to that. Thousands of violins.

———

I could feel the warmth of Dominic's body as I fumbled with the key to my door.

"I hope you'll get used to the dogs," I said, smiling confidently.

"Oh right, the dogs. I'll cope with them," he said. "If they don't bite."

I didn't answer because as the door swung open, I stared at a blizzard. My jaw dropped. Was it snowing inside? No wait. That wasn't snow. It was toilet paper. Miles of it. How did those tiny creatures get the toilet paper? I'm not a complete fool. I keep it out of their reach in my supply cupboard, with the door firmly closed. Had they learned to fly? Had they grown opposable thumbs? Hired an assistant?

Sweet Marie dashed by with a flamboyant streamer of double-thick premium quilted floating behind her. She glanced back over her shoulder provocatively before rounding the corner into the bedroom. Truffle smirked from the sofa where he sat surrounded in billowing white, like a tiny black dog angel on a huge curly cloud.

I was trying to make sense of the surreal scene and barely noticed the thud of footsteps on the stairs.

Dominic yelped.

"Hey, sorry," Jack said. "I didn't know you had company, Charlotte."

I narrowed my eyes at him. Any doofus would know that meant "get out of here, this is a private moment." But Jack was not just *any* doofus. He was special.

"Wow," Jack said. "What happened here? I thought I heard strange noises coming from your place. I came up in case something was wrong." He gave Dominic a look indicating he might fit the category of something *very* wrong.

Truffle and Sweet Marie had just noticed Dominic too. Sweet Marie lost interest in her white streamer. She bared her teeth at Dominic. Truffle leapt from the sofa and streaked straight for his ankles. Luckily, I grabbed the little angel in time. He squirmed in my arms, snarling and yipping. Sweet Marie growled.

Dominic turned a snowy white, much like the toilet tissue. "Maybe this isn't the best time. I'll call you, Charlotte."

Seconds later the downstairs door clicked behind him.

"Huh. What kind of guy is afraid of toilet paper?" Jack said.

"Very funny. And don't think I don't know what you're up to."

"What am I up to?" Jack said. *"What?"*

—※—

Tuesday morning I decided to buckle down and pay attention to my dying business. I put Miss Henley and Olivia, and yes, Dominic, out of my mind and answered my messages. I called my on-and-off laundry client and left a message. I contacted half a dozen others who had indicated some small interest in my services. I flinched as I listened to their excuses. I spent an hour pondering what it would take to get my life going again. I made a list of actions to kick-start business, but every one of them had some kind of obstacle. When the phone finally rang, I snatched it up.

"Charlotte?" Dominic sounded nervous.

I said, "Allow me to apologize for my noisy dogs and my nosy neighbor."

"Don't worry about the nosy dogs and the noisy neighbor," he said.

"Hmm. That works too," I said with what I hoped was a casual little laugh.

"Did I get you at a bad time?"

"No. Just trying to salvage my career."

"Hey, I'm a freelancer too. I know all about the ups and downs. Those downs can be scary."

"Tell me about it. My biggest hitch seems to be that most people think I'm implicated in the murder of an elderly client. How's that for a scary down?"

"Bad break."

"Until Miss Henley's murder is solved, I'm going to be one lonely little organizer."

"That's why I called you. I was just at Henley House, catching the house in the morning light, and I observed something that you should see."

"What?"

"I can't really explain it. You have to . . . it's bizarre. But it may have to do with those documents you were supposed to look for. Or it could be just my artistic imagination."

"Really? Oh, but I can't be seen going in to Henley House."

"I suppose not. And you shouldn't go by yourself anyway. I can meet you there, but I've got appointments set up all day."

"Lucky you," I said bitterly.

He laughed. "Okay, jealous lady. How about seven? Park around the side so you're not seen if you don't want to set off the gossips. What I have to show you may be nothing, but even if so, it won't take long. And I can fill you in about my photo session with Olivia at the same time."

"That sounds terrific."

"Maybe we can have a glass of wine together afterward. Your place, not Henley House. Does that sound good?"

"It does."

"I'll pick up a bottle of something nice. Oh, and by the way, I've found a source of organic dog biscuits here in Woodbridge. You deal with the nosy neighbor, and I'll make friends with those fierce guard dogs of yours."

---

I snapped open my umbrella and exited the Miata with my head held high. I kept my spine straight and sailed into the library, past the circulation desk and into the reference room. I did not make eye contact with anyone in the room, although I felt the stares on my back and I was very conscious of the soft gossipy buzz. Never mind. I was in a good mood. I smiled at the idea of the organic dogs biscuits. The dogs would adjust to Dominic instantly. Jackie Boy would just have to cope with the new man in my life.

Ramona's eyes sparkled. "Thanks for the other night. All the excitement outside the library. Tension, trouble, television cameras. That's as good as it gets for publicity. Prime time. Breaking news. Shots of the front of the building. It's already been pumping up business. I bet our stats will be stratospheric this month. We are calling it the affair of the dramatic digit."

"Glad I could help. Um, do you have that obit handy?"

"Oh right, the item that sparked everything." She picked up a thin file and handed it to me. "I'm real sorry about that. I had your information tucked right over here. I made copies of the documents for you, and I guess my colleague didn't realize it. Things got a bit hairy here on Saturday, and I must have stuck your envelope in the wrong place. We were up to our patooties in . . ."

I borrowed Dominic's word. "Jackasses?"

She threw back her head and laughed. A few readers glanced up in surprise. "We call them patrons. But that particular group is a bit special."

"I figured that out. So do I owe you anything for the copies?"

"All part of the service."

I took the envelope to the nearest table, carefully keeping my back turned to a man I suspected of being in the crabby crowd from Saturday. I sat down and opened the file, with a mounting sense of suspense. The first photocopy was an article about Crawford titled "Woodbridge's Wandering Son Dead at Thirty-Six." The second was a copy of an obituary.

My reading was interrupted by a strident voice from across the reference room. "That's her, all right. I'm surprised she's not in jail."

"Just a matter of time, I hear," another voice answered, then sniffed.

Luckily my spine was already straight. I raised my nose and sailed out. That would be my last trip to this particular library.

As soon as I passed through the door to the fresh air, I lifted the obit, reading as I went. My hand stopped in midair. My mouth went dry.

**Henley, Crawford Lincoln.**

Accidentally in San Diego, CA, Dec. 3, 1970, in his thirty-sixth year. He was predeceased by his parents James Washington Henley and Cecily Beryl Crawford of Woodbridge. He is survived by his wife Laura (Lo Bello), his infant son, Dominic, and his cousins Helen Henley, Randolph Henley, and Olivia Henley Simonett. Private services will be held in Woodbridge and in San Diego at a later date.

# 17

I gripped the steering wheel of the Miata so hard it should have bent. What a dimwit I'd been, letting Dominic Lo Bello lead me on. Just plain empty-headed.

Take our time, indeed. Meet his *mom*. Oh yeah, *right*. And would she be Laura Lo Bello? Mother of Dominic Henley? Crawford's infant son would be now in his late thirties. You didn't have to be a detective to figure it out.

I hated to think how far things might have gone if I hadn't found out Dominic was probably the Henley heir. Correction: I mean if I hadn't found out he was a lying slacker who *wanted* to be the next Henley heir.

I zigged and zagged a block from the library then decided I'd better pull over before I rammed an eighteen-wheeler to let off steam. I sat in my little car and yelled. I pounded that poor steering wheel until my hands hurt. A passing dog walker gave me a startled look and scuttled off toward the wooded hills at the end of town. I took a long series of deep breaths. Was there something about me that attracted cheating creeps? And why did Dominic lie in the first place? What could he gain by hiding his relationship to the Henleys?

A new and awful thought hit my brain like a grenade. Dominic had already been in town when Miss Henley died, clearing a serious impediment to Olivia's fortune. Had he killed her? Had I given him some information that would make whatever nasty plan he had even easier? I'd told him about Pepper. Maybe *he'd* tipped off the police and alerted the media.

I closed my eyes and leaned back on the headrest. It gave my bruised fists a break, but it didn't help much. I needed someone to talk to, but everyone I might expect to vent to was unavailable. I left long crabby messages for Jack, Sally, and even Margaret. I gave my opinion about Dominic's character and shared what I intended to tell him to his face at the Henley House at seven. The calls didn't dissipate my anger; in fact, they helped me to develop a few new choice phrases to fling at the dirty little liar.

I'd no sooner hung up from leaving the last message when Jack called back.

"He wants you to meet him at Henley House?" he said. "Have you forgotten you found a body there? Listen, I'm meeting a guy at five thirty about some security installations for the shop. I should be free before seven. I'll meet you at Henley House. Don't go in without me."

"I need to do this myself. I'm a big girl."

"You're a tiny little big girl. I don't plan to hold your hand when you tell that spotted snake what you think of him, but I'll be there for you. Make sure you wait for me."

"Yeah, yeah."

"Uh, promise."

"Fine, I promise."

Spotted snake? I liked that.

Ramona must have tried to call while I was talking to Jack.

"Charlotte? Ramona here. You sure stormed out of here

like your tail was on fire. I hope you weren't sick or something. Anyway, you left the rest of the file I had for you. I'm not sure if you read it. It has some additional information about Crawford Henley and his family. Interesting, if tragic. It's at the information desk with your name on it. Tell them it's on the second shelf, in case I'm not around and they're playing three blind mice."

I was steeling myself to drive back to the library when I caught sight of Lilith loping along on the other side of the street. She looked more forlorn than ever. Her hair had wilted in the drizzle. She bent forward under the weight of an over-stuffed backpack. I had a pretty good idea what that meant: obviously, some people had way more trouble than I did. So what if I'd been deceived? Big whoop. Lilith had been fired unjustly, she'd lost her car and had her bike stolen, her education was threatened, and unless I was wrong, she'd lost her apartment. I made a U-turn and pulled in beside her. Up close, her eyes were swollen and red. Not such a good look with the purple hair. The stench of smoke clung to her.

"Hop in," I said.

She gave me a sullen look. "I don't need you taking pity on me."

"Actually, I'm kind of hoping you'll feel sorry for me."

"You? Why?"

"Total absolute betrayal. I need a shoulder to cry on. Are you available?"

She brightened. "Bring it on."

Together we barely managed to stuff Lilith's backpack into the Miata. I had a sick feeling we were carrying everything she'd been able to salvage. I raised an eyebrow.

She shrugged. "My apartment's toast."

Before I could say anything, she said, "And I'll survive."

She lowered herself into the passenger seat and we spun off. For obvious reasons, I wanted a café where I hadn't gazed into a certain person's cheating eyes.

"How about Betty's?" I said. "It's far enough out of town that I might not be recognized."

"Sounds good." Lilith managed a pale smile. "I love diners. And no one recognizes me anywhere anyhow."

I smiled back at her. Whatever problems I had, I had family, luckily far away, friends, luckily close by, a career, which might someday recover from the setbacks of the last week, a lovely secure place to live, and two velvety dogs to snuggle up with over the next couple of days as I sulked over Dominic's duplicity.

Who did Lilith have aside from me?

As far as I could tell, not a single soul.

---

Betty's was a happening spot for truckers, retired guys, and anyone who liked a genuine retro bargain. Inside was an ongoing homage to 1956.

"But why would he lie about who he was?" Lilith said, as we raced a pair of long-haulers to the last empty booth.

"I have no idea." I slid onto the cracked red leather banquette. Betty herself began her slow shuffle over to take our orders.

Lilith picked up the plastic-coated menu. "Would you have avoided him if you knew he was one of the Henleys?"

I didn't even need a menu. Betty's club sandwiches are the stuff of legend. "Probably not. It wouldn't have made any difference to me. So why the deception?"

"He's a scumbag, for sure. Some guys are like that. But you were bound to find out."

I nodded. "I guess that didn't matter to him. He planned to move on."

"That's real sleazy."

Betty might be pushing eighty, but she was quick enough with the famous club sandwiches. Unfortunately, by then, just thinking about Dominic's deception had ruined my appetite.

Lilith picked up one of the giant hand-cut fries. "Would he inherit from Miss Henley too?"

"She wasn't really wealthy and she left most of her estate to St. Jude's for the scholarship fund."

"Oh right. I hear they're calling it the Helen Henley Memorial Scholarship Fund."

"Then her own home and Henley House go to the historical society along with some money for renovations. Maybe Dominic could challenge the will. I'm not sure. But you know what's worst of all?"

She shook her head and popped the fry into her mouth.

"I actually sent him out there to Stone Wall Farm."

Lilith interrupted. "What do you mean, you sent him? He's been around before, taking pictures."

"But I told him to cozy up to Olivia."

"He's already spent lots of time with Olivia."

"What?"

"Sure. She liked him just fine. He brought her flowers once. Another time he took her for a spin in her wheelchair in the garden. I've seen them chatting."

I gasped. "That's his scheme. He gets to know her, then eventually she finds out who he is, and abracadabra, she changes her will in his favor. Maybe that's why he lied. He's keeping it a secret from *Olivia* until the time is right."

"Once again, I've got to ask, why deceive? Olivia would love to have a nice nephew to leave her money to. She's all alone in the world."

I said, "And the only reason she's alone in the world is because Helen died."

"Well, yeah. And Randolph, of course."

"But that was a while ago. Why did you mention Randolph? Did you know him?"

"Sure. He used to visit Olivia all the time. He made her laugh. He always made sure she got out of the building. For a walk, if she was stable enough. He'd wheel her in the chair if she was having a wobbly day. The same kind of thing that Dominic was doing recently, only it was a lot more fun with Randolph. Balloons on the wheelchair, party hats, noisemakers, that kind of thing."

"You're kidding me."

"You look surprised."

"I am. Miss Henley told me he was cruel and miserable."

"No way. He used to join her in the dining room for dinner. He'd play card tricks and tell jokes. We were all bent over laughing. He'd even take the time to talk to Gabe. He might have been a funny old guy in these weird suits that needed cleaning, but everyone liked him. Olivia was crazy about Randolph."

"I remember the suits, and the grubby ties. But I had a totally different impression."

Lilith curled her lip. "Consider the source. Originally, I think Olivia was planning to leave Randolph a pile of money. I heard that she changed her will to include Stone Wall Farm only after he died."

Lilith stopped talking and took a large bite out of her club sandwich. I had a pretty good idea she hadn't eaten that day at all.

After chewing and swallowing, Lilith said, "Olivia changed a lot after Randolph was killed. This last year has been very hard on her. And then Helen's death upset her even more. Helen didn't come much when Randolph was alive, but she did her duty afterward."

"Wait a minute. You said after Randolph was killed. He died before I moved back to Woodbridge. Did you mean that someone murdered him?"

"He had a terrible accident. He tripped as he was crossing the street and got hit by a truck. It wasn't anyone's fault, just a sad thing. But it's not like dying in your bed at ninety-nine."

"But it makes me wonder."

Lilith stared at me over her cup of hot chocolate. "You mean what if someone pushed Randolph?"

"Face it, with Randolph and Helen gone, there's no one between Olivia and Dominic."

"So what will you do? Go to the police?"

An image of Pepper, face skeptical and arms crossed, flashed through my brain. "I'm pretty sure they won't believe my speculations."

"And stay away from that guy, Dominic."

"I intend to after tonight. I'm meeting him tonight at Henley House, of all places. He's got something to show me, and I plan to tell him to get lost."

"Meeting him at Henley House? Real bad idea, if you ask me."

I chuckled. "It would be, but my friend Jack's riding shotgun."

"I'll come along too, if you want."

I smiled. "Thanks. I'll be fine with Jack. But in fact, I do have a small errand I need done. Can you pick up a file for me at the library? It's more information on Crawford Henley's family. Second shelf behind the reference desk. My name is on it. If there's any question about it, just call me. Does your cell phone number still work?"

She patted her pocket. "Yup. It's about all I have left."

"Excellent." I handed her a business card. "Can you drop the file off at this address later?"

"Piece of cake."

"Speaking of cake," I said, "Betty's known for her devil's food special. And chocolate is my drug of choice."

***

Just when I expected that nothing would ever go right for me again, my phone rang.

"This is Glenda Baillie."

"Oh!"

"You called about my mom, Wynona Banks?"

"Yes, I am very sorry for your loss. I am told that your

mother was a wonderful woman. That she was extremely kind and caring in her dealings with Mrs. Simonett."

"She sure loved Olivia." I heard a quaver in her voice as she spoke. "In your message you said that you thought her shooting had something to do with Helen Henley's death."

"Yes, I do. And I have some—"

"The police didn't seem to think that."

"No. They prefer to think it was random. But Olivia Simonett has a huge fortune, and I think someone is getting rid of anyone in the way of it."

She gasped. "You mean Mom was just in the way?"

"I don't have proof, but I am absolutely convinced the two deaths are related. And in fact, Randolph Henley died under mysterious circumstances not that long ago."

"Mom was so upset about that. Olivia was devastated."

"Did your mother comment about the fact that Olivia planned to leave a lot of money to the Stone Wall Farm Foundation?"

"She mentioned it. This was a new idea that Olivia got when the new director took over. We used to call her Miss Frosty."

"I understand why. Did she think it was a good idea?"

"Well, no, not really. My mom raised the five of us as a single parent. Every one of us went to college. Mom kept working with underprivileged kids afterward. She said it was a shame money didn't go to people who needed it."

"Hmm."

"Of course, Olivia was planning to leave a bundle to my mother too. So she didn't have to worry about a thing in her old age. Now she won't have an old age. What are you suggesting? That Miss Frosty was behind this? I can't stand the woman, but that seems far-fetched."

"I suppose it does. It's possible though, or it could have been someone else who stood to inherit."

"Like who?"

"I'm working on that. This must be so hard for you, but could you help again if I have questions?"

"You know what? I'm not sure what's worse, your mom being killed by a random shooting or being murdered because of money. It's all hard to believe. I still remember her cheerful voice when she called me on her way home that last day. I'll never have that again. So you're damn right I'll help."

———❖———

If you are planning to dump someone, no matter how excellent your reason for the dumpage, you absolutely need to look your best. I already knew this from previous experience. By the time I got home I had planned what to wear when I looked Dominic in the eye and told him he was a lying, money-grubbing weasel.

I always keep an outfit in my closet ready to go if something important comes up. Right down to new Swiss hose, still in the package. My teal blue cotton velvet jacket looked serious enough, and the swingy bias-cut skirt screamed style, but I thought a peek of a lacy camisole at the neckline might hint that I plan to continue to have a very eventful life that didn't involve any creeps named Lo Bello. I decided my black strappy stilettos would make that point too. So what if it was freezing out. And what the hell, since he didn't like dogs, I made a point of bringing along Truffle and Sweet Marie.

———❖———

The yellow police tape was gone when I pulled up in front of Henley House. And for some reason the gate was closed. Dominic's red Jeep Cherokee was parked at a confident angle at the curb. I avoided the fire hydrant and pulled up a half block away. I fumed in the car and waited for Jack. I'd mentally rehearsed the scene with Dominic and was ready to get it over with.

Fifteen long minutes dragged by. Where was Jack? I usually keep a project on hand if I find myself with time to kill, but it was too dark to read or make lists. I fished out my phone. I tried Jack. No answer. I called Sally and got her machine. I had no luck with Margaret either. I even gave Rose a buzz to see how she was doing, but her phone rang on and on. Finally, I left a message with Glenda Baillie asking what her mother had said in that last cheerful message.

I sat back and thought black thoughts about men in general.

"Turns out Jack's just one more male I can't count on," I snapped at the dogs.

They yapped either in agreement or protest, who knows? Who cares? I was pretty steamed and didn't really need emotional reinforcement from my pets. I stepped out of the car and started pacing. That's when I spotted the bicycle lying on the ground near the side of the house. Oh right. Was Jack already inside the house? Why the hell hadn't he waited for me? Had he planned to tell off Dominic himself? Punch him out? Really, what is it with men? Testosterone lunacy?

I stomped up the stairs to the verandah. I wished my red boots had been available to aid in the stomping. I planned to confront Dominic at the door, offer an assessment of his character, and tell him to stick his so-called information where the sun doesn't shine. Then I planned to whirl and make a dramatic exit back to my car and out of his life forever. And as for Mr. Wait Until I Get There, I would deal with him later.

Of course, Dominic didn't answer the door.

Goose bumps danced on my arms. The last time I'd knocked on that particular door, I'd gone in to find Miss Henley's body. I had no desire to set foot in the dank, crowded interior of Henley House, even if Jack was there too. Dominic was just going to have to get his lying backside out on the verandah. After five minutes of banging, I concluded that he didn't plan to do that.

I turned the handle and the huge oak door creaked open. I pushed it all the way and shouted into the foyer.

"Are you there, Dominic? It's Charlotte. I have something really important to show you." Meaning, I'd like you to get a good look at the contemptuous expression on my face. Then you can watch my backside as I walk away.

Rain dripped through the holes in the verandah roof and settled on my nose as I waited. I tapped my toes. I stamped my heels. I gave the door a little kick. Not such a good idea with strappy stilettos.

I shouted, "I don't know where you guys are, but I want to see you. Now!"

Theories competed in my head. They were duking it out in the back of the house? They were both afraid to talk to me? Dominic had given Jack some reasonable explanation and they were making friends? None of it made sense. Plus the rain had finished off my hairdo. I would have pulled the damp straggling remnants into a ponytail—always be ready with a ponytail holder or a scrunchie in your purse, another motto I love—but I'd been so rattled I'd forgotten my purse in the car. That's so unlike me, I don't even have a motto to deal with it.

Never mind. Time to get it over with.

I pushed the oak door open a bit more. I stuck my head in and bellowed, "Come out here and have the guts to look me in the face when I tell you what I think about you and your sneaky, deceitful game you miserable, lying, underhanded, money-grubbing lowlife. And as for you, Jack, we'll talk later."

It was the best I could come up with under my personal circumstances, which were mainly cold, wet, mad as hell, and with very bad hair.

Nothing.

Cowards.

I leaned further into the foyer and repeated my words, louder and meaner. Still nothing. My throat was getting sore from hollering, but I decided to give it one more try. I just wanted to yell it to his face. I pushed the door a bit farther but it wouldn't budge. Keeping my wet feet firmly outside, I stretched myself just far enough to peer around it.

Why was Dominic lying on the floor? It took a second before the answer hit me.

Pull yourself together, I told myself. That can't happen twice. This isn't the movies. I stepped in, looking more confident than I felt. I knelt down and touched the hand. It was still warm. Dominic lay there, legs splayed, arms outstretched, eyes wide and unblinking. It didn't take a detective to tell he'd been shot.

I gasped and struggled to my feet. I backed toward the door, still gasping and staring at the horrible sight. I twisted my foot and fell backward over the threshold. The fall knocked the breath out of me.

I tried to get to my feet but collapsed with the stab of pain in my ankle. I struggled to my knees, nothing wrong with them, and crawled forward, over the threshold. I stared once again at Dominic Lo Bello's body and his handsome lying face, staring glassily at the ceiling.

I hesitated before touching him. The memory of Miss Henley's cold stiff body was still fresh in my mind. He *was* warm. Could he be alive with a head wound like that? Call 911, of course. But my cell phone was in my handbag back in the car. I had to get to the car fast. As I got to my feet and limped forward, I spotted something odd, just beyond Dominic's hand. Without thinking, I reached down and snatched it up. How did the heel from my red boot get there? That didn't make sense. I stuck the heel in my pocket and whirled at a small rustle behind me, soft and sibilant. A rat perhaps? And just where was Dominic's killer?

*Two minutes spent organizing your handbag every night
will make its contents readily accessible, saving
you time and frustration.*

# 18

I hobbled in a panic toward the car, half expecting to hear the crunch of gravel behind me. I glanced back and tumbled again. This time I shredded my new Swiss hose in the contact with the driveway. By the time I reached the Miata, my hands were shaking. My knees were shaking too. They were also bleeding, but that was the least of my problems. Luckily, I had the keys with me. On the third try, I got the door open and crumpled into the car. I locked the door behind me and reached for my purse to get the phone. Truffle and Sweet Marie leapt up seeking kisses.

"Settle down," I shrieked. "Where's my purse?"

They cocked their little pointed heads and grinned. They love the "where's the whatever" game.

"Oh crap, not now. Tell me you didn't."

The contents of my perfectly organized purse lay scattered on the passenger-side floor of the Miata. Although not all of them, by the look of it. Some must surely be under the seat. When did they learn to open a zipper? Sweet

Marie upped the ante by picking up my large, soft makeup brush in her teeth and giving it a little shake.

Concentrate. You can boil the makeup brush later. What if Dominic can still be saved? All that matters is 911.

So where was the phone? I grabbed the spilled items from the floor and stuffed them back into the purse. Wait. Maybe the phone hadn't spilled out of the purse in the first place. I dumped everything back out onto the seat. Sweet Marie climbed in my lap. Truffle licked my ear.

Okay. I contorted myself to look under the seat. I felt around, practically dislocating my shoulder. No phone, although I did encounter my new Yves Saint Laurent compact, open and upside down. So much for that pricey little luxury.

Two pairs of beady black eyes gazed on with interest. Who would win this game? Not much chance for me at the moment.

I had failed to follow yet another motto: keep your phone handy because when you really need it, you need it right away. My mottos were dropping fast. My beautiful organized life had fallen apart. But at least I still had a life. I'd wanted Dominic sorry, apologetic, groveling, repentant, realizing what he'd done, understanding he was a miserable liar. Not dead.

But what if he was still alive?

I started the car, squeaked as pain raced through my ankle, and put the pedal to the metal. As the Miata shot down the hill, an ambulance peeled around the corner of North Elm Street and raced past, siren shrieking. A pair of squad cars careened after it, lights flashing. I pulled over, waved, and blew my horn hoping to attract their attention. They didn't even slow down. I watched through my rearview mirror as the three vehicles rocketed up the driveway of the Henley House. If by some miracle Dominic was still alive, they'd take care of him.

I screeched to a stop in front of Rose's yellow door. In the distance I could hear the wail of more sirens. Had the passing cops seen my bright little Miata? I backed up and eased the car along the narrow driveway by Rose's house. I kept going and turned into the backyard. I stuck a dog under each arm and limped back to the front of the house. I clattered up the stairs. The yellow door stood open.

"Rose!" I called.

I felt a wave of nausea. Was this what my future held? Every door I reached swinging open and then . . .

Sirens drew closer, a new batch of police cars shot up the hill, just as the ambulance sped down. I stepped inside and called again. "Rose."

I heard a moan from the living room. Rose sat slumped in her orange recliner. Her oxygen tank lay on the floor, out of reach. Her eyes were closed. Her lips were as blue as her hair, and her vibrant fuchsia jogging suit contrasted with her pale, grey face.

"Rose!" I shook her. Her breathing was raspy. And no wonder. The little cat paraded on the back of the chair, near her head, purring and spewing allergens. Truffle and Sweet Marie went into action, yipping like coyotes. The cat raced across the room and up the curtains.

Rose's eyelids fluttered but didn't open. That was probably a good thing. She would have hated to see her curtain rod collapse under the cat's weight and the orange draperies in a heap on the floor.

I reconnected her oxygen as best I could, muttering soothing words. I fumbled for the phone and dialed 911.

"North Elm Street," I shouted. "Send an ambulance."

"Thank you, ma'am. That shooting's already been called in."

"No," I said firmly, "it's not a shooting. I am calling from number Seven North Elm. An elderly woman is in respiratory distress. My, um, neighbor. She seems to have lost consciousness. Her oxygen is disconnected. Tell them to hurry."

"Sure thing. Oh, hang on, is that you again, Charlotte?" the dispatcher said. "Pretty sure I know your voice."

"No," I said, "it isn't. I told you I'm the neighbor."

I hung up. The dogs had the cat cornered on the kitchen counter. The cat hissed and spit. The dogs leapt and snapped. I raced to the living room and grabbed the fallen drapes. I flung them over the cat and wrestled the cat and drape combo into the bathroom well away from Rose and the dogs. The panicked creature spat at me. I got a nice scratch on my arm too, before I closed the door. But not before I caught a glimpse of myself in the bathroom mirror. My flirty little skirt and velvet jacket were beyond help. My hair hung in strings. There was a streak of blood across my cheek. Mine? Or Dominic's? My stomach flip-flopped. I looked down. My knees were bleeding.

I didn't really care how I looked considering what had happened to Dominic and Rose, but one glance at me and the paramedics would call the cops.

I fought a panicky urge to run. Instead I returned to the living room and squeezed Rose's hand. "Help is coming. You'll be fine." I figured Rose didn't really need to see me get arrested. I yanked clothes out of the gym bag I had left at Rose's a week ago. "I have to change my clothes, but I'm right here. You're not alone anymore."

One minute later, I'd changed into my beat-up jeans and hoodie and pulled my hair into a ponytail. I stuffed the clothes I had been wearing into the gym bag. The bathroom was off limits, so I hightailed it to the kitchen and washed my hands and face and headed back to wait for emergency services with Rose.

Two young paramedics arrived before I really got my breathing near normal.

Of course, I didn't know the answers to any of the

questions. "I'm just a neighbor. I saw the door open and got worried," I kept repeating. "I found her like this."

"You know her family?" The first paramedic was looking at me kind of funny.

"She has a daughter somewhere. California, maybe. Where will you take her?" I wiped away a stray tear.

"Woodbridge General."

"Should I come too?" I tried to sound normal.

"Sorry, ma'am. It'll be family only."

"But . . . okay, I'll try to find where the daughter is and contact her."

I was talking to the air by that time. The ambulance pulled away with Rose inside. I collapsed into the orange sofa and thought hard. Okay, first things first. One of my regular mantras.

So, find the daughter. One thing about organizing people's lives, you know how most of them operate. Telephone numbers, addresses, and zip codes are in address books. I hunted around for Rose's address book with the happy spaniel on the cover. I closed my eyes and thought back. Rose kept it right there by the phone. Never mind, this was a simple house, no clutter, no built-up junk. A place for everything and everything in its place. It didn't take long to conclude that Rose's address book wasn't anywhere.

Had it been in her pocket?

I didn't recall noticing any pockets in her jogging suit. A paranoid thought hit me. Had someone taken it? Had someone broken into Rose's house and pushed her down? Maybe knocked her out? Disconnected her oxygen?

Who would do that? The same person who killed Dominic? A horrible thought hit me. Where the hell was Jack? Why had his bike been outside Henley House?

"Be logical," I said out loud. "There can't be more than one demented attacker in Woodbridge. Can there?"

The thing was, did that person want to kill me too? Or was it more fun to frame me for the other murders?

On Rose's television, Todd Tyrell's teeth were flashing. "Breaking News" splashed along the bottom of the screen. At the sight of my own face, I picked up the remote and turned up the volume.

"Following the discovery of a second body at Woodridge's historic Henley House, police are seeking Woodbridge businesswoman Charlotte Adams, aged thirty, for questioning."

My image splashed across the screen again. This time, I was flanked by two police officers. My expression gave new meaning to "guilty as charged." You could practically hear the gavel coming down. But Todd wasn't finished.

"WINY has also learned that Adams has been placed at the scene of the recent uptown drive-by shooting of fifty-nine-year-old Wynona Banks, who died tragically last week in a hail of bullets. WINY has confirmed this information with independent witnesses." A clear shot of Tang's Convenience filled the screen.

"Adams's whereabouts at this moment are unknown, but caution is advised before approaching her."

"Oh puleeze," I shouted. "I am an organizer! I do not kill people. Caution is so not advised."

"Adams is known to drive a late model Mazda Miata." My license plate number flashed on the screen. "Anyone seeing her should contact Woodbridge Police immediately."

The pounding of my heart was also reverberating in my head. What could I do? Turn myself in? Was that the best thing? I hadn't killed anyone. But someone was going to a great deal of trouble to make it look like I had. I just had to think about the heel of my boot near Dominic's body to remind me of that.

I needed a few minutes to clear my head. So many things to worry about. Would Rose be okay? Would Wynona's daughter hear this awful lie? Would the police show up and arrest me? What if someone spotted my car in the backyard? Or Mona Pringle decided to mention my name? I locked the dogs in the bedroom and headed quickly to the back door. I lifted the blind and peered out first. I didn't see anyone, and it made sense that no one could see me.

In my car, I poked around under the seat until I finally located my cell phone wedged behind a seat belt. I stuck that in my pocket and got busy. I lifted the canvas from Rose's ancient Grand LeMans. I pulled off the tarp, then wrestled it over my little Miata.

I headed back to the house thinking of Todd Tyrell. His news announcement had been flashing before the last cruiser left Henley House. There was only one person who could have known that Dominic was dead and that I'd been at the scene. Had the murderer alerted the media? Had the person who made sure my pen was found near Miss Henley also stuck my heel near Dominic? Either way, someone who knew me had committed two well-planned murders. Three if Wynona Banks was part of the game. To say nothing of Randolph.

The front door banged. Truffle and Sweet Marie raced toward it, barking. I stood frozen. There was nowhere to hide; even the drapes were gone. I straightened my spine and prepared myself to face the police.

"Hello? Are you in here?"

A wave of relief washed over me as I recognized the voice. "Lilith?"

"Can I come in?"

"Sure. But how did you find me?"

"If you're going to try hiding out, you'll have to do better than this."

"What do you mean?"

"You told me you had a friend near the Henley House. You told me her name. You sent me to the library where there are directories. How hard was that?"

"Well, you shouldn't be here."

"What? You asked me to pick up an envelope at the library, remember?"

"But that was before I was wanted by the police. Oh, maybe you don't know about that."

"Well, I went by your place to deliver the envelope and the house was surrounded by cops."

"Oh boy."

"Yeah. I got the hell out of there. I hate cops. For historical reasons."

"I'm beginning to understand how you feel."

"Anyway, I headed off to the nearest bar and caught the news alerts."

"But how did you find me?"

"Process of elimination. Where else are you going to go? The cops are surrounding your house. I knew you weren't at the library."

"They're saying I killed people."

"Cops make mistakes, and I've learned that the hard way. So, I've decided to trust you."

"That's—"

"Because you trusted me. And I'm not sure if it was the right thing or not, but I opened your envelope from the library. You better sit down."

I sat.

She pointed and said, "Are you wearing two different shoes?"

I glanced at my feet. Sure enough, I was sporting one battered green and silver running shoe and one half of a pair of faded red Keds. No wonder the paramedic had given me that strange look. "Right, remind me to change. I have another pair just like them."

Lilith handed me the envelope. It wasn't sealed. I sat on the orange sofa and unfolded the papers inside. A Post-it note from Ramona saying "SORRY!" A few more items on the Henley family. I practically stopped breathing as I came across the newspaper article and another obituary.

I read the tragic account of a ten-year-old child killed in a house fire along with his mother, Laura Lo Bello. Poor little Dominic. He'd never had a chance.

*Sort your possessions using containers labeled*
GIVE AWAY, SELL, TOSS, REPAIR, *and* KEEP.
*Only organize what you're keeping.*

# 19

"But if he wasn't Dominic Lo Bello, then who was he?" Lilith asked.

I bit my lip. "I have no idea."

"This just gets weirder."

"No kidding, but you'd better leave, because it's just a matter of time until the cops do door-to-door interviews here. If you're found with me, you'll get hauled off to the police station. They'll probably decide you're an accessory. Having your face on WINY won't help you much in rebuilding your career."

She said, "What can I do?"

"We have to find Rose Skipowski's daughter. She's somewhere on the West Coast, I believe."

"Sure. What's her name?"

"I don't know anything about her. Rose's address book is missing, which is very weird. If you could get an address and a phone number, that would help." I glanced at the wall clock. "Too late for the library."

Lilith said, "I'll try the Internet café. Can't be that many Skipowskis to check out. Anything else I can do?"

"If you had your own place, I'd ask you to look after Truffle and Sweet Marie."

"I'd be happy to. They're so cute."

"They can be real . . . hey, where are they?"

"They met me when I arrived."

"Oh crap! The front door!"

The yellow door stood wide open. Outside, the wind whipped sodden leaves along the rainy street. Truffle and Sweet Marie were nowhere to be seen.

"We have to find them," I wailed.

"Let's go."

"They hate the cold. They'll come to you right away." Unless, I thought, unless they ran in front of a car. Unless a bigger dog got them. Unless . . .

Lilith grabbed me by the shoulders. "Don't panic. We'll find them."

"Right," I said.

Lilith glanced at my shoes but kept her mind on business. "Where will you go?"

"I don't know. If you find them, call my friend Sally. Tell her I sent you." I raced back to the living room, grabbed a flyer, and scribbled Sally's phone number and address. I reached for my purse and fished out twenty dollars.

Lilith looked offended. "What's that for?"

"Internet café fees. Cab fare. Whatever. Leave a message if I don't answer. Thanks for everything."

The wind picked up as Lilith and I headed in opposite directions, shouting the names of two small endangered creatures.

⸙

An hour later, I stood on an empty street and felt despair wash over me. There was no sign of Truffle or Sweet

Marie. No phone call from Lilith. Nothing but wind, cold, and slippery leaves. I couldn't give up.

I tried every driveway, every backyard, looking for some-place they would have taken shelter. I didn't dare knock on doors, since everyone in Woodbridge would have seen my face splashed across their television screen.

A thought hit me as I tiptoed into a stranger's backyard. These were spoiled little dogs. They could never find their way home. If they returned to Rose's, the door was closed. What would they do? They certainly knew my car; maybe they'd hide under it. Was that crazy wishful thinking? I turned and dodged into a driveway just as a squad car screeched in. A police officer emerged. "Stay right there," he said.

He drew his gun and said, "Drop your weapon."

What? The only thing that dropped was my jaw.

"Is that you, Nick?" I said.

Officer Nick Monahan said, "Charlotte?"

"What do you want me to drop?"

Nick crept closer. "What's in your hand?"

"It's my purse. What would I be doing with a weapon, Nick?"

"We got a couple calls about a prowler."

"Oh right, that would be dangerous little me," I said.

"Don't joke about. There's an all-points bulletin out for you. You're wanted for murder."

"Of course there is. Tell me, Nick. Do you think I killed people?"

"Don't matter what I think. I have to arrest you."

"For what? Looking for my dogs? Is that illegal now?"

"Your dogs?"

I reminded myself that Nick Monahan might be a very beautiful man, but he had never been known for his brains, which tended to reside in his pants. Even so, I marveled that he'd made it as a cop. Connections really counted in Woodbridge.

"My two little wiener dogs ran away. I'm really scared they'll get hit by a car."

"The thing is, we're in the middle of . . . are you wearing two different shoes?"

"Listen. You have to help me find them."

"Different shoes. Man, that's not like you, Charlotte. You are always really hot looking."

"Help me find them, Nick."

"I can't help you look for wiener dogs. I'm supposed to arrest you. I'm going to call for backup now. Then if you promise to go to the station, I'll come back to hunt for the dogs. What do they look like?"

I bit my tongue. Then I said, "Backup? For what? Protection from me? Big bad Charlotte Adams? Be a man for once, Nick."

"But there's an APB . . ."

I had only one card up my sleeve. I played it. "The only person you are going to need protection from is your wife."

Even in the dim light, I could see him blanch. "What do you mean?"

"I mean you better shoot me now, because if you arrest me, I am going to tell Pepper the truth about what happened between us. I kept my mouth shut before because she was so happy about getting married to you. She was my lifelong friend and I didn't have the heart to tell her how many times you made passes at me. But I bet the honeymoon's over now. I imagine she knows you better. I'll look her straight in the eye and fill her in on everything you tried to do and every cheating word that came out of your mouth."

"C'mon, Charley. You wouldn't do that."

Ew. Charley. I just hate that. "Sure I would."

"But you know what she's like," he said.

Oh yes. I knew what they were both like. A smart, ambitious, ruthless woman who happened to love a guy heavy on sex appeal and light on morals. In those circumstances, shit can happen.

"She'll kill me."

"Oh, I don't think she'll actually kill you. She'll hurt you, definitely. And make your life miserable for years, I imagine. She'll watch you like a hawk. You won't be able to—"

"But Charley . . . you were the one I had the hots for all during high school. Remember? It was you. I was crazy about you, babe. I couldn't help myself. It's not my fault. I still—"

"Yeah, whatever. Pull the trigger or let me go." I didn't think that Nick Monahan had the guts to shoot me or the brains to find a solution. The worst I could expect would be a grope. In his nervous state, I was pretty sure even that wouldn't happen.

I said, "Tell you what. I'll head off now and you call for backup. No hard feelings."

Nick stood there and slowly reholstered his weapon.

"There's an all—"

"I know, APB. So chances are one of your colleagues will get me."

"But listen, the other guys think you killed a bunch of people. They might really shoot you."

"I didn't kill anybody, but Pepper wants to think so."

"Well, Pepper's . . . hotheaded. And she can be kind of mean. But they still need proof to be able to charge you with murder. Why don't you just come into the station? No one's gonna be able to prove you killed anyone. I even think Pepper knows that. No one will get hurt if you come in. It'll just be a bit of inconvenience, and that Korean chick will get you out."

He had a point. It was a sensible approach. And I am almost always sensible. And no one would get hurt. Who was left at that point anyway? I must have gasped out loud.

Nick said, "What is it?"

"Nothing," I whispered. I'd just realized who else could get hurt.

A window squeaked open in the house near us. A quavery elderly voice called out, "Did you catch the prowler, officer?"

Nick turned toward the window. "No, ma'am. No prowler here. Just a nice lady, looking for her dogs."

"Sorry, officer, I can't hear you. Did you arrest him?"

Nick raised his voice. "No prowler, ma'am."

"You're putting him in the van?"

Nick moved closer to the window. "It's just a case of mistaken identity, ma'am."

"Do you need me to identify him?" she quavered.

Nick put his face right up to the window and shouted, "It's all right, ma'am. Nothing to worry about."

If only that were true.

He turned back to face me. He shrugged in a big, goofy, lovable way and flashed the famous Monahan grin at me. "Nothing to worry about at all," he repeated soothingly.

Even my tired, overwrought brain knew there was plenty to worry about. So many people dead. Would Olivia be next? I knew I had to do something. Fast. What were the chances that if I told Nick my crazy suspicions, he would do the intelligent thing? Nonexistent. In my heart, I knew that Nick would make it worse somehow. I couldn't let that happen.

Nick was back at the window again. Declining an offer of hot cocoa and s'mores. I heard genuine regret in his voice. If I hadn't been there, I was certain Nick would have accepted. He was always nice to old ladies and small animals. Those were his good qualities. He leaned in farther to reassure the woman in the window. I seized that opportunity to make a run for it. I raced along the driveway, hurtled over the broken-down fence, and dashed over to the next street.

---

I was grateful to Nick for being a spineless dimwit who was unlikely to shoot me and to Rose for living close by.

I found the dogs huddled in front of the yellow door, barking to be let in. I clicked the lock on the door behind us. I slid down to the floor and let the troublemakers scamper off to see if the cat was still in the bathroom.

Okay. I have a policy about doing the right thing. But what exactly was the right thing in a case like this? The idea unfolding in my brain was so wacky, I couldn't imagine even trying to explain it to any police officer, let alone Pepper, who was in charge of the case. First of all, I could no longer pretend I didn't know the police were looking for me. Even Nick would remember that he'd told me. I needed time to think my way through the mess of thoughts battling in my head. I needed peace and quiet.

Of course, the police were bound to put two and two together and start banging on Rose's door. In fact, I wasn't sure why the person who attacked Rose hadn't told them to look for me there, but that would probably happen. I thought I heard sirens in the distance, getting closer. I reached for Rose's key rack and grabbed keys. The neighbors might be in Florida, but their houses were available. With a dog squirming under each arm, I hightailed it out the back door and across the yard.

Luck was with me. The third key fit and I was in. I slithered along the floor through the kitchen and hallway and up the stairs. Of course, I couldn't turn on the lights. I definitely didn't want the police catching sight of my slithering backside. I felt my way through a bedroom. One of the beds had an extra blanket folded at the foot. I tucked it around the dogs, covering their heads. That always sends them to dreamland. I tried not to think of how far I'd sunk in life. How had I gone from being a helpful professional organizer to a furtive home invader? I promised myself I would do something nice for these neighbors of Rose's as soon as I got my head straight. Through the drawn bedroom curtains, I could see the pulsating lights of police vehicles. It sure made it hard to think calmly. Finally, I flopped on the bed, closed my eyes, pulled a pillow over my head, and tried to deal with the crazy questions in my brain.

Who could help me? Margaret? No, as an attorney, she'd have to advise me to turn myself in. Maybe she'd have to notify the police. Another thought hit me: even though Margaret didn't know about Miss Henley, her mother could have told her I was in the neighborhood when Wynona Banks was killed. Definitely no calls to Margaret.

A small, nasty voice in my head told me I had to be careful. Someone who knew me well was behind these killings. But who had known about my involvement in Miss Henley's project aside from my friends? Who knew I planned to meet Dominic at Henley House? I'd left messages for Sally, Jack, Lilith, and even Margaret. I'd even called Rose. Sally and Jack had both known Miss Henley was going alone to Henley House on the night she was killed. Sally, Jack, and even Margaret would recognize my formerly lucky pen. They knew from my phone messages that Dominic might be the Henley heir.

I couldn't remember telling Sally I'd been at Tang's that afternoon, but I'd certainly blubbered it to Jack. In fact, Jack knew everything. The same Jack who was supposed to meet me at the Henley House, so I wouldn't go in and meet with Dominic—or whoever Dominic *really* was—alone. The same Jack who never showed his face, although his bicycle had been there. The same Jack who was tall, fair, and blue-eyed, like Olivia and Crawford. Not short and dark and intense like his fond adoptive parents. The same Jack who had easy access to my car. My friend, Jack. Who was he, really? Could I trust him to help me now?

And what about Sally? She was blonde, tall, and graceful like Crawford. I remembered Sally's own mom as a small, grey, bitter woman, leading a joyless existence with the stepfather who treated Sally like gum under his shoe. Could Sally have been a Henley born on the wrong side of the blanket? Could she have plotted the deaths of Helen

Henley and Dominic because they stood in the way of her inheritance?

No one else made sense except one of these two. I didn't know Lilith well, but she hadn't been around at the early stages. She had no way to know what I'd been up to with Miss Henley or where I was when Wynona was killed. The same with Rose, who'd ended up a victim herself. The only two who made sense were Jack and Sally. If Esme Adams were writing this story, one of them would have been the guilty party for sure.

"Well, that's real nice, Charlotte," I said out loud. This isn't one of your mother's hyped-up tales, I reminded myself. And Sally and Jack are your lifelong friends. You know what's in their hearts. You know you can trust them.

A thought struck me. Sally keeps that television blasting on WINY day and night. She would have seen the news alerts. She'd be frantic with worry. All it would take was one quick phone call to reassure her. But Pepper would anticipate that. I didn't know how long it took to tap phone lines, but Pepper would know which ones to go for: Sally, Jack, and Margaret. All the misfits.

I was truly on my own.

The police would be taking Rose's place apart by now. It was just a matter of time until they found that gym bag with my bloodstained clothing. What if someone had seen me run next door? Plus my car was still in Rose's backyard, covered with the tarp. The cops would want to talk to the neighbors. They'd come here too. Would they kick the door down?

This kind of thinking gets your adrenaline going. I sat up, heart pounding, head buzzing, and front tooth aching. I could hardly call my dentist. Wait, there was something about dentists. Something I'd heard at the memorial. Something that may have been important. And better, something that might help me get out of this tight spot.

I crawled back downstairs. The flashing from outside gave off enough weird flickering illumination for me to see as I moved around. I located the phone and the phone book. Next I found a door in the kitchen and opened it, hoping it led to the basement. I made my way tentatively onto the stairs and pulled the door closed behind me. I felt for a light switch and flicked it on. If my luck was still holding, I could find what I wanted and no one would see the light from outside. I fumbled through the phone book until I found the telephone number I needed. My hands were shaking as I pressed the keys on my cell phone.

First I took my five messages. Sally sounded hysterical. Jack was just as bad. Even Margaret had a touch of emotion in her voice. Of course, I couldn't call them back.

The fourth message was from my laundry client, now the least of my problems. She said with a chuckle, "We'll be going ahead with that project now. He's been watching the news with his mouth hanging open. I said you were real ticked off at him. I told him I'd picked up a few pointers from you. He's looking at things a bit differently."

The last message was a welcome one from Glenda Baillie. I guess she hadn't caught the television news about me. "Hello, Charlotte. To answer your question, my mom said she was on her way to get some chocolate truffles for Olivia. Someone had asked her to pick them up. She was always happy to do something extra for Olivia and it got her killed."

Click, click, click. The pieces started to fit together: the prank phone call to Kristee, the closed chocolate shop, the presence of the Dominic Lo Bello impostor at Tang's around the corner so soon after the shooting. His sudden interest in me.

I needed to get the hell out of here and move fast.

Ramona was surprised to hear from me.

"Charlotte?" she said, for the second time.

I said, "At the memorial reception, you mentioned you saw Miss Henley on that last day. I really, really need to know exactly where she was going."

"The last time? Oh right. Let me think. I was going to the doctor's."

"And you saw her there?"

"I saw her heading down the hallway toward the office when I was on my way out. I told you she could still rattle me. But why do you want to know?"

I said, "Don't worry about a thing."

"But what have you got yourself into? The news . . ."

"It'll all blow over. I'll just head on down and see if I can figure out what was going on."

Ramona shrilled, "Head on down where? To the Medical-Dental Building? To Dr. Janescek's office?"

"No choice. Benjamin's my doctor too, you know. Thanks."

"Please, Charlotte, don't go anywhere. You have to turn yourself in before something terrible happens."

"They'll never take me alive," I said.

Ramona's sense of humor had deserted her. "Listen to me! You're up to your patootie in . . ."

I clicked off, secure in the knowledge that Ramona would have no choice but to call the cops. But just in case, I had one more number to look up.

"Yes, of course, my dear," Professor Quarrington said when he heard my request. "Of course, I'll be happy to help. You'll be where?"

"Miss Henley's home. Her own home, not the Henley House."

"Would you like me to meet you there?"

"No thanks. Just tell the police I'm on my way. I have to run now. I'm sorry for any trouble I've caused you."

"No trouble at all, my dear."

Don't be so sure, I thought, after I hung up.

I needed to speak to Lilith, but her number was in my address book. I'd left my purse in the bedroom. I switched off the light and headed back upstairs. I waited long enough to hear the slamming of car doors. I peeked through the blinds to see the cop cars careening off. That was my cue: I grabbed the blanket with the sleeping dogs and raced downstairs.

—◆◆—

I couldn't drive the Miata. With an APB out on me, I could hardly take a cab, and Stone Wall Farm was well beyond walking distance. That left Rose's old LeMans. At least I had the keys, and after my break-in, blanket snatching, and calls to mislead the police, what was a little joyride? Rose had said that one of her neighbors checked it every now and then. Was there a chance it was still running? It wasn't like I had a better plan. The engine sputtered, then coughed and turned over.

"Snuggle up and hang on," I told the dogs.

My heart rate skyrocketed as I passed a pair of police cars, facing each other, at the corner of the street where I'd last seen Nick the Thick.

My cell phone rang, and I held the wheel with one hand and answered, something I would disapprove of normally.

"I found her," Lilith said.

"Who?"

"Rose's daughter, of course. Isn't that what you wanted me to do?"

"Sorry, I'm a bit . . ."

"Anyway, she's an actress. She's shooting a movie in Vancouver, and she doesn't see how she could get back here right now."

"Oh boy."

"That's just plain bad," Lilith said. "People should take care of their elderly relatives."

I said, "Um, maybe you could . . ."

"Go to the hospital and pretend to be her daughter?"

"Yes."

"I'm walking over now. You can't believe the number of cop cars on the road."

"If you get in to see her and if she's conscious at all, ask her who she let into her home. She keeps that door locked. She must have opened the door to the person who attacked her. I have this crazy idea . . ."

"Where are you?"

"I'm on my way to Stone Wall Farm."

"You don't think anyone would go after Olivia? Oh my God, Gabriel would freak. What am I talking about? There's really good security at Stone Wall Farm. They have staff on twenty-four hours a day. Nothing can happen to her with Francie right in the room."

"I hope you're right. But two people were attacked today, three if you count me: Dominic's dead and Rose is in the hospital. We're talking about a killer with a lot of nerve."

"Call the police! They'll protect Olivia."

"The police are not going to believe me. Especially since I don't have everything figured out yet. The murderer will just take cover and wait for a better time. Let me do this now. Call me when you talk to Rose. I'll have my phone on vibrate. If I don't answer right away, it might be because I don't want anyone to hear me."

"Be careful, Charlotte."

"You too."

*With any kind of organizing project,*
*it's important not to give up,*
*no matter how bleak things look.*

# 20

The road to Stone Wall Farm is scenic and curvy in the daytime. The undulating hills make for a gorgeous drive. Translate that to nightmare as soon as the sun goes down. Add a high wind and occasional blasts of rain and it's a Tim Burton fantasy. My hands were frozen in the steering wheel grip by the time I reached the property. I wasn't dopey enough to park where anyone could see or hear me. I left the car near the edge of the property and told the dogs to keep sleeping in their new blankie. I called Lilith. She didn't pick up. I left a message saying that I'd left the dogs in the brown Pontiac sedan just past the gate. Just in case.

Without looking back, I crept along the hedge near the driveway, until I was even with the main building. Most of the rooms were dark, but here and there a corridor light shone. I tried the back door and found it locked. No surprise. I crept around to the side door, which I thought was the kitchen entrance. That too was locked. The same thing for the five sets of French doors along the wide verandah. By this time, I was near the front. I crouched down and peered through the glass at the staff desk in the front hall. There was no sign of a staff member. Surely there was a night nurse on duty. And what about security?

My phone vibrated in my pocket. Bad timing.

I slunk away from the house and took shelter behind a large cedar tree. It could be only one person. I called Lilith again.

"That was fast," she said.

"What happened with Rose?"

"You were right. I said I was the daughter. No one argued with me. No one asked for ID. Nothing. They just let me in."

"That's good," I whispered. "How is she?"

"She's unconscious still. I couldn't get any information from her. I'll try again in the morning. But now, I'm on my way to meet you. Don't do anything until I get there."

"Do you still have your key?"

"Don't need it. There's a keypad on the side door, near Gabe's room."

"I don't know where Gabe's room is."

"Main floor just off the common room. It's set up specially for his motorized chair. Got its own ramp and everything."

"The common room? The big sitting room off the front foyer? The parrots are there, right? Okay, how do I use the keypad?"

"Everyone has their own code. Mine was SWFL—so, like, Stone Wall Farm Lilith—unless they changed it after they fired me. They're planning to switch to security cards, but they hadn't installed the new system when I got the boot."

"Would they have changed your code?"

"Probably. But I don't imagine they'd expect me to break in. Watch out for the night nurse and the security guard."

SWFL didn't work. So much for the Stone Wall Farm staff not expecting Lilith to break in. I tried SWFF for

Francie and I was through the door. I crept along the hallway. Off in the distance, I thought I could hear the soft murmur of late-night television. As I approached the desk in the front foyer, I scuttled on all fours and hid behind the drapes. Life was turning into a hokey stage play. My heart froze. There *was* someone there. The night nurse sat slumped on the chair, her head resting on the desk. A spilled cup lay by her hand.

Her chest rose and fell. Definitely alive. I scurried up the stairs, hugging the wall. Straight out of one of my mother's wilder novels. The hallway was dim, but light filtered up from the lobby level as I crept toward Olivia's suite. The television noise seemed to be coming from it. Did that mean Olivia or her caregiver were awake? I edged closer. The television droned on.

I paused outside the door, breathing hard. Was that the soft thud of footsteps on the stairs? Or just my imagination? Without thinking I slipped into Olivia's suite. A ragged snore erupted from the daybed in the corner. Francie. How many people were involved in this crazy plot? Was Francie one of them? She seemed pretty dozy. Was that an act? I had two doors to choose from. Which one was Olivia's bedroom? I tiptoed through the closest door and found myself in the bathroom. My heart rate shot up when I heard the door open to the suite. A staff member checking up on Olivia? Why would they do that with Francie in the room?

I could see and be seen in the soft safety light. I hopped behind the shower curtain. Hard to believe, but that seemed like the most sensible thing. I tried to get my breathing under control. I looked around for something to defend myself with. There were also the usual rails and antislip guards that you might expect to find in an elderly invalid's bathtub. One door led to the sitting room; the other must have been direct access to Olivia's bedroom. Everything in the bathroom fit with Olivia's luxurious but limited lifestyle. I was surrounded by high-end imported bath products. Verbena shampoo, olive and sage conditioner, lavender shower gel, and French skin cream. Large soft towels were stacked on the spa-style shelf. I could toss one over someone's head and then make a run for it. Abandon my nutty, half-formed suspicion and hide in the woods. But after all I'd been through, I didn't plan to leave Stone Wall Farm until I found what I needed to know. And I didn't want to get caught first.

When I thought I heard the door to the suite close again, I crept out silently. Or at least silently until my foot struck the trendy metal flip-top wastebasket. It clattered across the ceramic floor and came to rest against the door, spilling its contents. I grabbed one of the towels and waited for Francie to check out the noise.

Eventually, I decided that Francie was still passed out. There was no sound from Olivia's room. I bent down to clean up the mess I'd made on the floor. Force of habit. Who cared about a few spilled tissues and toiletries at a time like this? My hand stopped at the contact-lens case.

Olivia might be old and fragile, but she hadn't lost her vanity. In the dim light, I squinted at the tiny empty container. So that was the explanation for her brilliant blue eyes.

I opened the door and peeked through. Francie still snored on the daybed. I crept toward Olivia's bedroom. Another soft night-light showed a mountain of bedclothes. I tiptoed toward the bed, holding my breath. I leaned in closer. The bed was empty.

I checked her sitting room again and whipped open the bathroom door. Olivia was gone. I moved softly and peered from the door into the corridor. No sign of anyone. I listened. No soft pad of footsteps. But there was something else. The distant, subtle smell of smoke.

I scuttled down the wide staircase. As the bottom, I sniffed again. Definitely something burning. The woman at the desk continued to sleep, mouth open, a trickle of drool pooling on the desktop.

I swallowed. The smell of smoke was faint but distinct.

Fire? Oh crap. Why hadn't the alarm system gone off?

Lilith had told me that Gabe's suite was on the main floor because of his motorized wheelchair. I could probably get him out, but how many other people were sleeping upstairs and downstairs?

It didn't matter what happened to me for breaking into Stone Wall Farm. I had to get help. I shook the sleeping woman's shoulder. She groaned but didn't wake.

"Open your eyes," I whispered. "There's a fire."

As I let go, she slipped from her chair to the floor. I grabbed the desk telephone and pressed the button for emergency services. No dial tone. I jabbed the buttons in panic. Nothing.

Okay, no phone. By this point, I would have welcomed the security guard, but there was no sign of him. Where was the fire alarm? I vaguely remembered seeing one in the common room. I raced toward it, past the covered parrot cage.

A voice from the cage croaked, "Stupid boy, stupid boy."

A second said, "Cripple."

I stopped. The last pieces of the puzzle fell into place. My nutty idea was not so wild after all. I stared at the figure across the room. She stood erect in her pink and silver silk dressing gown, her long white hair hung in a braid around her shoulder. She moved quickly and confidently toward the window, the dressing gown flowing behind her, the braid now glowing silver in the moonlight. She bent and peered out the window. My heart thundered in my chest. I caught sight of a blur of motion outside. An owl? No, definitely human in shape. I thought I recognized the dark spike of purplish hair.

The smell of smoke was growing stronger. Where was it

coming from? The kitchen? I spotted a fire alarm on the far wall and dashed toward it.

"Take your hand off that," the voice said.

Like hell. I was surprised by how fast she could move. I found my hand in her steely grip and gasped. I wrenched my hand away from her. "Don't you smell that smoke? Something's burning. We have to warn people."

"I don't think so," she said.

"Listen," I said. "You have to . . ."

"You listen," she said in her familiar voice. The gun in her hand glinted in the dim light. "I told you to step away from the alarm."

I knew nothing about guns except that this one had probably killed Dominic, or whoever he was. "The people here have never done anything to hurt you. You can get away, but we can't let the building burn."

Behind her in the window, something moved again. Lilith again? No, the wrong shape. I couldn't be sure. I didn't want to take my eye off the gun and the woman who was holding it.

She said, "*I* can get away. You'll be staying. In fact, you may find things too hot to handle."

"But Olivia . . ."

"You can stop this ridiculous charade. It's perfectly obvious that you know who I am. It no longer matters. Time to get moving."

"It won't work, Miss Henley," I said.

"But it has worked. Perfectly."

I stood tall and met her blazing blue eyes. "Not really. You slipped up a few times."

"Don't bother to prevaricate. It won't get you anywhere. Now step away from that alarm."

If anyone but Miss Henley was going to survive the night at Stone Wall Farm, I had to stall. To do that, I had to appeal to her famous ego. If Lilith had arrived, she needed to know what we were dealing with. Even two of us were no match for a gun. I said loudly, "The truth is that I am not the only person who knows it was you, Miss Henley," I said loudly. If Lilith was coming, she'd had time to get into the building by now.

"I'm not deaf," she said. "And if you thought you can wake the nurse by shouting, you thought wrong."

"Other people know."

"I doubt that. I've eliminated anyone who would. Now march toward the kitchen. Get moving."

"Not so fast. You gave yourself away on several accounts. The visit to the dentist just before your so-called death. You were seen."

"Circumstantial blather. There's no law against going to the dentist."

It was time to trot out my wilder speculations. I didn't have much to lose. "You made sure you upset the receptionist enough so that she left you alone to switch your dental records with your cousin Olivia's. That was brilliant."

She smiled. "It was. I'm quite proud of it. It's a shame you are the only one who figured it out."

"I have to admire the way you pulled it together," I said. "Must have taken a lot of planning. Letting your own hair grow out long and natural, but wearing a short wig in your familiar style and color. The blue contacts. Even if poor nearsighted Francie spotted the contact lenses, she would put that down to Olivia's vanity."

Miss Henley smirked. "Olivia always wore contacts, the vapid creature. I enjoyed turning that against her. And as for Francie, she's a fool and that's why I chose her."

"Of course, that made perfect sense. Wynona Banks was no fool. She would have known you were not Olivia at once. But Dominic was there to take care of that problem. Very well planned. What did you do then? Offer Francie the job?"

"Thick as a plank, that woman." Miss Henley sneered. "To stupid to live."

"But just in case, you kept her doped with sleeping pills. She'd never know who you were calling or whether you were in or out."

"I told you to get moving."

"I must commend you on using Dominic Lo Bello. What was he? An actor? A small-time criminal? An illegitimate child of Crawford's? Whoever he really was and however you found him, he turned out to be an excellent choice.

"I met a lot of nasty children in my teaching career. Unlike you, some of them came in handy. Dominio was one of them. I met him one year when I taught summer school upstate, before he went to jail the first time. He came in very handy over the years."

"I imagine he did. He certainly was able to charm Olivia into a drive in the country on the evening she died. I am guessing here, but I suppose he suggested a visit to Henley House. Then a sharp blow to the head. Dominic was strong enough to maneuver the beam and drop it on her. Olivia ended up under a stack of moldering papers at Henley House, her face damaged beyond recognition, so that only dental records could confirm who she was. Of course, you'd already switched those. How did Dominic cut Olivia's hair and put the wig on before he obliterated her face? The cops and the pathologist would put the wig down to a small vanity. No one would ever question that the body wasn't Miss Helen Henley."

She smirked.

I said, "But I figured it out, and I have made my deductions known to the police."

"Oh spare me. The police won't listen to you. They consider you a suspect in my death. I've seen to that."

"And that was inspired too. Setting up the contract. Making the unreasonable call to my home the night before. Taking my pen during our meeting and leaving it under Olivia's body. Placing the heel of my boot at the scene of

Dominic's murder. Nice touch. Did you get Dominic to take that from my car when he was at my place? Very devious. You set him up to leave a clue implicating me in his own death. But of course, he didn't know it was to be his death, did he?"

"He was useful, right to the end," she said. "Until he got too greedy."

"I'm not surprised he got greedy, with all he had to do including that nasty hit and run. Phoning in the tips to Pepper and to Todd Tyrell. I suppose he did everything in return for his piece of the pie. And what a pie it was: all of Olivia's lovely money. A few months of planning, maybe longer, a couple of weeks of relative risk, some boredom here at Stone Wall Farm, and then you'd be off to revel in the millions instead of living with quiet dignity on your sensible investments and teacher's pension. Unfortunately for you, I was able to get the message about who you really are not only to the police but also to your media flunky, Todd Tyrell."

"Not that I believe you for a moment, since I know you are a bluffer. But even if you did, it's still too late for you."

"Don't count on it. The world will learn what happened to your cousin Randolph. Olivia liked Randolph much more than she liked you, didn't she? Perhaps you found that annoying, as well as the fact she would have left him a bundle." I hit the mark with my guess.

"Randolph was easily taken care of. Not much of a challenge."

It dawned on me that she was enjoying this. She wasn't going to shoot me before she could exult over her crimes, revel in her cleverness.

I said, "Randolph, as peculiar as he was, had many people who liked him. There was quite a crowd at his funeral."

"Shut up, you stupid girl. People just came to gawk at a pathetic old fool. There was no respect for him. None."

"Oh yes, respect. Always important to you. That's why

your bequest to St. Jude's specified the big memorial reception for Miss Helen Henley and the scholarship in your name. You could attend the church pretending to be poor demented Olivia and enjoy seeing the church full of people paying their respects to Miss Helen Henley. No wonder you planned it. Just as well you missed the speeches. So many jokes about 'Hellfire.' But then I guess you can't have everything."

"Once again, you are mistaken. I *will* have everything."

"But, of course, not while you're stuck here being Olivia."

She smirked again, definitely not a pretty sight. "That's right. And after tonight, I won't be. You do not have to worry about that."

I spoke as loud as I could without raising her suspicions. "Well, I am worried, since you have a gun trained on me. I know you plan to set fire to Stone Wall Farm. You've already started something smoldering. Francie and the night nurse have been drugged. I imagine the security guard too. They'll never make it out. The other patients will be trapped. You don't care about that. Because Olivia will escape. Let's see, you'll be found hysterical, lying on the lawn. Maybe you'll wake one or two other residents to join you to avert suspicion. Olivia could be a bit of a hero."

"This whole crowd of drooling fools will be better off dead. No one cares."

I felt a wave of nausea. I thought of Gabe and how much his mother and Lilith both cared.

She said, "And of course, I don't care about you, Charlotte Adams. Although, your snooping and bumbling have been godsends to me. Even though I'd planned it, you made a much better suspect than I could have ever hoped for. Running around like a rabbit. Especially tonight. I couldn't believe my good fortune when I heard you were eluding the police."

Oh crap. She was right. I supposed she'd been following

the APB on television this evening. Had she seen me come in to the building as she was making her deadly preparations?

I said, "I'm telling you, it won't work."

She paid no attention. "I hadn't planned it this way, but when I realized you'd come here, I thought, perfect. Francie was already out like a light. It was easy enough to slip something into the night nurse's tea. You'll be blamed for the fire here, naturally. Not that you will survive it, but no one will doubt your culpability. It was really unwise of you to break in. But it's most convenient for me, as I no longer have to depend on the fire looking accidental. So much easier."

"Couldn't Olivia just express dissatisfaction with the services and move away? Why does anyone else need to die?"

"A few loose ends. Medical files, that kind of thing. Better to have them destroyed. Olivia will survive, but naturally after such a disaster, she will no longer leave her money to Stone Wall Farm. No one will know."

"I knew. And I knew it was time for you to make a move. I certainly wasn't foolish enough to come out here alone."

"You're bluffing again, of course. I remember that about you when you were one of my students. Always trying to protect that motley crowd of pathetic friends. Your tactics didn't work then and they won't work now."

I dug in my heels. "The people here are helpless, but you can't really eliminate the library staff, the historical society, and more important, the media, especially your tame toady, Todd Tyrell. I've let him know."

"I doubt that. But since you know so much, are you aware they have a wine cellar here? Quite extensive. I think you should take a little tour." She gestured with the gun.

Yeah right, I thought. And you'll lock the door and I won't be able to get out. They'll find my crispy bones along with the staff and residents when they sift through the smoldering wreckage of Stone Wall Farm.

"I don't think so," I said.

"Then I'll shoot you. And I'll enjoy it."

"If you shoot me, that will poke holes in your story about me setting fire to the place. Why would I also shoot myself? For that matter, how and why would I have locked myself in the wine cellar?"

"By the time anyone shows up here, I will have thought of a very good reason. Perhaps the gun will be at the feet of the night nurse. Shot you to protect me, then was overcome by smoke. How sad. I will enjoy working it out."

Where was Lilith? Had she gone for help? Stone Wall Farm was miles from anywhere. Would she be back before I was full of holes or the building a smoldering ruin? I said, "Leaving aside the ridiculous notion that night nurses have guns, the autopsy will show that she's been drugged."

"Well, of course, you drugged them."

"But I would have had to be here earlier to do that. I was elsewhere, having a conversation with a police officer."

"Nice try."

"Another question: Why harm Rose?"

"You don't know everything, do you?"

"Here's what I think. You had someone drive you into Woodbridge, ostensibly for a visit—maybe Francie, she'd never catch on. Inez might have questioned that after your hissy fit the other day. Then if Francie headed off for a break—and she's the type—you were five houses away from Henley House. You could meet Dominic, ambush him, and head back to be picked up at Rose's. But I'm betting Rose figured out you were Helen and not Olivia. She probably couldn't stop herself from saying so. She had to go. You wouldn't want that to be tied to Dominic's death, so Rose was left to die, with the cat you knew she was allergic to tossed in for good measure. You figured someone would find her in a day or so. Natural causes, this time."

To the side through the window, a flash of movement, a familiar lanky body, and the glint of rimless glasses, ducking down out of sight. Not Lilith. Jack! My heart leapt in my chest. What was he doing there? Where was Lilith?

"What's out there?" she said, turning to follow my gaze.

I decided I had nothing to lose. Every wild speculation whirling through my brain was fit to mention. Why not keep bluffing? "It was always you all along, wasn't it? So many deaths. Fires, drownings. Crawford, then later his widow and son, dead in a fire."

"No great loss, that crowd," she sneered. "A stain on the Henley name."

I said, "Lilith's job, her bike, her apartment building. I imagine Dominic handled all that for you too. You had to get rid of her, didn't you? But you couldn't risk killing her. Two caregivers from the same facility within two weeks; that would draw unwelcome attention. But Gabe knew who you were as he saw you. And Lilith could communicate with Gabe. What if Gabe ended up with someone else like Lilith? Someone who made an effort to understand him. Someone who might discover your secret before you'd managed your move. For sure, you'd need to get rid of Gabe. You couldn't resist tormenting him. The parrots picked up your words. 'Stupid boy. Cripple.' No wonder his mother said he had lost interest in them recently."

"This has been entertaining," she said. "And you're right, of course."

She stood with her back to the foyer. I don't know how I did it, but I kept my eyes on her bright blue ones. I didn't look past her.

"I'm right about something else," I said. "Your murder game is over."

"Not just yet."

I said, "Actually . . ."

As Miss Henley lifted the gun, Lilith raced toward her from the foyer. She raised her arms high and brought the heavy black vase from the table crashing onto Miss Henley's head.

The blue eyes widened and rolled upward, the gun tumbled, and Miss Henley crumpled on the floor. Shards of pottery, water, flowers lay around her.

Lilith sank to her knees sobbing. "My God, she was going to kill Gabe and everyone here. Oh God, I hope she's dead."

"You don't really." My legs turned to rubber. "I'm sure she's not."

Lilith whispered, "The things she said. She was proud of it."

I looked around wildly. My voice shook. "We have to find the source of the smoke."

Lilith said, "I think your friend put it out."

"Well, what are friends for?" Sally said, appearing around the corner. "I'm the one who told you to stay away from Hellfire in the first place. But did you listen?"

"How did you get here? How did you know?"

Lilith said, "I was worried about you coming out here. You weren't thinking clearly. I didn't have any way to get out here on my own. You gave me Sally's number for the dogs. Here we are."

Sally said, "Didn't I tell you that project was a trap? But did you listen? Nooo."

"But who could imagine anything like this?"

"You know what I can't imagine? Why you didn't call *me* tonight. Were you deranged?"

"I was worried Pepper might tap your line and Jack's. And my idea about Miss Henley, it was so crazy. I couldn't imagine anyone believing me. I was in a panic. I suppose I thought you and Jack would stop me."

Sally said, "Jack loves crazy ideas. Why do you think he got those philosophy degrees?"

I said, "I saw Jack through the window. I was afraid she'd shoot him."

She nodded. "I got in touch with him on his cell phone after Lilith called me and told him you were coming here. Dominic had knocked him out. Lucky he didn't get killed, or arrested. He got away before the cops spotted him. I didn't tell Benjamin any of this. He would have stopped us. I just left a note. Oh boy, he'll be totally devastated about Olivia."

Lilith interrupted. "Charlotte, you saved Gabe. If you hadn't kept her talking, all those evil plans, we never could have . . . it's just so unbelievable."

I wanted to see Jack. "But where is Jack?"

"I knew my way around the building, so Sally and I tried to find the source of the fire. Jack went to put Gabe into his chair and get him out. He was calling the police and the fire department. I was going to wake up the people on the second floor when I heard what that evil woman said about Gabe. I never hated anyone so much in my life. I never felt fear or anger like that, not even back when I was living on the street."

Sally said, "Jack was trying to get Pepper on the line so when the cops showed up, they didn't shoot the wrong person, like, say, you. We figured Jack would have the most impact talking to the cops. We thought Pepper would listen to him. That Hellfire is such a fiend that she could probably convince them that you were the dangerous one."

"She'd already managed that."

Lilith moved across the room and flung open the French doors. In the distance sirens shrieked. This time I was glad to hear them.

I hugged Sally and tried to keep from crying. "Thank you both. You saved my life and all these others."

Sally's eyes were full of tears too. "I think you did that, Charlotte."

My voice wobbled. "I really want to see Jack. I have to thank him too." Neither of them would ever know the black suspicions I'd harbored after I spotted his bike outside Henley House.

Lilith said, "Come on in, Gabe. She can't hurt you now." I heard a hum as the motorized chair rolled up the ramp and into the room.

Jack appeared in the door, behind Gabe. He was holding two squirming creatures and grinning in his Jack way. One eye was swollen shut and there was a sloppy bandage across his nose. "Truffle and Sweet Marie were howling out there in the car, so I figured it was safe to let them out now." He set them on the floor and they torpedoed toward me.

Out of the corner of my eye, I spotted a movement on the floor. While we watched openmouthed, Miss Henley's hand shot forward and grabbed the gun.

"Well," she said, sitting up, "four miscreants for one. I can see the news headlines now. Badly beaten elderly widow shoots murderous gang in effort to save fellow patients."

Why had we left the gun there? Why hadn't we picked it up? How dumb was that? We knew who we were dealing with.

Truffle and Sweet Marie smelled trouble and began to bark.

"I imagine the police will think you four were all in it together," she said, straightening herself out. "I'll make it sound plausible."

"It won't work," I said. "Too many people know."

She ignored me. Maybe the blow from the vase had affected her hearing. The dogs raced toward her barking and snapping. She turned to fend them off. Perhaps that's why she didn't react immediately to the sound of the motor. Gabe's face contorted as the wheelchair hurtled across the carpet. Miss Henley jerked her head away from the dogs and toward the wheelchair. Too late. I leapt forward and knocked the gun from her hand just before the wheelchair hit her, full force.

Lilith hugged the shaking figure in the chair and wept. "Good for you, Gabe. Good for you."

This time it was really over. I grabbed the dogs and collapsed into Jack's arms. And Sally's arms too, of course.

Outside the open French door, I saw the first police car squeal to a stop. From the safety of our group hug, we watched Pepper step out.

# 21

Jack opened the door to his new shop to me and my dogs. "Hey, that bruise on your chin is clearing up. Your teeth look great," he said.

"They should," I said. "They cost enough."

"Money well spent."

"You're right. It's a good thing And your eye is less swollen and your nose looks like it will be okay soon. No one will be able to tell Dominic clobbered you with a board. I'm so glad we're getting past all that terrible stuff. It was a fabulous idea to have a preopening party for CYCotics."

Jack said, "But it was your idea."

"It was fabulous anyway. Speaking of fabulous, I brought the chilled champagne and the chocolate truffles. And I have champagne glasses in the Miata. You can help me with those."

Jack said, "Excellent. But plastic would be fine, just this once."

I shuddered, thinking of plastic glasses for champagne.

"Please, it's the least I can do. Anyway, they're from the Dollar Do! Margaret called to say she'd be along shortly. Apparently she has an endless source of Ben & Jerry's, and she said we can count on it. I brought dishes and spoons. Benjamin's going to pop in with the kids for ice cream. And Sally is picking up Rose." I looked around the cycle shop. "I suppose we should find them somewhere to sit."

Jack looked around and frowned. "Sit?"

The large, shaggy unspecified breed of dog that had been sniffing around sat on command.

I said, "Good boy, Schopenhauer. You sure showed up the resident brats." Truffle and Sweet Marie, who are familiar with the word "sit," ignored the comment as well as the command. Big surprise.

Jack said, "Isn't he great? And look at how well he sits."

I said, "He's magnificent. But since most of the people at this preparty party are no longer teenagers, you'll find they prefer not to sit on the floor. I'm just saying."

Jack said, "If you're talking about Rose, I can restack some boxes, I guess. You think she'll mind?"

"Stack enough for all the girls. Have a chocolate truffle. It will help you cope."

"Mmm. Kristee's finest. How's she taking things?"

"Being Kristee, she'll be bitter about losing her best client. That bothered her a whole lot more than all the death and destruction Miss Henley caused."

"You think she suspected all along? When Hellfire left instructions that Olivia get her favorite kind of chocolates every week?"

"I can't let myself think about that," I said.

"We'll never know everything, will we?"

"No. I've been waking up nights and wondering about so many things. Like Olivia's husband and children. Helen was supposed to be away at college, but now that we know the lengths she would go to, maybe she came back. She was a strong swimmer, and now that we know about what a psychopath she is, well, it makes you think."

Jack said, "Don't think."

"You're right. Not tonight anyway. Tonight is for being happy," I said. "Let's just celebrate."

Jack's face lit up. "This place is something, isn't it?"

I glanced around at the space full of bikes, helmets, accessories, and other gear. "All that coverage on WINY will be good for your business. I still can't believe you're opening tomorrow. It all happened so fast."

"That Lilith was amazing. She can move like the wind, and she has a real feel for bikes. I'd give her a job here any day."

"I'm glad she's back taking care of Gabe and finishing her courses. Speaking of Gabe, I hear he's pretty excited about getting out to his first party in years. Stone Wall Farm might be fancy, but it has no nightlife. That might change under the new administration. I'm glad that the ice queen got the boot."

"Gabe's amazing. Guy's in a wheelchair and manages to knock over a killer and save all our lives. Of course, he had a nice distraction thanks to Truffle and Sweet Marie. Man, he sure had a major hate on for Hellfire."

"Don't call me *man*, Jack. Sally's pulling up with Rose now."

"You think Rose will like Schopenhauer?"

"Pretty sure she will. Rose is allergic to cats, but not dogs. Miss Henley knew that too."

Jack said, "Big dog like Schopenhauer will be good company and protection for her. With Lilith moving in upstairs, Schopie will get his walks too."

"And with Lilith in the house, Rose will be able to stay in her home for years."

The door opened. Sally and Rose arrived, Sally shrieking. Rose was resplendent with freshly blue hair and a black jogging suit with shiny silver stars on it. She carried a tray of Toll House cookies. Margaret followed them through the door with a cooler. Behind them, I could see the Stone Wall Farm van pull up. Lilith got busy letting down the ramp for Gabe. Gabe's wheelchair had balloons attached to it.

All three dogs began to bark.

Jack popped the cork on the champagne and turned to Margaret. "I don't suppose you know anyone who wants a nice little grey cat?"

I guess we were back to normal. As normal as it gets.

**Mary Jane Maffini** is a lapsed librarian, a former mystery bookseller, and a previous president of Crime Writers of Canada. In addition to creating the Charlotte Adams series, she is the author of the Camilla MacPhee Mysteries, the Fiona Silk series, and nearly two dozen mystery short stories. She has won two Arthur Ellis awards for short fiction, and *The Dead Don't Get Out Much*, her latest Camilla MacPhee Mystery, was nominated for a Barry Award in 2006. She lives in Ottawa, Ontario, with her long-suffering husband and two miniature dachshunds.